Shame On It All

Other books by Zane

Addicted

The Heat Seekers

The Sex Chronicles:
Shattering the Myth

Shame On It All

Read the excerpts at:
http://www.eroticanoir.com

Address inquiries to:
Strebor Books International,
P. O. Box 10127, Silver Spring, MD 20914
or
email the author directly at: zane@eroticanoir.com or visit
Zane on the web at http://www.eroticanoir.com.

A sneak preview of the Heat Seekers appears at the end of this
novel.

Shame On It All

Zane

A

PUBLICATION

STREBOR BOOKS INTERNATIONAL LLC

distributed by

A&B DISTRIBUTORS INC
BROOKLYN, NEW YORK
11238

Published by
SBI

STREBOR BOOKS INTERNATIONAL
P. O. Box 10127
Silver Spring, MD, 20914
streborbooks@aol.com
http://www.streborbooks.com

ISBN 0-9674601-2-3
LCCN 99-91609

Distributed by
A&B Distributors Inc
1000 Atlantic Ave.
Brooklyn, NY 11238
(718) 783-7808

COVER ILLUSTRATION: © *André Harris*
TYPESETTING & INTERIOR DESIGN: *Industrial Fonts & Graphix*

Manufactured & Printed in Canada

To Carlita and Charmaine
As sisters, you have been forever supportive
of my efforts and goals
It is a blessing to have you both in my life
and while our lives are nowhere near
as dramatic as the Whitfield Sisters,
we do have our differences.
Despite that fact, when it comes down
to the wire, we are always there for
one another. For that, I am
eternally grateful.

Peace and Much Love,

Zane

Acknowledgments

With every new release, my list of acknowledgments gets longer and my blessings grow ten-fold.

As always, I must thank the Lord for not only everything He has given me but also for everything He has taken away for without failure and a great deal of loss, one can never truly be inspired.

Thanking my parents is a must, for without them there would be no me. They deserve a thousand nights of praise for that mere fact alone. Their understanding, their support, and their love have nurtured me into the woman I am today and I could not possibly express my appreciation in words.

As for my children, they are my inspiration in day-to-day life and come before anything and anybody in my life. Thank you for giving me a reason to struggle on in the face of adversity and stress. Remember that Mommy loves you more than life itself.

To my sisters, Carlita and Charmaine, thanks for just being you. Thanks for the long conversations, the babysitting you put in on the weekends, and for treating my children like they are your own. The same goes for my brothers-in-law, David and Rick. I have this tremendously large family. Our family reunions involve hundreds of people so I won't begin to go down the list. However, I do appreciate everything you have all done for me.

I would like to thank my agent, Sara Camilli, for her support and efforts on my behalf and for reading the five hundred Word documents I have loaded up her computer with. I realize that I get a bit carried away at times with my writing but you are always understanding and willing to read my words. Thanks for keeping my best interest at heart and for telling me to get some rest when I throw caution to the wind in regards to my health.

Now this is a book about sistergirls so I have to do a quick run-down of mine. Big shout outs to: Shonda Cheekes, Pamela Crockett, Esq., Michelle Askew, Esq., Pamela Shannon, M.D., Cornelia Williams, Janice Jones Murray, Janet Allen, Karen Black, Dee McConneaughy, Judy Phillips, Sharon Johnson, Gail Kendrick, Lisa Fox, Dawn Boswell, and Tracy Jeter. Some of you I have known since I was in diapers and others I have only known a little while, but I just want you to know that you have all support-ed me or inspired me in some way.

Thanks to my fellow writers who have supported my efforts and to the numerous bookclubs, both online and offline, that have selected either one or both of my previous novels as their Book-of-the-Month including: The Ebony Expressions Book Club, The RAW SISTAZ Book Club, The Black Bookshelf, The Nubian Chronicles, Read Sistah Read, and The G.R.I.T.S. To the African-American Authors Helping Authors Organization, I look forward to great things.

Thanks to all the bookstores and distributors that have taken it upon themselves to spread the country with my books. I would like to especially thank Eric, Maxwell, and Wendy from A & B Books and Learie and Gail from Culture Plus.

Thanks, Rahni (Ronald Shanderson) for using the term "Shame On It All" so much that it stuck to my ribs.

Last but definitely not least, thank you to the thousands of sub-scribers to my ezines, the hundreds of thousands of visitors to EroticaNoir.com from around the globe, and those of you that flood my email box on a daily basis with your support and encouragement.

I hope you enjoy *Shame On It All*. Email me at Zane@eroti-canoir.com and tell me if I should go for it and write Shame On It All Again.

Preface

Chester Whitfield was practically in stitches from laughing so hard at Huggy Bear. *Starsky and Hutch* was by far his favorite television program. He never missed an episode.

Huggy Bear had just strutted into a bar wearing a pair of gray polyester bell bottoms, a white velour button-down shirt, and an ankle-length paisley-print coat with red faux fur on the lapels. He leaned on the bar, flashed the bartender one of those infamous Cheshire-cat grins, sucked on his tongue, and ordered a *drank*.

"Boy, that Huggy Bear sure is a cool ass cat." Chester chortled. When he got no response from his better half, he glanced over at his wife, Rachelle, who was cuddled up beside him on the sofa. He was disappointed when he noticed she was too enthralled in the latest issue of *Ebony* to pay attention to the program. Or him, for that matter. "Rachelle, you're not going to watch the show with me?"

"I will in a few minutes," she replied, not lifting as much as an eyebrow in his direction. "I'm looking at the fashion section. I was thinking about buying the girls some of those dashikis all the young people are wearing on the East Coast. They have an address in here I can order them from."

"Aw, hell naw, Rachelle," Chester protested. "That's the *last thing* you need to do."

"Why do you say that, Chester?" Rachelle finally lowered the magazine so she could leer at him. "There's nothing wrong with a little black pride."

"Of course not! You know good and well that's not what I'm saying, woman! If I were any blacker, I'd be damn near invisible."

Rachelle fell out laughing. Chester did have a valid point. He was as dark as they come, but that's one of the things that attract-ed her to him the most. There was nothing sexier to her than a man with an abundance of melanin in his skin.

"So why can't I get the girls some dashikis?"

"Bryce and Harmony might be okay with them, but Lucky is out of the damn question!"

Rachelle glowered at him. "Hold up now! That's my baby girl you're talking about. You better watch yourself."

"Last time I checked, Lucky was my baby girl, too." He reached over and started stroking her hand. "After all, I did donate some sperm to the cause."

Rachelle clucked her tongue, yanking her hand away from him. "Yeah, but I did all the hard work. I just wish you could feel *one contraction* and you would see me in a whole new light."

Chester put his arm around her shoulders, pulling her to him. "You know I adore you, woman." He kissed her gently on the fore-head. "All I'm saying is that Lucky is into enough cultural stuff already without adding on the clothing accessories. Have you lis-tened to that child lately? I mean *really, really* listened? She sounds like Malcolmenia X!"

Rachelle cackled. "I think her interest in African-American history is a good thing. It's better than her being interested in boys like Harmony and Bryce."

"Lucky better not be interested in any knuckleheads!" Chester snapped. "She's only twelve and I'm not even having that. I can tell you that much right now. Let one of those anorexic, pea-shaped head boys come sniffing around here. I'll break out my ninja suit and pull a Bruce Lee on his ass."

Rachelle shook her head. "Chester, you're fooling yourself. Our little girls are growing up and there's nothing we can do about it but let nature take its course."

"Speaking of the junior Supremes, where are they anyway? Why is it so quiet around here?" Chester got up off of the sofa and walked out into the foyer. He peered up the steps onto the second landing. "I haven't seen any of those chaps since dinner."

"You should be glad!" Rachelle yelled from the living room.

"You're always complaining about never getting to watch *Starsky and Hutch* in peace."

Chester headed back into the living room. "Good point, Sweetheart." He plopped back down on the sofa next to Rachelle. "But, that still doesn't answer my question. Where are they?"

"Well, Lucky and Bryce went next door to help Mrs. Harris make cookies for the bake sale tomorrow at the church and Harmony had a date with Zachary."

"A date?" Chester's eyes jutted out like he had never heard the word before. "A date where?"

"The movies I think. Some new one came out last week called *Fame*." Rachelle started reading the magazine again; wishing Chester would get quiet so she could read an article about Billy Dee Williams. Ever since *Lady Sings the Blues*, she'd been having intense sexual fantasies about him. "Chester, relax and watch the show. Harmony and Fatima are double dating so there's nothing to worry about."

Chester sat up on the edge of the seat with worry lines across his brow. "Hmph, Fatima is not exactly the portrait of virtue. The fact that she's with Harmony only makes it worse. What about that raggedy ass car of Zachary's? It looks like it's held together by duct tape. What if they break down in the middle of nowhere?"

"Chester, relax!" Rachelle rolled her eyes at him. She knew Chester always took stuff to the extreme. "Zachary's car is parked in the drive. I let them take our car."

"You let them do what?" Chester yelled, almost knocking the coffee table over when he jumped up and headed out into the hallway.

Rachelle got up to follow him. She discerned trying to read about Billy Dee was a lost cause. Chester would undoubtedly pace the floor; ranting and raving until the girls came home and were all accounted for.

She was trying to think of something to say or do that would placate his nerves when they heard the kitchen door slam. Chester half-ran to the rear of the house, startling Lucky who was searching the fridge for something sweet to drink.

"Where's Bryce?" Chester demanded to know without so much as a hello.

"Oh, hi Daddy!" Lucky glanced at him for a second and then stuck her head back in the fridge.

"Lucky, I asked you where Bryce is? Is she still next door?"

"Actually..." Lucky began hesitantly, running a series of possible cover-up stories through her mind. "Bryce didn't go over Mrs. Harris' with me."

Rachelle jumped in then. "She didn't? Then where did she go? She hasn't been here all evening."

"Umm, she went over to Brenda's house to get her history book. She accidentally left it over there yesterday and she needs it to do homework this weekend."

"That does it!" Chester hissed. "Rachelle, I'm not going to have these chaps running the streets at all times of the night. Where's the phone book?"

Rachelle went to the living room to retrieve the phone book while Chester lit into Lucky. "Why didn't you make Bryce go with you? You knew good and well the two of you were supposed to be together."

"Daddy, Bryce is older than me! She won't listen to me! *I tried to tell her!*" Lucky threw her most virtuous look at him, sitting down at the kitchen table to gulp down her cup of juice. She could tell he was *past* pissed off. It looked like steam was coming out of his ears. "Daddy, guess what?"

"What?" Chester snapped back at her, not really interested in hearing anything that didn't pertain to Bryce's whereabouts.

Lucky was determined to change the subject. "Did you know that W.A. Lavalette invented the printing press?"

"Naw, I didn't know that," Chester mumbled.

"Well, he did." Lucky wrapped her pint-size hand around the glass, hoping that Bryce would show up soon. She hated lying to her parents. "I have a book upstairs about it, if you want me to go get it."

Chester was about to yell at her and tell her *"Hell naw!"* but caught himself. After all, it wasn't Lucky's fault that Bryce was a fast ass. As much as they showed out, Chester loved his three daughters undeniably. He gazed at Lucky, sitting there with the smooth caramel skin, sepia eyes, and cinematic smile Rachelle had passed on to all of their children. "No, that's okay, Sweetie," he replied. "You can show it to me tomorrow."

"Okay, Daddy. I will." Lucky bit her bottom lip, contemplating whether or not it was a good time to ask him if she could cut her hair short, wear an afro, and get a nose ring. "Daddy, if it's okay with you..."

Before she could finish her sentence, all hell broke loose in the Whitfield household. Chester heard the front door slam and a car screeching out of the driveway at the same time. He peeped out the kitchen window and saw the taillights of Zachary's tin can car moving at the speed of light.

"Bryce, I'm going to kill you!" Harmony blared from the front hall. "I'm going to rip your eyeballs out and shove them up your nosy ass!"

Chester ran to the front, screaming on his way. "No one uses the word ass in this here house but me! What the hell is going on here?" he demanded to know.

"Daddy, I'll tell you what's going on here," Harmony began, shoving Bryce into Fatima and knocking them both down on the steps. "Bryce hid in the back of the station wagon while Fatima and I were out on a date."

Chester's eyes ballooned as he glared at Bryce. "Say what?"

Bryce jumped up off of the steps so she could exonerate herself. "Daddy, before you go off, you really should be thanking me."

"Thanking you for what?" Harmony questioned, wondering what kind of bullshit Bryce was shoveling this time.

"Thanking me for making you keep your drawers on for one thing," Bryce blurted out, rolling her sepia eyes at Harmony.

Rachelle jumped all up in the mix at the mere reference to undergarments. "What's all this about drawers?"

"Bryce, I swear if you say one more word, I'm going to make you wish you were dead!" Harmony screamed at her, pinching her arm and almost drawing blood.

"Let go of me," Bryce insisted, pulling her arm away. "You're the one who was about to get busy in Daddy's car. Then we all would've had to pile in there to go to church tomorrow and sit on Zachary's cum."

"What the hell do you know about cum?" Chester demanded to know. Before Bryce could answer him, he decided he was getting a bit more information than he cared to. "That's it! Everybody upstairs to bed!"

"But Daddy..." Bryce pleaded.

"Did you hear me? All of you get your little asses to bed!" He glanced over at Fatima. "You too, *Miss Thang*! Wait till I tell your parents about all of this!"

"But I didn't do anything!" Fatima protested.

"The hell you didn't!" Bryce snapped back at her. "You were about to suck Tony's wigger until the cops showed up and flashed that light in the car."

"Police? Lights? Sucking wiggers?" Rachelle couldn't take any more. She was likely to faint at any second.

Chester started taking off his wide-leather belt. "Did I stu-stu-stu-stutter? Every one of you better get upstairs now or I'm going to start whupping ass and taking names!"

They all knew he wasn't playing. Talking about sucking dick was the last straw. Harmony took off up the stairs with Fatima in fast pursuit. Bryce lagged slowly behind.

Chester yelled up the stairs after them. "In the morning, I'm laying down the law in this here house! All types of punishments! No more telephone time for you, Harmony, and I better not catch that Zachary around here again! I should've known that fool was only after one thing! Always coming over here, smiling all up in my grill! Tell him I'm going to drop kick his ass on sight! Just consider yourself grounded, Missy!" He heard Bryce chiding Harmony and went after her next. "As for you, Bryce, it will be a cold day in hell before I let your mother spend another dime of my hard-earned money on one of those floor mats you wear on your head! You've got that pretty head of *real* hair and you're always trying to cover it up with a wig! I never said it before but you look ridiculous! *Ri-di-cu-lous!* Now go to sleep!"

They all went into the bedroom that Harmony and Bryce

shared and slammed the door. Harmony and Fatima started talking trash about Bryce's wig.

"Damn, he said you look ridiculous!" Fatima cackled.

"Bryce does look stupid," Harmony concurred. "She looks like she stuck her finger in an electrical socket."

They gave each other high fives and guffawed while Bryce told them both, "Bite me, heifers!"

Lucky reluctantly went to bed, too. She and Bryce shared a room when they were younger but Bryce said she was sick of listening to Lucky preach about black power and moved her stuff in Harmony's room. Lucky didn't mind a bit. She appreciated the privacy because it gave her quiet time to read. Plus, she could hang up all the black posters she wanted. She grabbed a book about Black inventors off of her bookshelf, crawled up on her bed, and started reading. She knew the drama was far from over. Harmony and Bryce just loved to argue with each other.

Harmony, Bryce and Fatima changed into their nightclothes, smacking their lips and ridiculing one another the entire time. Bryce climbed on her bed while Harmony and Fatima managed to crowd onto the other twin bed together. Harmony reached over and turned off the lamp on the nightstand between the two beds. As soon as the lights went out, the tempers flared back up.

"Bryce, I want you to know that I will never, *ever* forgive you for this shit!" Harmony blared out in anger. "Tomorrow, I'm taking all those ugly ass wigs, especially the one you have on because it looks like Dorothy's house from the *Wizard of Oz* fell on your damn head, and burning them out behind the barn."

"You and what army, hoe?" Bryce questioned. "Touch my wigs, Harmony, and I'll tell Daddy what *really* happened."

"Hell, you might as well had already. You told him just about everything anyway."

"Not *everything*," Fatima interjected, worrying about whether Mr. Whitfield would carry through with his threat and tattle to her parents.

"Hmph, close enough," Harmony uttered with disdain. "Daddy's going to ground me for sure and it's all your fault."

"I didn't tell him you actually *did* do the nasty with Zachary on the hood of the car and that Fatima really *did* suck Tony's dang-a-lang," Bryce countered.

Harmony clamped her eyes shut, trying to hold back her anger. She was so sick of Bryce following her every damn place. There was only a three-year difference between them, but it was a significant one since Harmony was a junior in high school.

"Bryce, all I have to say is I can't wait until I go away to college. I'm leaving you, California, and all of your drama behind. I'm going to the East Coast. Probably Howard University in D.C."

"So am I," Fatima added. "Harmony and I are going to take Washington, D.C. by storm."

"That's cool," Bryce hissed. "So, you'll have a three year head start, but I *will* follow you. You'll never get rid of me. *Not ever!* When you take one of those big, gigantic, elephantine dumps like the ones you have after you eat Momma's sticky oatmeal for breakfast, I'm going to be there to smell it!"

"If you don't shut up in there, I'm going to whup all three of you!" Chester yelled through the closed door, startling them because they hadn't heard him come upstairs. "And Bryce, stop talking about your momma's cooking! You can't even make a bologna sandwich without almost cutting off a finger! You have a lot of damn nerve! Talking about somebody's cooking! Just for that, I'm making you cook dinner tomorrow! I want a roast with *all* the trimmings and a homemade apple pie! Since you thought you were too good to go over Mrs. Harris' tonight and bake, I'm *making* you do it tomorrow! I'm going to make sure I have some antacid on hand because I know it's going to be all burnt up and nasty!"

Bryce was about to say something sarcastic, but thought better of it. The last thing she wanted or needed was one of her daddy's whuppings. She wasn't even sweating the menu. She knew her mother wouldn't ever allow her to cook a Sunday dinner or dinner *period* for that matter. She let out a heavy sigh and stared at the silhouettes of Harmony and Fatima sprawled out on the other bed. As much as she hated to admit it, she adored Harmony. Harmony was like a goddess in her eyes. Bryce always wanted to look just like her. Even though they favored quite a bit already, Bryce didn't have the same style and demeanor as Harmony. Besides, Bryce knew Harmony would be a success at whatever career she chose. Bryce was determined to follow in her footsteps and she had the sneaking suspicion Lucky was just as determined to do the same.

"Chester, leave those girls alone and come to bed," Rachelle ordered from the master bedroom down the hall. "Enough is enough!"

"Enough is enough nothing," Chester mumbled and strutted down the hall to join Rachelle in bed. He turned around and made a group announcement to the entire house. "I missed the ending of *Starsky and Hutch*, I've got hard-headed chaps running the damn streets at all times of the night with fast ass boys, and Lucky thinks she's Malcolmenia X! I can't wait till breakfast! Some heads are gonna roll around here! You can take that to the bank! Shame on it all!"

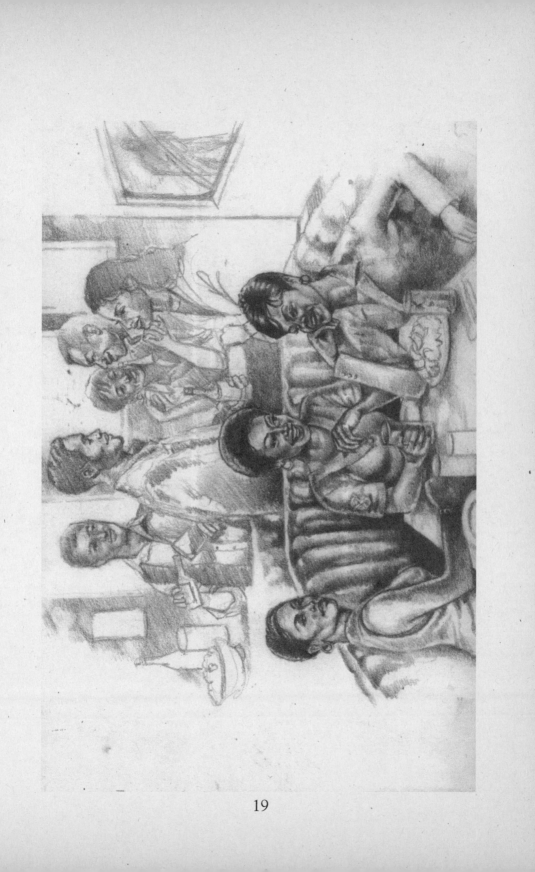

Ten Years Later

Part One:

Memorial Day Weekend

Chapter One

The Whitfield Sisters

Harmony was strategically positioned at the bar so she could view the front entrance of the BET Soundstage in Landover, MD. As usual, both of her trifling ass younger sisters were late. That's the very reason she never agreed to meet them for lunch during the week. She knew they would be at least a half hour late, take damn near an hour to eat because they would be too busy running their loud mouths, and spend another fifteen minutes on long ass good-byes in the parking lot.

However, it was a Saturday so it was all good. Besides, Harmony took pleasure from chillin' at the bar alone. Her frozen daiquiri was the bomb, she'd spent the early morning hours at the salon getting her hair and nails hooked up, and the brotha working magic behind the bar was so handsome, she wanted to give him a candlelight bubble bath and then lick him dry. She was wearing a new black designer pantsuit and sporting that bad boy with some gold hoop earrings and black pumps. All things considered, what more could a sista ask for?

She was pondering that very thought and halfway mesmerized

by Ginuwine's fine ass doing his rendition of Michael Jackson's *She's Out Of My Life* when someone slapped her upside the back of her head.

Harmony swiveled around on her stool, ready to give some sorry mofo a tongue-lashing and possibly a knee to the groin. Instead, all she encountered was her crazy ass sister.

"Bryce!" Harmony exclaimed as she gave her a love-slap across the cheek. "*Gurlllll*, I was about to go the hell off!"

"Harmony, give me a break." Bryce rolled her eyes. "You know good and damn well your ass is not about to go off on a complete stranger. Lucky and I, yes. Stranger, no."

"Hmph! You never know. I've been doing those Tae-Bo tapes. I might drop kick a nucca every now and then."

"The hell you say!" Bryce plopped down on the stool beside her, looking exhausted.

Harmony eyed her sister up and down in awe, wondering how in the hell she got into the skintight white bodysuit she was profiling in. "Damn, Bryce! You wear the tightest ass clothes I've ever seen. Who are you supposed to be? Lil' Kim or Foxy Brown?"

Bryce flipped her the finger with one hand and waved the sexy ass bartender over with the other one.

"What can I get for you?" he asked. Bryce was immediately turned on by his deep voice.

She leaned up over the bar and was all too obvious about peeping the dick size. "Well actually, I'd like two drinks. A sloe screw followed by an orgasm. Unless, of course, you want to break a sista off with the real thing."

"Damn, Boo!" He flashed a happy grin, realizing that freaks don't always come out at night. "So it's like that, huh?"

"And you know this."

He sucked his teeth like a death row inmate about to receive his last meal, a pussy burger with no mayo, and walked to the opposite side of the bar to retrieve the bottle of gin.

Harmony gawked at their Ghettoized version of *Romeo and Juliet*. "Bryce, have you no tact?"

"No tact at all," Bryce proudly announced and leaned up further over the bar so she could peep the ass.

He glanced at Bryce over his shoulder, licked his lips, and blushed.

Harmony had a streak of jealousy in her, but hell would freeze over before she ever fessed up to it. She secretly admired the fact that Bryce was so outgoing with the male species. Harmony was the shy, conservative type but, then again, there was an aggressive side to her. She proved that on Memorial Day weekend. She bit her bottom lip, reminiscing about the wickedness she'd done and wondered if either one of her sisters would even believe her if she spilled the beans over lunch.

"Here are your drinks," the bartender said provocatively, placing two glasses in front of Bryce along with a number scribbled on a cocktail napkin. "And here is my number. Give me a call sometime so we can discuss the real thing."

He winked and walked off.

"You know he's a playa," Harmony remarked. "He didn't even ask your name. What are you gonna do? Call him and say, '*I'm the hoochie who had on the white outfit so tight you could see my pubic hairs?*' "

"You're just jealous cause he wants me."

"I doubt that, Sis! That man probably has more bitches than the electric company has switches."

"Whatever!"

Bryce and Harmony were busy checking out a matronly-looking woman on the video screen when Lucky pranced in sporting a Negro League baseball jersey and black wide-legged jeans. Bryce thought it was so cool for the BET Soundstage to put people on the screens that were celebrating their birthdays and anniversaries. Most people only get ten minutes of fame in their entire lives and that was one of them.

Before Lucky could even attempt to hug one of them, Harmony was whisking towards the hostess station to see if they could get a table right that second and Bryce was up and running with a drink in each hand.

"Well, damn chicas! I guess I'll just show ya'll some sisterly love later!" Lucky clucked her tongue in disgust.

Bryce had a change of heart, turned around, and managed to hug Lucky without spilling the drinks. "Hey, Baby Sis! How's it going?"

Lucky returned the embrace and kissed Bryce lightly on the cheek. "Just chillin, Sis. Med school is kicking my ass though."

"You're a Whitfield and Whitfields never quit."

"Gurl, you ain't never lied."

"Are you two coming sometime today or what?" Harmony brushed past them, following the hostess to their table.

"What's with her?"

"Hell if I know, Lucky," Bryce responded. "You know how Harmony gets when things aren't picture perfect. She lets emotions ball up inside her like a knot and then explodes."

Lucky nodded in agreement. "True that!"

Once they were comfortably seated in a booth with their own little personal video screen kicking out various music videos, Harmony suddenly became peppy and almost scared both Lucky and Bryce half to death.

"So, what's new with you ladies?" She gleamed at them with her big, sepia eyes and her natural beauty was never more forthcoming. "How's school, Lucky?"

"Fine." Lucky only spoke one word because she sensed Harmony's demeanor was the calm before the storm. She'd been through the ordeal too many times not to recognize it.

"That's great!" Harmony opened her menu and then glanced over at Bryce. "How are things going at the investment firm?"

"Everything's cool," Bryce answered, waiting for the other shoe to drop, too.

"Marvelous!"

Bryce and Lucky, who were seated on one side of the booth opposite Harmony, gave each other that *ut-oh* look.

Harmony ignored the interchange between them. "I think I'll have a crab cake sandwich with some black beans and rice. I love their rice recipe."

Other than ordering their food and another round of drinks,

there was silence at the table for a few minutes. Lucky spent the quiet time checking out all the brothas walking past their table or lounging at the bar.

The lack of conversation became too much for Bryce to handle. "How are things at the temp agency, Harmony?"

"Marvelous," Harmony reiterated.

Damn, not that marvelous again. Bryce sat there trying to figure out a way to break the ice.

"I may not tell you this often enough, Harmony, but I'm extremely proud of you. Starting your own temp agency and everything."

Harmony crossed her freshly-manicured hands on the table in front of her. "Thanks, Bryce. I'm very proud of you, too. Both of you."

Lucky was only halfway paying attention. She was caught up in Jon B's *They Don't Know* video.

Harmony ignored her blatant disregard of the compliment. "So, what's the younger generation been up to lately?"

That comment hardly went unnoticed. Lucky put her hands on her hips out of pure habit, even though no one could see them underneath the booth, glared at Harmony, and objected. "You're always on this younger generation kick. You're only three years older than Bryce and five years older than I am. Geesh!"

"Well, I'm still older," Harmony snapped back. "I would implore you to remember that."

"Implore?" Lucky put her elbows on the table and rested her chin on her palms. "Now I'm positive Bryce and I are in for it. You only start acting prissy and using big words when you're pissed off."

"I'm not pissed off!" People in the adjoining booths began to stare so Harmony lowered her voice to a near whisper and repeated, "I'm not upset."

"Whatever," Bryce stated and went back to watching videos.

Harmony decided that she wasn't even going out like that. She would show them. "For your information, I did something over the Memorial Day weekend that I'm very elated about." *Well, kind of elated about.*

"Really?" Bryce questioned with skepticism. "What might that be? Did you volunteer to feed the homeless or some other *holier-than-thou* activity?"

Harmony threw daggers at Bryce through her eyes. "Very funny!" Bryce and Lucky both snickered. "Actually, I had sex. *Wild, freaky sex.* The sort that makes your hair frizz up and look like you lost a fight with the lawnmower."

Bryce and Lucky eyed each other before they both inquired, "And?"

Lucky added, "You've been fucking Zachary since Momma thought Billy Dee Williams was the sexiest man alive. Big deal."

"Um, pardon me, Gurlfriend," Bryce interjected. "But Billy Dee is *still* the sexiest man alive. Did you see the way his ass cheeks looked in those suits in *Mahogany* and *Lady Sings the Blues?*"

"Zachary and I broke up over a month ago," Harmony blurted out while she had the nerve.

"Say what, Sis?" Bryce was all ears, completely forgetting about Billy Dee. "You and Zachary broke up? Fa *realllllllllllllll?*"

"Yes, we mutually decided the most feasible solution was to part ways."

"Could you kill the big words and just get jiggy with it," Lucky snapped. "It's hard enough to understand your ass half the time as it is. Why did you guys split? Was he going downtown to only window shop and not actually buying anything?"

Bryce and Lucky started snickering again.

"You are so nasty," Harmony hissed.

"Hmph, if you only knew. Wait till you hear what *I* got into Memorial Day weekend. Better yet, it was more like what got into me."

"Well, what *I* did tops everything the two of you hoochies did put together," Bryce boasted with pride. "Harmony, your hair might have been messed up and mine would have been tore da hell up too if I didn't have this fly ass weave."

"It's fly all right." Harmony chuckled. "Fly if the person looking at it is half blind in one eye and can't see a damn thing out the other one."

Bryce flipped Harmony the finger. "Whatever, heifer. "

Lucky reached over the table, giving Harmony a high five. "Good one, Sis!"

Bryce rolled her eyes and smacked her lips. "Like I was saying, what I did put whatever you two did to shame. My hair was straight, as always, but my makeup was smeared like crazy afterwards."

"What is this? A hoe competition?" Harmony shook her head and added, "Shame on it all!"

"Come off it, Harmony. So you got some wigger. Big fucking deal," Bryce chided as she took another swig of her orgasm.

"Okay, Bryce, forget it. I was going to tell you all the freaky shit I did, but I wouldn't want to bore you."

Lucky's eyes widened as she jumped up in her seat. "I wanna hear about the freaky shit you did! *Who'd you fuck? Huh, huh? Who'd you fuck?*"

Harmony curtained her forehead, trying to hide her embarrassment while one of the male wait staff dispersed their plates to them off a large, brown tray.

After he was out of earshot, Harmony glared at Lucky. "Calm the hell down!"

"This is so damn silly." Bryce added her two cents. "Harmony may have gotten some dick, but her ass didn't do *nothing* freaky."

"Are you sure about all that, Bryce?" Harmony challenged her.

"I'm damn sure." Harmony started throwing eye daggers again. Bryce added insult to injury. "Hell, Zachary probably dumped your ass because you were boring the shit out of him in bed."

Lucky punched Bryce in the ribs with her elbow. "That's a low blow, even for you."

Bryce turned her attention to her steaming platter of baked fish. "Whatever!"

Lucky started chowing down on her Cajun shrimp, but Harmony didn't even pick up her fork.

"Harmony, could you stop staring at me like that while I'm trying to eat?" Bryce rolled her eyes and stuck out her tongue. "You're getting on my last nerve. Geesh, if looks could kill."

"If looks could kill, you'd be one dead hoochie. And keep that nasty tongue of yours in your mouth. We don't need any germs floating all over our food. There's no telling where your tongue has been lately."

"Whatever!" Bryce took a swig of her drink. "It's been some-place your tongue hasn't. That's for *damn* sure. Licking all over a big, juicy, elephantine dick. Your ass is too prissy to suck dick. That's why Zachary flew the coop."

Harmony pushed her untouched plate to the side. Lucky wished she had a hair weave like Bryce to use as a protective hel-met from the verbal bullets about to be fired. Much to her surprise, Harmony's voice was rather calm. "All right, Bryce. Since you think you're sporting the bomb ass pussy between your legs and have such an exciting sex life, amuse me. Tell me, tell *us,* what you did Memorial Day weekend."

"No, you go first, Harmony," Bryce replied. "Age before beauty."

"What, you're scared now? You're worried that I might have actually done something more erotic than you?"

"Erotic? Chile, please! The closest you ever get to erotic is ordering lace drawers from the Victoria's Secret catalog."

"Hmm, just like I figured," Harmony lashed back. "Chicken!"

Lucky laughed and started flapping her elbows, almost knocking Bryce's plate onto the floor.

Bryce caught it. "Okay, since you seem to be so damn interested, I'll gladly tell you. *But,* there's one condition."

"Which is?" Harmony asked with a lifted brow.

"If I tell the two of you what I did Memorial Day, you *both* have to do the same and not hold anything back."

"Deal," agreed Lucky.

Harmony nodded and also agreed. "Deal."

"Cool! So, we don't leave here until all the dirt flies. Period!" Bryce pushed her own plate aside so she could have some elbow room while she was relating her erotic adventure. "Aiight, here it goes. Ironically, it all started when this nucca called me a bitch."

Harmony smirked. "Figures!"

Chapter Two

The Feeling's Mutual

"**Y**ou stupid bitch! Can't you fucking see?"

I just knew this man was not talking to me. I glanced over at Colette, my homegurl who was sitting beside me in the passenger seat, searching for some sort of reassurance that the silly mutha fucka didn't mean me. I don't know what it is about *the B word* but the shit sets me off.

I yelled out the window of my car back at him. "Fuck you! You fucking piece of shit!"

He yelled out, "Deez Nuts!" flipped me the finger, put the pedal to the metal, then screeched off in his red Mazda RX-7 with the personalized license plate that read "THE MAN."

I was cursing under my breath while he pulled off from the light, trick ass. "I hate it when people cut me off in traffic and then pretend like it's my fault and shit! Men can't fucking drive anyway! They're only good for one thing!"

Colette laughed, trying to calm me down some. "Bryce, don't sweat it, Girl. Shit happens, ya know?"

That didn't help much. "I know shit happens, but *still*. He pulls out in front of me, when I had the right of way, and then has the audacity to call me a bitch! Fuck him!"

"Now that you mention it, Sis, I wouldn't mind." I glared at Colette. She was grinning from ear to ear. "Well damn, Bryce. He was fine as all hell. If I met him in a club or something, I would tear his ass up."

"You know what, Colette? You're getting too old to be thinking with your coochie-coo. You need to start thinking with your mind."

"Damn, what crawled up your ass and died? You're in such a bitchy mood today!"

I left it at that cause I didn't want to have to get medieval on her ass. I turned the radio up so loud the bass was making my gas pedal vibrate. Colette got the hint that I didn't care to discuss it any further. First, the asshole in the other car calls me a bitch and then my own friend calls me bitchy. The day was getting off to a messed up start and I didn't like it. I didn't like it one iota.

Truth is, they were both correct about me being bitchy. George and I had a big quarrel the night before on the phone. He called me from his so-called *business* trip talking trash and asking me a bunch of questions about what I was doing while he was away. That pissed me off because I read somewhere that over eighty-percent of men, married or not, take condoms with them on business trips just in case they get lucky. On top of that, it's a commonly known fact that men only ask a bunch of questions and throw accusations when their asses are guilty themselves. They figure the woman must also be cheating since they are.

I had been through the scenario too many times before and I knew George was nothing but a playa. I laid awake the night before musing over it and decided it just wasn't worth it. As soon as he returned from his trip, I was calling it off. After all, the only way to get respect is to demand it and accept nothing less.

I almost missed my turn because my mind was wandering. I came to my senses and started concentrating on my driving instead of my shitty ass man. Colette and I were on the way to a Memorial Day cookout at our friend Lamar's house out in Upper Marlboro, MD. I was more than ready to get there. I was stressed and needed to sit down underneath a shade tree with a brewsky and chill. A small part of me was hoping I might find a decent man there, but I wasn't about to hold my breath. Good men are like good hair-dressers. Hard as hell to find.

We made the last turn before getting to his house and could see all the cars parked up and down the street. Colette broke the silence and turned the radio all the way down. "Damn, look at all these peeps. I know I'm going to find me some action up in this piece."

I rolled my eyes at her, not wanting to divulge the fact I was halfway hoping to find me some action, too. I turned the radio back up while I looked for a place to park cause my cut, *Untitled* by D'Angelo, was on. I just love the way he grins at his dick during that video. Talk about power of the imagination. I can just imagine him slinging it this-a-way.

You ever notice how people turn the radio all the way down or completely off when they start approaching their destination instead of waiting till they park? It's almost like they're trying to creep up on the place and the radio will somehow give them away. Makes no sense because it's not like people can't hear the car motor and besides, why creep anyway? I think it's just one of those subconscious things people develop a habit of doing.

I was looking for a spot, listening to my cut, and wondering why Colette had turned it down in the first place when I saw it. "Fuck! Ain't this some shit!"

Colette had no idea what I was talking about. "What's wrong, Girl? You okay?"

I could only manage to point. Colette looked in the direction my finger was aiming and immediately saw the problem. A red RX-7 with a tag saying "THE MAN" was parked in Lamar's driveway. I wanted to scream.

I drove all the way across town for this cookout, thinking I would at least have a halfway decent time, chilling out with friends, playing cards, eating some grilled chicken and corn on the cob, whatever. Why did that trick ass have to be at the same cookout? Shame on it all!

Colette reached over and started patting my shoulder. "Bryce, it's all good. Just ignore his ass. Hell, I'll keep him occupied so he won't bother you."

I jerked my shoulder so her hand would let loose and started parallel parking in the one space left on the entire block, other than in front of the fire hydrant. I wasn't about to get a ticket so I squeezed my car into the cramped space.

Colette was getting on my last nerve but neither she nor "THE MAN" was going to ruin my day. I'd come to have a good time and that's exactly what I planned to do. Let's face it. There was no point in even going unless I was willing to put forth some effort to have fun.

After I successfully maneuvered into the space and cut the engine, Colette and I did *the female thing*: looked in the mirrors and primped. I used the rear view mirror while she utilized the one under the sun visor. We had to make sure our lipstick and eyeliner weren't smudging, there was no lipstick on our teeth and, of course, we had to make sure there was not a single strand of hair out of place.

After we both made sure we were looking *foine*, we got out the car and started walking the half block to Lamar's house. The scent of BBQ ribs and chicken was in the breeze. I could hardly wait to sink my teeth into a little sumptin' sumptin'. I skipped breakfast on purpose so I would be good and hungry by the time we got to the cookout.

We could hear people laughing and talking loudly as we got closer, along with the faint noise of some music playing. Probably from a little boom box. We walked past the front door and headed straight for the gate leading to the backyard. I know the feeling when people start tracking through the inside of your house when the party is really outside. So other than going inside to use the restroom, I always stay outdoors.

There is always an exception to the rule. My exception came when I went in the back yard and that trick ass started bothering me. We spotted each other at the same time, both of us had that *I'm-gonna-kick-your-fucking-ass* expression on our faces. I had him at a disadvantage because, after seeing his car out front, I knew he was there already. He was in a state of shock. I was hoping he had a weak heart and would keel the fuck over right then and there.

He was on the opposite side of the yard from the gate, talking to some hoochie with long, fake nails and a weave that looked like one of those you can put on layaway. It figured he would be into women with no class since he had none his damn self. I have a weave, but my shit looks good.

Colette broke my damn concentration. "Bryce, I see Lamar over there. I'm going to go speak and see what the haps are."

"Okay, I'll be around here someplace. I'm about to grab sumptin' to drink and find an available chair in the shade."

"Kewl!" With that she switched off, utilizing the walk she spent years perfecting. I really should've gone with her to speak to Lamar since he was the host, but he was on the other side of the lawn near that *thing* and I wasn't about to go anywhere near him.

I saw a group of guys standing around an oak tree and figured that must be where the beer cooler was located. I was right and asked one of them to hand me a Miller Light. They all started looking me over and not even trying to fake the funk. Men and women are totally different. Women check men out, too. Everything from their shoes to their fingernails to their dicks, but we do it with style.

I found a nice spot in the shade and plopped down on a comfortable lounger. I was sitting there minding my own damn business when "THE MAN" came walking straight towards me.

Before he could even open his mouth, I got in his ass. "Look, I'm really not in the mood for this. We had a near miss car accident, we were both angry, and the shit is over with now. So just take your ass back over there and it's all good."

He laughed at me, the trick. "First of all, I was coming over here to apologize to you and introduce myself, but I can see you're in a foul ass mood."

As mad as I was at him, seeing him up close was not such a bad thing. Colette was right. He was fine as hell. He looked to be about 5' 9" and he was cut. He had hazel eyes and a caramel complexion. I was thinking of lowering my guard, allowing him to apologize and all of that. Then, I remembered him calling me a bitch and flipping me the finger.

"You're right. I'm in a foul ass mood. As far as an introduction, I don't wanna know your ass. You already called me bitch, so that's my name. Go back over there and talk to that frog-faced hoe and leave me the fuck alone."

"*Okay, BITCH!*" he spewed at me.

I was about to get up off the chair and ram my foot up his ass, but he walked away too fast.

We managed to avoid each other until I got in the long line of peeps rushing to fix a plate once the food was ready. I felt someone breathing down my neck, turned around, and his skank ass was in line behind me.

I was starving and all that jazz, but I wasn't about to be anywhere near him. I admit I was acting immature about the entire thing. However, there was something about him that irked the hell out of me.

I told the guy I had been chatting with most of the afternoon, who was standing beside me in line, that I wasn't hungry after all and would catch up to him later.

As I walked away, I turned around and rolled my eyes at the trick. I went inside Lamar's house through his living room patio doors, on my way to the powder room on the first floor. I didn't have to go. I just wanted a moment of peace without having so many people around.

George had obviously gotten to me on the phone more than I realized. I felt so stressed, every muscle in my body seemed tense.

I went in the powder room and glared in the mirror. I looked at myself, wondering why I always got all the losers. It isn't like I'm ugly. In fact, far from it. I'm 5'4", 128 lb. with a deep caramel complexion and sepia eyes. I spend a lot of time making myself look nice and hours and hours at the gym keeping my body in shape.

I turned sideways to look at my physique in the mirror. My tits were firm and so was my ass. They both looked succulent in the mocha, skintight spandex dress I was wearing. My hair was straight. I even peeped my toes and they looked good to go.

Still, for the life of me I couldn't figure out why all the maggots of the world gravitated in my direction. After I made sure my makeup was all in place, I opened the bathroom door, planning to return to the cookout. I figured the food line was probably down to a minimum by then and the asshole should be sitting down some-where feeding his face.

I was glancing down at my purse, replacing the lipstick, when I bumped right into his trick ass. He'd apparently been waiting to take a leak.

He snarled at me. "Well, excuse you!"

"Let me tell you something! You don't know me, but *I am not the one* and this isn't the day to be fucking with me, aiight?" I start-ed to walk away from him when he grabbed me by the arm and swung me around.

"Listen, Baby, I apologize okay? I shouldn't have acted so ugly towards you this morning in the car or after you got here. I'm real-ly not a bad person."

I rolled my eyes. "Can I have my arm back?"

He let go, extending his hand to me. "I'm Troy."

I took his hand and shook it, but still didn't tell him my name.

"Let's try this again. I'm Troy and you are?"

"Bryce." I threw him half a smile since his eyes were kind of turning me on.

"Nice to meet you, Bryce."

"Same here." I pulled my hand away from him, not even real-izing he still had a firm grip on it. "Well, I'm going to go get some food now. Peace."

With that, I walked away. I could feel his sexy eyes boring a hole through my ass until I hit the patio doors and went back outside.

Colette came rushing up to me. "Uh huh, I saw your fresh behind in there talking to him. Spill it, Girl!"

"Colette, please calm the hell down. He just apologized. That's it." I headed towards the food table, leaving her standing there in all of her hoochiness.

"Yeah, right. Whatever, Bryce."

I finally got my eat on and was sitting under a shade tree talk-ing to Lamar and downing another brewsky when I noticed Troy pointing at me. He was standing in the middle of a group of skeez-ers and making hand motions, as if he was turning a steering wheel. I couldn't believe his trick ass had apologized, then turned around and starting talking shit about me to other people.

My head started aching something fierce so I asked Lamar, "Baby, do you mind if I go lie down in your basement for a little while? My head is killing me. I think it's just the sun."

"Sure, Baby! Want some Tylenol?" Lamar was a sweetheart, as always. He and I had almost gotten a little thing going on when we first met, but things never panned out. Just one of those things.

"No, thanks. I'll be fine." I got up and started walking towards the house.

"Shit, you're already fine!" I turned around and winked at Lamar. "You can go upstairs and lie down in my bedroom if you like. It's more comfortable."

"Naw, Boo, the basement is fine. It's cooler down there and I think it will make my head clear up faster."

"Okay, Boo."

I walked past Troy, profiling for his hoochie harem, rolling my eyes at him on my way into the house. I went down in Lamar's basement and noticed he'd gotten a pool table since the last time I'd visited. I've always loved playing pool. My sisters and I used to play pool in my grandparents' basement when we were kids.

I flipped through Lamar's extremely diverse CD collection, discovered a compilation of slow jams, put it in, and turned it on. After a couple of minutes, I realized I was too excited to lie still and got up. I didn't know why I was excited. Just was. George had been away a few days and dick is like oxygen. You don't miss it till it's gone. I was mad horny.

The pool table seemed to be calling out my name so I went over and racked the balls. To me, playing pool alone is just as much fun as playing with someone else.

I was seriously out of practice. I had a hard time getting the first three balls in. It was then that I heard the basement door open and close, followed by footsteps coming down the carpeted stairs.

I figured Lamar had decided to come check on me. "Lamar, I'm knocking around a few balls. Hope you don't mind."

"Knocking balls around, huh? Sounds kinky!"

I couldn't freakin' believe it. It wasn't Lamar. It was Troy's trick ass again. "What *is* your problem? Now you're following me around and shit?"

He laughed. "Don't flatter yourself. I was just coming to see if you're all right and to find out if I'm the reason you came inside."

"*NEE-AH-GRO, pleasssse!* Now who's flattering themselves?" I igged his ass and went back to playing pool. "You have some serious issues."

"Can I play?" He was standing right beside the pool table, peeping my ass while I was bent over setting up my next move.

"Hell no, you can't play trick. What you can do is leave."

"You know what? I thought you and I might be able to work things out at first but I can see now, you're a lost cause." He turned around and headed towards the stairs.

"I don't say this often." I was really pissed off at that point. Pissed off with a wet pussy. "I get along with most people, but I hate your fucking guts."

He reeled around quickly, walked up to me, pushed his hips up against mine, forced my ass up against the pool table, looked deep into my eyes, and snarled, "Yeah? Well the feeling's mutual."

I reached my hand up to slap his trick ass across the face. He caught my wrist before impact. I tried to slap him with the other one. He got a hold of it also. Then...

...We started tonguing the shit out each other. Don't get me wrong. I did hate his ass at that very moment. I just wanted to fuck him unconscious, too.

We tore into each other like animals. Troy let go of my wrists. I threw my arms around him, pulling his tongue deeper into my mouth. I've never wanted anyone as bad as I wanted him. Trick ass.

He pushed my dress up over my hips and lifted my ass onto the table while I straddled my legs around his back, using my calves to pull him onto the table with me.

We were both breathing radically heavy as we continued the kiss. He elevated me and sat me further back on the table, darting his eyes back and forth while he pushed all the balls out the way. He grabbed my wrists again and forced my back on the table. The entire time, we never stopped kissing. It was like our tongues were stuck together.

We both shut our eyes and got lost in each other, letting all the passion mixed with anger erupt through our tongues.

My legs were still straddled around his back when Troy finally decided to take a breather. He started ripping at my dress, pulling both spaghetti straps down at the same time so he could get at my nipples.

He starting sucking on my left one, burying his nose completely into it. I was moaning loudly, which was unusual for me. I'm normally extremely quiet during lovemaking. It was different with Troy because we weren't making love. We were making hate.

He was holding me down. The shit wasn't even necessary cause my ass wasn't going anywhere. We heard some footsteps overhead, someone bound for the powder room probably. I broke one of my hands loose and started pulling his shorts down from the rear. I wanted some dick and I wanted it bad.

Troy stopped sucking on my breast and helped me get his shorts down and off. He didn't take the time to pull my panties down over my legs. He ripped those suckers clear off. He got down off of the table, leaving me there breathing shallow, walked around to the other side, and started sucking my breasts upside down while he climbed on top of me.

He grabbed both of them, squeezed hard, and pushed them upward towards his face. He released them, moved his head further south, and bit all over my stomach on his way down to my pussy. His body began to overshadow mine until his dick knocked me slap in the forehead.

I grabbed a hold of it like a leech and started deep throating that bad boy. He spread my legs open and began sucking on my clit, digging his entire face in. I lifted my hips up off of the table, grinding my pussy onto his face while he pumped his dick in and out my mouth.

He paused just long enough to make a lewd comment. "That's right. Knock them balls around."

I pushed his dick out of my mouth and reconfirmed what I'd said earlier. "I fucking hate you."

He laughed. "The feeling's mutual." Then, he started sucking on my pussy again. I decided to fix his ass and tried to suck his dick the hell off. I thought he would scream out in pain but he loved the shit. So, I bit him. He retaliated and bit me.

I pushed his ass off of me and came up swinging. He pinned my arms down and hollered, "Chill! DAYUM!"

I wasn't taking any more of his shit. I started kicking and hitting him with all the strength I could muster. He finally managed to get control of the situation again. I submitted to him, but only because he had rammed his dick inside me and it was all that.

He wasn't hung like a bear but his dick was thick, just like I prefer them. I favor dicks that won't knock the bottom out the well but will rub the hell out the walls. He tore my little coochie coo up.

Troy pushed my legs up as far as they would go and I wrapped my ankles around his neck. He started pounding his dick in and out of my pussy walls. I came the first time about two minutes into the act.

I was kind of repentant, fucking a stranger in a friend's basement and all, but not disgraced enough to stop. He pulled his dick out and whispered in my ear. "Turn my pussy over so I can hit it from the back."

I obediently turned over and got on my knees. He started catapulting his dick in and out of me. "Your pussy? Fuck you, Troy. You trick ass."

He laughed again. I hated it when he laughed. "Yeah, fuck me. Fuck me like you hate me." Then as an afterthought, he added, "Oh, that's right. You do hate me."

He snatched my hair, compelling me to arch my back and bring my pussy further back onto his dick. I could feel his balls slamming up against my thighs. My pussy juice was dripping down on the felt cover of the pool table.

We fucked for a good hour. I had never seen a man who took so long to bust a nut before. I think some extra blood must have dashed to his dick cause he was so full of anger.

Finally, and I do mean *finally*, he detonated inside me like a nuclear bomb. By the time he came, my pussy was inflamed and my knees were stinging from being in the doggy position for so long.

We fucked for so long, the CD I put on had finished playing and the changer had switched over to the next one.

Lamar opened the basement door and shouted down the steps. "You okay down there, Bryce?"

After catching my breath, I hollered back. "I'm fine, thanks! I'll be up in a minute!"

We heard the door shut and Lamar's footsteps as he walked away. Lamar was no fool. He knew the deal.

I somehow regained my self-control, got my clothes adjusted, scooped my torn panties up off the floor, and shoved them in my pocketbook. I didn't say another word to Troy. I left his ass lying there, half-naked on the pool table.

When I got back outside, I grabbed Colette by the arm and told her it was time to go. She didn't put up a fight. We told everyone goodbye and left. She tried to grill me in the car about what happened in the basement. I cranked up the radio and refused to comment.

The Response

"Why are you looking at me like that?" Bryce was pleased with herself, knowing there was no way in the world that they could top that. "I warned you it was some wild ass shit."

"Hmmm, that was mediocre," Harmony stated snidely.

"Mediocre?" Bryce was astonished.

"It was aiight," Lucky wholeheartedly agreed, taking another bite of her food.

Bryce took a quick inventory of the expressions on both their faces and it was painfully obvious that no one was impressed.

"Bryce," Harmony interjected. "Sleeping with roughnecks and playas is nothing new for you. Less than an hour ago, you were throwing yourself at the bartender."

"Whatever!"

"I'm serious. You slept with a guy at the BBQ, totally disrespected yourself, and the messed up part is you will probably fuck him again the second he comes sniffing around."

"I'm getting tired of doing this, but here goes." Bryce vehemently flipped Harmony the finger. "First of all, Troy doesn't even have my phone number. Secondly, I'm living with George and thirdly, I wouldn't fuck Troy again if my life depended on it. Not in this lifetime."

"You know that mofo is destined to get your number from Lamar so he can make some late night booty calls at your crib," Lucky commented, as if from experience.

"I'm dead serious," Bryce insisted. "That was a one shot deal. I hate his trick ass. I was just horny as hell that weekend. I would fuck a nucca with a peg leg before I let Troy tap this again."

Lucky and Harmony exchanged looks. They both knew Bryce was lying her ass off. They knew if the nucca showed up at her door with a Happy Meal and a Coke that she would spread 'em.

Especially the way she was bragging on his dick.

"N-E-Way, I refuse to believe ya'll outfreaked me. I'm willing to keep an open mind about this, *but* I won't believe it till you lay it all out."

Lucky and Harmony grinned at each other as if they shared some deep, dark secret.

"A deal is a damn deal. Your turn, Harmony. Let's hear about how Sista Harmony, Grand Priestess of the DC Chapter of the Sexually-Repressed, got her freak on."

"Yeah, let's hear it." Lucky chuckled.

"Fine. You both know Fatima," Harmony stated more as a comment than a question.

"Hell yeah, we know Fatima. Ya'll been best friends forever." Lucky was getting impatient. "Can you just tell your story sometime today please?"

"I'm about to tell it right now, but you might want to hold onto your seats. What happened to me is unfuckinbelievable!"

"Whatever," Bryce snarled, hoping Harmony wasn't about to take her *Freak of the Whitfield Clan* title away from her.

Chapter Three

That's What Friends Are For

"**H**armony, will you fuck my husband for me?" When Fatima blurted it out, over club sandwiches and chips in the cozy cafe where we meet for lunch twice a week, I thought my ears were playing tricks on me. I took a good look at the expression on her face and realized she was as serious as a heart attack.

"What the fuck are you talking about, Sis?"

"I want out of this marriage. Javon is nothing but a low down, cheating ass dog and I'm sick of it." Fatima was all but in tears as she continued. I was speechless. "I know he's cheating on me. I've been trying to catch his ass in the act for over a year now. Spying on him, going through his pockets, listening in on phone calls. I even hired a private detective. All to no avail."

"Then how do you know he's cheating if you've never caught him?"

"I can smell the bitch all over him. He comes home covered in her perfume, smelling like pussy. I hate his ass *soooooo* much. You're my last resort."

"Fatima, I can't fuck your husband. What's wrong with you?" I didn't realize our waiter had just walked up to the table to ask whether or not we needed anything else. His eyes widened. I knew he had overheard my last statement.

After we told him everything was delicious and we didn't need anything else, I went on. "You and I have been friends since junior high. How in the hell are you going to sit here and ask me to do some shit like that?"

"That's exactly why I'm asking you, because you're the only one I can trust. I thought about hiring some hooker or call girl, but I'm not sure it would work. He may not go for it and I need him to go for it. You see, if I set his ass up and get proof, I can get out this marriage and walk away with everything. If I just up and leave him, I'll get nothing at all. I fully intend to live the lifestyle to which I am accustomed. Minus the asshole, of course."

I couldn't believe she was saying such things. Talking about it so casually, you would have thought she was talking about the next meeting at the garden club. My best friend, my sister-in-arms, the light of my life who has always been there for me through thick and thin. Fatima has always stood by me, through the darkest of times, when no one else was around. "Fatima, I don't think you're thinking clearly, Sis. Don't get me wrong. I love you more than life itself and would take a bullet for you, but *fuck your husband?*"

"Please, Sis. I'm begging you." The desperation on her face and the panic in her voice made me want to break out in tears.

There was nothing else for me to do at that point but agree. I always said I would do anything for her. It was time to put up or shut up.

We left the restaurant and took a walk in the park nearby. We sat down on a bench and hashed out the plan while pigeons waddled all around us looking for some sort of nutritional substance.

I asked the obvious question first. "You said you don't think he would go for a hooker or a call girl, so what makes you think he would go for me?"

"I see the way he looks at you and, besides, the danger of it all will turn him on. I know his skank ass!" She did have a point. I had often caught him staring at my breasts and trying to make eye contact. In all the years they had been married, he had never made an obvious pass at me though.

"But doesn't Javon know if he makes a play for me, I'll run straight to you and spill it?"

"That's the tricky part. You have to make a play for him and make him go for it at all costs. Convince him you want him so bad, you are willing to betray me for the dick."

To say I was in shock would be an understatement. My best friend and I were sitting on a park bench talking about the best way for me to seduce her husband. The craziest part was my acceptance of the challenge. I'd never done something so raw before. "Fatima, you sure there's no other way?"

"Harmony, you know I would never put you in this position unless I had to. Please, Sis. It has to be like this. It has to."

With those words, it was a done deal. She and I talked about it for another half-hour or so before we hugged and kissed each other on the cheek and parted ways. It was Wednesday.

Thursday and Friday, my mind was wandering all over the place. I started to pick up the phone and call Fatima a thousand times to tell her there was no way I could go through with it. Then I thought about the pain on her face and how, over the years since her marriage, she seemed more and more depressed and I never knew why. If she was hell-bent on getting a divorce, she deserved to walk away set for life. He could afford it and there was no reason for him not to pay. He should pay for hurting her, for cheating on her, for disrespecting her.

Then Saturday rolled around, Memorial Day. The day another close friend, Camisha, was having a surprise birthday party for her boyfriend. I attended the party alone that night since Zachary and I had broken up the month before. We were in the process of trying to work things out but, technically, I was unattached. I wouldn't be the one cheating; Javon would.

I was a nervous wreck, hoping I could pull it off. Would a man really attend a party with his wife and sneak off to get a quickie? With his wife's best friend at that? There was only one way to find out. Only one of two things could happen. He would go for it and get mad busted or try to run back to her and accuse me of trying to get with him. Either way, I had nothing to lose.

When I arrived at the party, most of the guests were already there, including Fatima and Javon. Camisha greeted me and I gave her the wrapped present I bought for her man, a nice tie rack and two silk ties. We chatted briefly as she escorted me out to the backyard where everyone was having cocktails by the poolside. She had hired a disc jockey that was playing some old school jams for us baby boomers. There were a few couples dancing but most people were just chilling. I figured, like most parties, the situation would change once they got a few drinks in them. After the alcohol kicks in, people forget about acting prim and proper and start shaking their asses like they're back in high school.

Before Camisha walked off to find her lover man, she hugged me, whispering in my ear. "Everything is set-up in the pool house, just like we planned." All I could do was manage a slight grin.

I needed a drink with a quickness. I thought Fatima was going to take care of everything herself. Come to find out she had Camisha involved in the shit, too. I began to wonder who else knew about the plan and wondered if Camisha had told her man. Hell, for all I knew, everyone at the whole dayum party was in on it except Javon. I located the bar and asked for a double scotch.

Fatima and Javon were standing on the lawn talking to another couple when I went over and hugged them both. Everything had to appear normal. If she and I avoided one another, Javon would have picked up on it. I started flirting with a few men who also came to the party alone, some friends of the honoree who are all pro football players like him.

The night went on without a glitch. It was all good. As suspected, people started getting freaky on the dance floor. They even got a couple of Soul Train lines going. As planned, Fatima went into the main house to make an imaginary phone call home to ask the nanny if the kids were okay and in bed. It was time for me to make my move.

I pretended to be tore up from the floor up and strutted right over to Javon with a bottle of scotch in my hand. Fatima had left him sitting alone on a lawn chair. I leaned over and whispered in his ear. "Meet me in the pool house because I need to talk to you. It's important."

I walked off towards the pool house, which was set off by itself away from the central party activities. In fact, it had gotten cool outside and most people were migrating towards the house anyway. Things were working out even better than we planned.

I reached the pool house and searched for the camcorder I already knew was there. I had to get it on before Javon showed up, *if he showed up*. You see, the strategy was for me to seduce him, get the entire thing on tape, and then Fatima was going to lie and tell him Camisha had later unearthed the tape. She was going to tell him Camisha left a camcorder in the pool house so they could make home pornos from time to time and somehow, it must have been voice activated and started taping all by itself. It was a far-out plan but, often times, it's the unthinkable shit that actually works because people never see it coming.

I located the camcorder hidden in an armoire between some rolled up beach towels. It was aimed directly at the bed, which was bejeweled with tropical printed blankets and pillows. The camcorder would be able to pick up everything in the small, cozy place. I didn't plan to make it a long drawn out process. Just do the dirt and get out. It couldn't last long anyway because Javon would have to rush back and find Fatima so she wouldn't be worried about him. All of it was dependent on whether or not his ass showed up though.

I was just about to presume Javon wasn't coming when I heard the door slowly creak open. He entered the pool house. He was obviously drunk as all hell, which would make things a lot simpler. Fatima said she would get him to down several drinks since she knew he lost his senses when he was drunk and didn't handle liquor very well.

Time was of the essence. As soon as he closed the door behind him, I went for it before I lost my chutzpah. I threw Javon up against the door and started kissing him. At first he hesitated, but then started to reciprocate. After a few seconds of tongue-tangling, he pushed me away, moved away from the doorway with his back to the bed, and asked, "What the hell is this? I thought you wanted to talk about Fatima?"

"I want to talk about me *and* you!" I started pushing him backwards until he stumbled and his ass hit the bed. I climbed on top of him, pushed his back onto the bed, and started unbuttoning his shirt and grinding on his dick.

"Hol-hold up, Harmony. We can't do this shit."

"But I've wanted you for so long, Javon. I can't take this shit anymore. I want you to take this pussy right now." I managed to get his shirt unbuttoned, exposing his chest. He didn't put up much opposition, despite his words to the contrary.

"What about Fatima? She's your best friend." He was a man torn between doing what felt good and doing what he knew was right.

The little bit of fight he had left in him perished once I lowered the straps of my party dress, exposing my hardened nipples. Simply put, he was a defeated man.

Javon grabbed a hold of my left tit and started sucking for dear life. I thought he was trying to suck the thing clear off my chest. I cut the breast-sucking down to a minimum. It had to be all or nothing on the videotape and I was getting sick to my stomach. The lengths I will go to for a friend.

Javon is an attractive man so it wasn't *all* that bad. It was the mere fact he was so willing to betray Fatima that disgusted me most of all.

I stood up on the bed, with my feet on the sides of his chest, pulled my satin panties down, and stepped out of them. Then, I sat down on his face and pushed his hands over his head, holding then down on the bed pillows while I ground my pussy onto his willing tongue. I purposely sat on his face that way instead of getting in the sixty-nine position because I was not about to suck his dick. A sista does have her limits.

I must admit the pussy-eating did turn me on a smidgen and I was reluctant to get off of his face. He was quite a hungry man that evening. But it had to be quick so, after my pussy had done its job and left his face looking like a glazed doughnut, I climbed off.

Javon was lying there, basking in the afterglow, while I started taking his pants off. "Dayum, Harmony. You have no idea how many times I have dreamed of fucking the shit out of you like this. This is unreal."

Little did he know that it was *unreal*. His ass was being set-up big time. I played along. "Just enjoy the ride, Baby. I wanna ride this big, juicy dick of yours."

Truth be known, I was highly discontent when I did get the dick out. He wasn't holding much. I found it hard to believe that Fatima even married his ass. Gurlfriend must have really loved the man at some point.

I sat on his dick and got it inserted after much maneuvering. Like I said, he was seriously lacking in the dick department. I rode the hell out of him, pretending like his dick was so mammoth it was knocking the bottom out of my pussy. *Ha! What a crock!*

As if to confirm my suspicions of him being a lousy fuck, Javon held true to form and came in about 3-4 minutes. I wanted to laugh my ass off but held it in. I told him we better hurry up and get back to the party. I started fixing my clothes and got a revelation. *Why not seal his fate for sure?* Instead of putting my panties back on, I stuffed them in his pants pocket and said, "Keep these to remember me by!"

I gave Javon some quick tongue action, jumped up off the bed, and left him there in the pool house, clothes hanging all off him, dick all limp, and a look of astonishment on his *caught-in-the-act-without-even-knowing-it* face. How pathetic!

When I returned to the party, everyone had gone into the main house by that point. The weather had gone from cool to downright chilly. Fatima was standing by the patio doors and I gave her the success signal we had decided upon. I gave her the finger. I know that sounds silly. We couldn't think of anything else at the time.

Fatima grinned but I sensed she was a bit upset, halfway hoping Javon did have some scruples after all. It is never easy letting go.

A few moments later, Javon rejoined his wife after cleaning himself up. He evidently took the time to wash up in the pool house because there wasn't a drop of pussy juice left on his cheating ass face. The rest of the evening was uneventful. He grinned at me across the room a few times, raising his glass to me once, but purposely avoided coming close to me so he wouldn't give himself away.

The man just knew he had gotten him some pussy on the sly. If he only realized his entire world, as he knew it, had just come to an end.

When I went to get my blazer from the closet in the front hall so I could leave, Fatima followed. "How did it go?"

I simply told her, "He went for it, Sis!" Then, I told her about the panties in his pocket so she could accidentally come across them. That was all she wrote and it was done.

Just as planned, Fatima rescued the panties before he could hide them. I knew he would keep them because just like serial killers, men like to save souvenirs belonging to their victims. They regard dogging out a woman as the end-all and be-all of manhood.

Also as planned, the incriminating videotape was found. I figured out why Fatima had brought Camisha into the plot. Strictly for climactic effect. Camisha showed up at their house a couple of days later with the evidence in hand and the concocted story rehearsed to the tee. Camisha came into their home, confronted Javon right in front of Fatima, slapped him across the face, and threw the tape in the living room VCR so Fatima could see what low-lifes her husband and best friend were.

That all got the ball rolling. Fatima called me on the phone, politely asking me to come over as if she was setting me up for a downfall. When I arrived, Camisha was still there and Javon was sitting on the couch looking like a sick puppy.

Fatima cussed me out and threw accusations like wildfire. When I denied it and pretended to be caught off guard, she turned on the VCR to play back the tape for my benefit. "Now bitch, what you got to say?"

We both had to suppress the laughter building up inside. Camisha did, too. The shit was getting rather ridiculous, but I played along and begged her for absolution.

Fatima went on and on about how she should have suspected it because she had found some panties in the pocket of the pants he had worn to the party the other night. She pulled them out of her purse and started waving them around in the air. She really drew the impromptu play out. Javon was on the verge of tears. I made a mental note to get my panties back from Fatima later. They were one of my prettiest pair.

Finally, I told Fatima I was sick of her calling me a bitch and stormed out. Camisha also excused herself, insisting that she need-ed to get home. Instead, she pulled her car up beside mine at the bottom of the long, curvy driveway as we were both exiting the property.

I rolled down my window, as did she, and we had a good laugh. Then we both expressed concern over Fatima's welfare. While she was putting up a spectacular front, Camisha and I both knew it was tearing her apart inside. But, we love her and had proven that love by doing as she asked. The rest is between her and her shitty ass husband.

The Response

"*Eww!*" Bryce felt like her baked fish might come back up at any second. "*You fucked Fatima's husband? And you say my ass is foul!*"

"*Oh my goodness!*" Lucky jumped in. "*I can't believe you fucked your best friend's husband!*"

An utter stillness came over the restaurant and for a second, it even seemed like the people in the music video were watching them. "Lucky, lower your voice!" Harmony glowered at everyone as if to say *mind your fucking business*. "Damn, Lucky!"

"Well, I still can't believe you did that shit," she replied. "No wonder I couldn't get in touch with either one of you on Memorial Day. Ya'll were out hoeing."

"What I did was an act of pure love unlike *Miss Knocking Balls Around On The Pool Table* over there."

"Whatever! That's some nasty ass shit," Bryce said, going off. "Ain't no camaraderie worth all that. He could've at least had a big dick, but you fucked a pencil dick cause someone asked you to and let them videotape your ass at that. You better not ever run for a political office cause..."

"Shut the hell up!" Harmony was infuriated. "Both of you can kiss my black ass with all of your self-righteous bullshit."

"Well, I can't really talk," Lucky said, diverting her eyes away.

"I bet not," Harmony hissed.

Bryce got cynical. "What did you do, Lucky? Fuck one of those white boys you go to school with?"

"Bryce, you know Lucky won't fuck a white man. Get real," Harmony said.

"I'm for real. A dick is a dick, especially when you're going through a drought season and you need to hop a ride on the first available dick that comes bouncing around."

"Yeah, but Lucky is into this entire Afrocentric, Black Power thing. No way!"

"Excuse me," Lucky interrupted. "I can speak for myself."

They both shut up.

"I did go out with this one white guy from my anatomy class, but only because he kept sweating me and calling me a racist."

"Say whaaaaaat?" Bryce asked, her eyes full of astonishment.

"Chill out, Bryce. Dang!" Lucky held her palm up to Bryce's face. "I didn't fuck him, *although* I must admit I thought about it one night when I was drunk. I was on my period though."

"Alleluia! Thank goodness for the menstrual cycle!" Harmony exclaimed. "The last thing we need is for you to start breeding mulatto children and dressing them in dashikis."

"He didn't care," Lucky continued. "He wanted to fuck me raw dog, blood and all. Then he told me if I was too offended by that idea, we could have anal sex instead."

"Shame on it all," Harmony uttered.

"Naw, make that a double shame on it all," Bryce added.

"Can I be honest with you guys?" Lucky was a bit apprehensive of the repercussions her next statement might bring about.

"That's what this lunch is all about," Harmony said. "Honesty and sisterly bonding."

"Okay, the idea of anal sex was kind of a turn on to me and I almost went for it, but..."

"But?"

"Once he took his clothes off, I was completely turned off. He looked like a ghost, his skin was so pale. He had a tan so I really couldn't judge his lack of melanin until he was butt naked. *I couldn't even hang.*"

"I'm as happy as a fag in Dickland that you didn't fuck no white boy," Harmony stated. "However, if that's not what happened to you on Memorial Day, then what did?"

"Well..." Lucky said hesitantly.

Bryce and Harmony looked at each other, both hoping Lucky didn't write a check her ass couldn't cash.

"We're listening," Bryce said, prodding her on.

"Well, I kind of, sort of fucked someone from med school."

"What is a kind of, sort of fuck?" Bryce asked sarcastically. "You either did the nasty or you didn't."

"Aiight, I fucked him. In fact, I fucked the living daylights out of him." She glanced at Harmony. "You might have messed up your hair and Bryce might have ruined her make-up, but let me break it down for you like this. When I was finished doing what I did that night, I went home, took off my panties, and threw them at the wall." Bryce and Harmony wondered what the big deal was about throwing panties at a wall when Lucky added, "And those bad boys stuck to it."

"Damn, you came like that?" Bryce speculated what would happen if she threw her panties at a wall the next time she and George got finished doing it.

"One of your classmates?" Harmony asked with a look of concern overshadowing her face. She didn't like the sound of Lucky's story already. It gave her an uneasy feeling and usually when that happened, it meant nothing but trouble. Lucky shook her head in the negative. It took a moment for it to sink in before Harmony reached over the table, grabbing the sleeve of Lucky's baseball jersey. "Aw, hell naw! Don't tell me you abandoned your damn mind and fucked one of your professors?"

"Nope. Actually, it was the dean."

Chapter Four

Intellectual Sex

I spent the majority of Memorial Day weekend cramming for exams. After awhile, I was at the point where I couldn't absorb another word in my brain so I took a well-deserved break.

Most people on campus were hanging out. Exams or no exams, it was a holiday. They were determined to get their eat and drink on regardless. I tried to call around to see if I could find someone to hang out with. I must have called too late because I didn't get anything except voice mails and answering machines. I was about to just call it a night and crash, but I really felt like doing *something*. I decided to take a ride and headed over to the Takoma Station.

As usual, the place was packed. Even more so because of the holiday. The band and the ambiance were awesome, more than worth the aggravation of struggling for breathing space.

By the time the band started its second set, I had downed quite a few of those $8.50 Long Island Iced Teas. Okay, scratch that. I was tore the hell up. I was so drunk, I lost my balance on the way to the ladies room to output some of my input. I tripped on the carpeted ramp and almost fell flat on my ass.

I felt someone's hands on my waist and realized they were the only things holding me up. They were big, warm, and powerful. I turned around to express gratitude to the gentleman who had been considerate enough to prevent me from making a spectacle of myself.

Much to my surprise, it was the dean of my med school. I was so ashamed, I could have cried. I lowered my head, hoping he wouldn't recognize me, and mouthed the word, "Thanks!"

I brushed past him, seeking out the sanctuary of the bathroom. When I got in there, of course there were wall-to-wall sistas up in that bitch. Sistas primping in the mirrors putting on makeup, sistas waiting for the phone, sistas waiting to tinkle, sistas talking about all the sorry ass mofos in the club they were hitting up for free drinks. Sistas every damn where.

They only have three stalls and I didn't think I would make it if I waited out the line. I debated about sneaking in the men's room across the hall. If there were fifty women in the ladies room, you know there were only two or three brothas in the men's room. It's always like that. I wonder how they get in and out so fast. *Half of them nuccas must not be washing their hands.*

I was in serious jeopardy of losing my bladder control and shifting my weight from leg to leg trying to prevent a boo-boo when one sista further up in the line was kind enough to give me a break.

"Gurl, you look like you're doing an African tribal dance or something! Go ahead in front of me. I have to go, but not *that damn bad.*"

I giggled and told her, "Thanks!"

I got in the stall and there was urine all over the damn place. On the toilet seat, on the floor, even on the wall from drunk ass sistas who missed their bull's eye when they tried to squat.

"Umm, can you hand me some tissue?" This question was directed to the sista in the stall next to me. I couldn't see her face but I knew her ass was there for two reasons. First of all, I could see her nasty ass, corn-infested toes hanging over some gold sandals she had on that were at least two sizes too small and secondly, because she was dropping bombs in the toilet and her shit was foul. Contrary to popular belief, *our* as in females, shit does stank.

She handed me a roll of tissue under the ceramic wall of the stall. For the third time in five minutes, I was compelled to issue another, "Thank you!"

Damn, everyone was being so pleasant to me, I almost broke into a hip-hop rendition of *Kumbaya*.

When I came out of the ladies room, I glimpsed around the corner to see if my dean was still there. The place was so crowded, it was like doing a *Where's Waldo?* puzzle.

I didn't see him anywhere so I decided to haul ass before he spotted me again and figured out who I was. It wasn't that I was breaking any med school rules by being there but, for some reason, I just didn't want him to see my ass drunk. I felt like a derelict and just wanted to head home, get in another hour or two of studying, and then turn in about 2 A.M.

It was cool outside and the brisk air sobered my ass up with a quickness; or so I thought. I was walking to my car and searching through my purse for my keys when his voice froze me in mid-step.

"Have a good evening, Miss Whitfield!"

Oh shit, so much for lack of recognition!

I looked behind me and he was leaning on the *biggest damn, shiniest damn, blackest damn* Mercedes I had ever seen.

"Hello, Dean Mitchell. I didn't think you knew who I was in there."

He started walking towards me. It had never hit me before but looking at him under the mixture of the moonlight and street lamps, I realized he was truly a sexy ass older brotha.

It was one of those fleeting thoughts though. I didn't give it too much credence because smoking boots with the dean of my med school was out of the damn question.

Next thing you know, he was standing right beside me on the sidewalk.

"Of course, I know who you are Miss Whitfield. I take pride in the fact that I keep tabs on all of my students."

"That's marvelous!" There I was in the middle of the night, sounding like Harmony and shit. Using the word she uses whenever she's really pissed off but wants to hide it from the world. Her *pissed off* word became my *nervous* word.

"Your first name is Lucinda, right?"

"Yes, but I hate that name so everyone just calls me Lucky."

"Lucky! How cute."

"Thanks!"

"You all ready for exams?"

"I sure hope so. I put in hours and hours of studying. I just needed to take a little break."

It felt like I was talking to Daddy, explaining why I left the library early in high school to go to a movie with friends. I started having flashbacks and shit.

"No need to explain that to me, Lucky. Everyone needs to relax; even medical students. Besides, they say cramming is not the solution to good grades anyway."

"I totally agree." I nodded. "Either you know it or you don't, right?"

"Absolutely!"

The next two minutes seemed more like ten because of the silence between us. We could hear the thumping of the music coming from the Station. Both of us kept glancing at the cars driving by like we were sitting on a porch in the country, drinking iced tea out of Mason jars and playing *Cars*.

I wanted to leave but didn't want to be the first one to say goodbye for fear of appearing impolite so I waited for him to say it.

Finally, I got my wish.

"Well, Lucky, it's getting late and I have to get going."

I glanced at my watch, but didn't pay any attention to the time. "Yeah, it is rather late. You take care, Dean Mitchell. I'll see you around campus."

"Goodnight!"

"Goodnight!"

I was about two cars away from my own, ready to break out in a run like the people trying to hop that train at the end of *Rosewood* to get away from his ass, when my head started spinning and my knees gave out from underneath me. The next thing I knew, I was ass out!

When I came around about an hour or so later, I was laying in a huge waterbed with crisp white sheets on it. A bad ass faux fur comforter with a leopard-skin pattern was covering me. I sat up and thought I was in a mansion or some shit like that. I mean, this bedroom was laid da hell out.

There was a wall that was completely glass and overlooked the Potomac River with all the lights from Virginia twinkling on the water from the other side. It reminded me of the view from the rooftop of The Kennedy Center. It was spectacular.

On the opposite wall, were several paintings by African-American artists. I recognized most of them right away. Wak, Poncho, Vanderzee. The ceiling over the bed was covered with mirrors and there was a blue neon sign on the wall over the doorway that read *Marvin*.

Marvin? Who the fuck is Marvin? Then it hit me. *Oh shit, I was in Dean Mitchell's bed!*

I jumped up off of the bed, checking to make sure my panties were still on because you know that's the first thing a sista needs to do after an alcoholic blackout.

I used to have them all the time when I was at Spelman. One night I was so drunk after going to a happy hour at *VIP's*, I didn't even recollect these guys from Morehouse giving me a ride home. The next morning, I couldn't find my pants from the night before. I was afraid I had told the Morehouse men to *"Come On, Ride The Train."* I was relieved when my roommate told me that the worst thing I did was miss curfew, cuss the dorm mother out, throw up in a trash can, and put on a strip tease show in the community room. Sure enough, my pants were right there in the middle of the floor.

But this wasn't Spelman and Marvin Mitchell was not a Morehouse man. He was my med school administrator and I had just woken up in his bed. I panicked.

I thought about jumping over the balcony rail and scaling down the wall like Spiderman, but had to think twice about that once I realized we were about ten floors up. It left me no alternative but to be a woman, face the fact that I had made a fool of myself, and go talk to him about it. Beg for his forgiveness if need be.

I tiptoed out into his living room. Much unlike my panties, my shoes were missing in action. I didn't see him anywhere but I was captivated by his place. I mean, his shit was really hooked.

Black leather furniture, a bearskin rug, a huge fireplace, marble tables, and more African-American artwork for days. I was standing there wondering why I couldn't find any younger brothas who had it going on like that when he walked up behind me and tapped me on the shoulder.

I jumped like I was about to do a pole vault in the Summer Olympics.

"Sorry, I didn't mean to alarm you."

"No, you didn't alarm me. It wasn't you. I'm just quite embarrassed about this whole thing."

"No need for that." He walked past me, headed into the kitchen. "Things happen. That's a part of life."

"Yeah, but getting *so* drunk I black out and you have to bring me to your place? You have to admit, that's a bit much."

I heard him running some water in the sink before he came back around the corner. "Well, maybe just a little bit," he said and held his hand up with a little space between his thumb and forefinger.

We both snickered.

The man is sexy. S-E-XXX-Y. The diminutive lines around his eyes are the only things on him that give away the fact he's about fifty. I felt my kitty getting moist and decided I needed to direct my thoughts to something else. *Anything else.*

"I took the liberty of putting on some coffee."

"Thank you. That's very kind. Bringing me here and all of that was really not necessary."

"Would you rather that I left you out on the middle of the sidewalk so people coming out of the Takoma Station could step over you, mistake you for a homeless person, and drop quarters on you?"

I put my hands on my hips, chuckling. "Good point."

I sat down on the leather sofa and grabbed a toss pillow, hugging it in front of my chest so he wouldn't see my nipples getting hard through the black halter top I had on.

"Would you like to watch some cable or listen to some music while the coffee is brewing?"

"Sure!"

"Which one?"

"It's up to you."

He put on a Maxwell CD and then sat down beside me on the couch. The moment I got a whiff of his cologne, I knew my ass was in trouble. It was strong yet subtle, sweet yet masculine. Such a damn turn on.

I moved my leg back and forth, causing friction on my clit. You know how we women do when the horns start poking out our heads. Now ordinarily, the young nuccas I deal with don't know what it means when a woman moves her leg back and forth, but this man was cultivated. He looked over at me and the way I was shifting my leg and blushed.

Shit, he knows I want him to lick my belly button from the inside out, I notioned.

Never in one million years did I think he would go for it but within seconds, his strong, manicured hand was gently rubbing my knee. I trembled so he backed off.

"Do you play chess, Lucky?" he asked, much to my astonishment.

"Umm, chess? No. I tried to learn once or twice, but I didn't have the patience for it."

"Understandable. It's quite a disciplined game."

We both got lost in the music.

"You like poetry?"

"Yes, I love poetry."

"Would you like me to recite some poetry to you?" he inquired.

"No!" I exclaimed. I didn't want any more fuel added to the fire that was burning inside me.

Fortunate came on and he grabbed my hand. "I know you dance."

I didn't respond. I didn't take exception either when he pulled me up off of the couch. He took me in his arms. I prayed that I could hold out. Once I felt his dick against my belly button, it was futile.

"You know, I really like the cute little Afro you have," he said, gazing seductively into my eyes. "Most black women today feel the need to process their hair when natural beauty is so much more engaging."

"Yeah, I agree. They either get perms, curls, or hair weaves like my sister Bryce. You should see her hair. I'm willing to bet you could bounce a basketball on it."

We both fell out laughing. I was still recovering from the joke when he took me by the chin and kissed me gently on the lips.

I was dumbfounded. I didn't pull away so he kissed me again, this time letting his thick tongue wander inside my mouth. I reciprocated.

Before the song ended, we were in his bed, ripping off clothes on top of the waves. I felt like I had died and gone to heaven when he started suckling on my nipples. I knew it had to be heaven when he started suckling on my clit because I came about five times in fifteen minutes.

I heard through the grapevine that older, more experienced men are fantastic lovers. I'm willing to give testimonial to that shit now.

After he had eaten his fair share of *Pussy a la Lucky* and polished off his meal with *Ass a la Lucky* for dessert, he flipped me over and took me from behind.

His dick was long and thick, but he was ever so gentle with the pussy. He took his time and made the rest of the world vanish. It was just me and him. Him on top. Me on top. *E-ve-ry* which way.

After he came all over my ass cheeks, we both fell asleep for a couple of hours. When we woke up, the sun was rising. It was about 5:30 AM.

I was planning on making a quick departure. I knew I was dead wrong for fucking him but shit happens. Instead, he took me into the bathroom and ran a bubble bath for us in his whirlpool garden tub.

He took a huge bath sponge and washed every inch of my body in slow, circular motions. He even washed my hair. The feel of his strong fingers on my scalp turned my ass out.

I washed him and then told him to stand up. There *it* was, right in front of my face. His big, scrumptious, juicy dick. I hungrily took it in, trying to deep throat the whole thing. Anything else wouldn't have done it justice.

To be frank, whenever I suck dick it is never for the benefit of the brotha. Sucking dick is all about me. I love sucking some damn dick and *suck a damn dick I did*. Marvin Mitchell may be experienced, he may have had a lot of women, but he has *never* had a dick-sucking like the one he got that morning.

His cum got me hooked. It was so damn delectable, I could drink that shit by the gallon. But like all good things, it had to come to an end so about 11 AM, I had him drive me back down to the Takoma Station to get my car.

I haven't seen him since and I'm not quite sure what will happen when I do. It's a tricky situation but all I can say is he can have him some *Pussy a la Lucky* anytime and anyplace just like that Janet Jackson song.

The Response

"No he can't have some Pussy a la Lucky anytime!" Harmony snapped. *"Have you lost your fucking mind?"*

"I have to agree with Harmony." Bryce jumped in. "Harmony and I might disagree on a lot of shit, *Lawd knows we do,* but she's right on point with this one."

Lucky poked her bottom lip out at both of them like a little girl about to throw a temper tantrum. "You guys!"

"You guys nothing," Harmony said. "You're not going to carry on some scandalous affair with your dean. I don't care if I have to call Daddy in Cali and tell him to come here and whup your black ass."

"Forget Daddy," Bryce proclaimed. "I'll whup her black ass myself."

"Amen to that," Harmony added.

"I don't know why ya'll jocking my bra strap. You were both out hoeing that weekend, too."

"Yeah Lucky," conceded Bryce. "But the shit you did could very well damage your future. Do you have any idea what will happen if this gets out?"

Lucky rolled her eyes.

Harmony leaned up over the table and gave Lucky the most angry, hurt look she had ever seen on her sister's face.

"You listen to me, Lucky, and you listen to me good."

"Aw hell," Bryce said. "Here it comes."

"Lucky, if you don't put an end to this shit right now, I will. If it means calling Momma and Daddy in Cali and telling on your ass. If it means taking your car back that I'm paying the damn car note on. Even if it means refusing to make up the difference between your scholarship amount and the full tuition for next semester so you have to switch schools."

"Harmony, you can't be serious?" Bryce queried.

"I'm *dead serious*. As much as I'm busting my ass running this temp agency, working eighteen to twenty hours a day sometimes to make sure that Lucky has an opportunity for a secure future, and she's going to turn around and jeopardize it all over some dick?"

Tears started to build in Lucky's eyes as the culpability set in. She never thought about all of that the night she did it. Harmony painstakingly struggled to ensure she had a bright future. She never asked for anything in return but hard work and dedication.

"No way! There's *no way in hell* I'm standing for this!" Harmony looked around the restaurant. "Where is that damn waiter with the check anyway?"

Harmony got up from the booth to go search for the waiter and Lucky grabbed her by the arm. She looked up at her with soggy eyes. "Harmony, I promise you that I'll never do it again. *I promise!*"

Chapter Five

Chillin At The Mall

"Ya'll some nasty ass heffas!" Harmony had listened to enough and was on her way out the door of the Soundstage after putting their bill on her platinum AMEX card.

"Hold the damn phone!" Bryce was right on her tail. Lucky was lagging behind a little because she ran into one of her male friends from high school in Cali on the way out. "Harmony, how in *da hell* you going to call us nasty when you fucked Fatima's little dick husband?"

Harmony sifted through her purse looking for her Ray Bans. The sun was kicking. Felt like hell had opened up. "What happened between Javon and I was totally different."

"Yeah, right." Bryce crossed her arms, striking her *I-can't-wait-to-hear-this-bullshit* pose. "What's the damn difference?"

"Hmph, I'll tell you the damn difference. You fucked some man at a BBQ on a pool table. Other people were outside sucking the meat off of ribs and you were inside sucking the skin off a nucca's dick."

"Whatever!" Bryce rolled her eyes and shifted her weight to her other leg. "You always try to play this *holier-than-thou* role when you're a bigger freak than Lucky and I put together."

Harmony finally located her shades and put them on, sighing out of disgust partly because she realized she had too much superfluous shit in her purse and partly because Bryce's hair weave was giving her problems. "Bryce, I can't really expect you to comprehend this being that you hang out with hoochie mamas like Colette. That skeezer would use food stamps to get some dick if she could."

"Oooooooh, I'm toooooooo scared of you," Bryce stated sarcastically and then covered her mouth to emphasis her boredom with an executed yawn.

"What I did with Javon's skank ass was done out of a commitment to a friendship that has withstood the test of time. If the shoe were on the other foot, Fatima would have done the same for me."

"Well, the shoe wouldn't ever be on the other foot because I know your ass is not moronic enough to marry a little dick man."

"You don't know who the hell I would marry!"

Harmony's bottom lip started trembling. Bryce knew she was taking it to the extreme, but it had been a long time since she raked on her sister's nerves so bad. Bryce was relishing every minute of it so she kept it going. "Shit, just admit it. You're a freak! F-R-R-E-A-K-K-K. You get two R's and three K's cause you're twice as raunchy and three times as kinky as a normal day-to-day freak."

"Ya'll still going at it?" Lucky barged into the convo after completing her mission of getting the brotha's digits from high school. "You sistahs are *unfuckinbelievable*. Take a damn dead issue and try to perform CPR on the shit."

Harmony and Bryce both leered at Lucky and told her to, "Shut the hell up!"

"Geeesh! Whatever!" Lucky sauntered to the edge of the sidewalk and lit herself a cigarette. "Fuck it. I know when I'm wasting my time on a lost cause."

They started to draw attention, but Harmony was not about to drop it. Lucky was right to an extent. Both Harmony and Bryce always coveted the last word and would spend hours, if need be, trying to get it.

"I'm not a freak. You and your entourage of hooker friends are freaks. I'm a grown woman. If I want to fuck my best friend's husband so she can take his ass to the cleaners, that's my business."

Everyone was staring by then. People even started coming outside from the waiting area to see what the deal was.

Harmony and Bryce just glared at each other like two Sumo wrestlers getting ready to pulverize each other.

"Please forgive my sisters." Lucky chuckled as she scanned the converging crowd of onlookers. "You remember when St. Elizabeth's let out all those crazy folks because they were low on funding? This is the result. You all need to write your congressman and lobby for a new bill to protect society from *bitches with attitudes*."

"Lucky, shut the hell up!" Bryce forgot about Harmony and came over to confront her baby sibling. "You don't *even* need to be talking. Look at your *Pam-Grier-wanna-be* ass trying to playa hate. You are such a..."

"Before the two of you get started, I'm about to bounce. Call me later this week." Harmony was twirling her key ring on her finger and not about to stand there and listen to her sisters trade snide remarks.

Harmony was halfway to her convertible Jaguar when her sisters came rushing up behind her. Obviously, they didn't feel like causing a ruckus any further either. "Where are you going, Harmony? I thought you were going shopping with us?"

Harmony turned around to look at Bryce, wondering if the chica was actually serious about going shopping after all of the insults. "Shopping? Didn't nobody say a *damn thing* about shopping today."

"I mentioned it to you on the phone. You don't remember? In fact, Colette's meeting us at Landover Mall."

"Colette?" Harmony resumed her pace and hit the button on her key chain to turn off the car alarm. "Now I know your ass is trippin' hard. The last thing I want to do is spend the rest of my Saturday afternoon with Colette."

"See, now you're insulting my friends."

"I'm not insulting jack. I'm just telling you like it is. Besides, I always insult your friends. It isn't like it's something new."

Lucky grabbed a hold of Harmony's right elbow as she was unlocking the driver's side door. "Come on, Sis! I don't get to spend that much time with you lately because med school is kicking my ass. Please! I want you to come shopping with us."

Harmony looked at Lucky's fallacious smile, immediately sensing some ulterior motives and then it hit her. "Uh huh, the only reason you want me to go shopping is so you can hit me up for some cash or run my credit card bills up. Your game is old, Sistahgurl."

"Damn, you're being straight up bitchy today." Lucky stomped off and got into her red '99 VW bug. She rolled her window down. "Bryce, I'm heading on over to the mall. I'll meet you there. Harmony has something stuck up her ass and the shit is starting to smell foul."

Bryce laughed. Harmony didn't say a word. Just got in her car and revved the engine. "Aiight, Lucky. I'm meeting Colette on the bottom level, near Sears."

"Cool." Lucky drove off with her music blasting and bopping her head to *Silly Hoe* by TLC.

"Silly hoe! How appropriate. If it weren't for me buying her that car, she would be ass out and digging for quarters for the Metrobus." Harmony was fuming. Bryce began to get concerned. Harmony was always playing the *uppity* role but she was almost never altogether rude unless something was really wrong in her personal life. Now that she was lashing out at Lucky, who was the sunshine of her life, Bryce knew Harmony had some deep-rooted issues.

"Wanna talk about it, Sis?" Bryce leaned on the car. "I know you're upset about Lucky and the dean. I know you're upset about fucking Javon, whether you want to admit it or not, and I know you're upset about the break-up with Zachary. Give it some time and you two will be back together."

"I *seriously* doubt that!"

"There's something else riling you, though." Bryce shook her finger at Harmony, trying to figure it out. "You know I can always read your ass. So you want to talk about it? Just me and you?"

"I've heard enough of your mouth for one day. Thank you."

Harmony took off, accelerating too quickly and almost jumped the curb turning out of the parking lot.

"Whatever's wrong with you, Big Sis, it's gonna be aiight. Nobody fucks with a Whitfield woman and gets away with it." Bryce spoke the words, but the only ears they fell on were her own.

"Bryce, we're over here!" Colette was standing in the middle of the lower level atrium waiting for her to come out of Sears.

One of the little Rugrats playing in the indoor playground threw a plastic ball at Bryce when she walked past. Bryce was about to school his little rude ass, but spotted a woman who outweighed her three to one heading towards him and pegged her as the proud mom. Bryce reconsidered her next move, muttered *Damn, BeBe's Kid* under her breath, and concentrated on catching up to Colette.

Colette was dressed in her typical get-up. Leggings and a crop top, leaving very little to the imagination. She had gotten a little tan since the last time Bryce hooked up with her so she was two shades darker than her usual high yella self.

"Where's Lucky? She catch up to you yet?"

Colette pointed at the Karibu bookstore. "You know your sister. She's in there collecting black literature."

Bryce went into the store and Colette switched in right after her. "Nothing wrong with reading. A mind is a terrible thing to waste."

"Yeah, well, so is a good dick."

Bryce laughed but she was glad Harmony wasn't there to hear it because she knew it would cause another fight. Harmony couldn't stand Colette and Bryce thought it was terribly unfair of her. Bryce accepted just about all of Harmony's friends. Lucky's too, for that matter, but it seldom worked the other way around.

"What are we reading today, Sis?"

Lucky glanced up from the Ernest Hill novel she was flipping through. "Hey, you made it!"

"Yeah, what did you think I was going to do? Make a detour?"

"No. I just figured you and Harmony would probably still be standing there cussing each other out until nightfall."

"Something's up with Harmony."

"Shit! You don't even have to tell me. That was *tooooooooo* obvious."

"You think it's about the whole sex thang with Javon or something else?"

"Hell, I'm not her freakin' analyst. I'm studying to be a pediatrician, not a shrink."

"*Wait! Wait!*" Colette had to lean against one of the bookcases to catch herself from falling out due to shock trauma. "Are you trying to tell me Harmony fucked *Javon*? Javon as in Fatima's hubby?"

"Yeah, Gurl!" Lucky confirmed her suspicions.

Bryce punched Lucky in the arm. "Why the hell did you say that?"

"Hmph, no point in faking the funk about it. She already figured it out and it's not like you weren't going to tell her later anyway. You tell her every damn thing. You're the Oprah of the D.C. area."

"Lucky, you're always so quick to judge everyone else. What about the shit you did?"

"What did Lucky do?" Colette cut in.

"None of your damn beeswax!" Lucky rolled her eyes and looked back down at the copy of *Satisfied With Nothing* she had in her hands.

Bryce pulled Colette to the side and whispered in her ear. "Don't worry. I'll tell you everything later."

"Aiight, Gurl."

They started giggling and Lucky igged them because she knew Bryce's big mouth was going to put her business out everywhere except on BET.

Fifteen minutes later, Lucky came out of the store with a shopping bag full of books. Everything from Marcus Majors to Walter Mosley. She also bought a copy of *Chocolate Star* by Sheila Copeland since all the black sistas at med school swore up and down it was the bomb.

Bryce only found one book that piqued her interest, *The Sex Chronicles: Shattering the Myth* by Zane. The men at her job were crazy over it and she was curious to know what kind of book had the *one-track-mind-can-I-feel-your-booty* nuccas at her job so mesmerized.

Colette didn't have a damn thing but the phone number of the dark-skinned brother with dreadlocks behind the counter.

"So where to now?" Lucky asked.

"It doesn't matter to me," Bryce replied, still in a foul mood because of Harmony's outburst at the restaurant.

"Well, I got here about an hour before you two," Colette stated with emphasis on the fact that she didn't appreciate having to wait on them. She looked down at her feet, which were crammed into a pair of mid-heel slingbacks. "My dogs are killing me. I wish I had a real man in my life right now. I would go home and let him suck my toes for me."

"Eww!" Bryce squeezed her nose as if to prevent a pungent smell from gaining access. "I don't mean any harm, Colette, but I have seen and *smelled* your crusty ass feet. I can't imagine any nucca being hard up enough for some pussy to suck them bad boys."

Lucky started crying laughing.

"Fuck ya, Bryce." Even though the derogatory comment was directed towards her, Colette couldn't help but break a smile.

"Sheeeeeeeit, sometimes you can smell those fungus breeders clear across the room."

They stood there in the middle of the mall, sharing a good laugh and babbling on about nothing in particular.

"Dammmmmn, look at her." They were sitting on a bench on the upper level, after hitting all the women's clothing stores twice, when Colette started pointing at this sista with an outfit on that looked like a Band-Aid. "And Harmony calls us hoochies. She needs to be here to see this shit."

Lucky and Bryce nodded their heads in agreement.

"Oh, shit!" It was Lucky's turn to point. "Look at that nucca over there with the black knee-high, dress socks on with Jordans, and jean shorts."

Bryce shoved her elbow deep into Lucky's side. "You're horrible," she asserted. "Talking about peeps like that."

"I was just making a comment. Besides, men like that can probably suck the lining out a pussy. Anyone who dresses so fucked up better be the mofo bomb in the bedroom or they ain't getting no play."

"I disagree." Colette smirked. "It is painfully obvious that Negro ain't had puddy since puddy had he."

Lucky and Colette gave each other a high five while Bryce tried to hold back her embarrassment. For a brief moment, sitting there in between Lucky and Colette while they were acting fuckin' stupid, she could almost relate to how Harmony felt at times.

"Speaking of eating pussy, did I tell you guys about this sista at my job who asked if she could lick my coochie?"

Lucky and Bryce both glared at Colette in disbelief.

"Get da fuck out of here!" Lucky's eyes lit up with interest. "Are you for real?"

"Hell, yeah!

"What did you tell her?"

"I told her that I love a good pussy-licking just like the next woman, but I would have to be going through serious dick deprivation to let a woman eat my nana."

"Haha! You go, Gurl!" Colette and Lucky reached over Bryce and exchanged high fives again.

Bryce shook her head and muttered, "Shame on it all!" She told Lucky and Colette she had to run because there were a few stops she had to make on the way home. The fact of the matter was that Harmony's attitude had ruined her day. There was something wrong with her big sister, but she knew better than to try to invade her space. When and if Harmony wanted to discuss it, Bryce knew she would reach out to her or Lucky. It was all a matter of time.

Bryce hung out another ten minutes or so listening to Colette and Lucky talk trash. One of the brothas Colette used to date walked past them with another woman and pretended like he didn't notice her. She yelled out at him for the whole world to hear. "Two-minute brotha!"

The woman with him turned around, eyeing Colette like she wanted to rip her a new asshole.

"Don't look at me! You're the one with the limp dick mofo."

Bryce jumped up, having had enough drama for one day, hugged them both goodbye, and hauled ass.

A Word From Our Sponsors

Niagra

PARDON ME, I KNOW YOU'RE all enthralled in the drama of The Whitfield Sisters but this will only take a moment.

My name is Dr. Ripuoff Formoney. *I know, I know!* I have quite an usual name but that's not why I'm here.

I'm here to tell you about a marvelous new discovery made exclusively for African-Americans who are suffering from the disease my boys and I affectionately call *Limpdickitus.*

Everyone should stock up on this product, including those brothas suffering from *Limpdickitus* and sistas who have *Limpdickaphobia.*

The product is called *Niagra.* I invented it myself in the basement of my row house in Southeast Washington, D.C.

Some of the brothas from the neighborhood were sitting around kicking it one day, shooting the breeze, and downing a couple of forties when the idea hit me.

It came to my attention that some brothas have a problem getting or keeping it up. Especially when they're under the influence of alcohol or a dime bag of weed.

Even one of my homeboys who's doing five to ten in Lorton for armed robbery called me collect, that trifling Negro, and told me he was having trouble staying hard while his shemale was sucking him off.

Being the super hero of the ghetto that I am, I decided I had to do something to save the brothas some face. I walked around the neighborhood collecting samples of crack, heroine, weed, and some other shit you've probably never heard of from every drug dealer I've known since way back in the day when *Car Wash* and *Flashlight* were the jams.

After a couple of hours of melting controlled substances on spoons with a lighter and mixing them together in a grape jelly jar, I came up with something *very* interesting.

I poured it into a pitcher of Cherry-Ade and guess what happened? My dick stayed hard for three whole weeks. I was tearing pussy and ass up right and left. Sistas I didn't know were banging on my door begging for me to knock them off a piece. Even my mother's best friend and her husband came through trying to get me to fuck them both. I told them I didn't get down like that, but I fucked the shit out of her fat ass though.

Well, my time is almost up so let me tell you like this. All of my friends are using *Niagra* now. I can't make the shit fast enough. The drug dealers supply me with their goods as long as I hit them back with a jar of my soul creation.

My boy in Lorton is talking about hooking me up with some business up there as soon as he finds a woman who is willing to put some in a balloon and squeeze it up her ass so she can deliver it during visiting hours. He swings both ways so he has mad bitches on the outside. He said just send him the base and the brothas up there in prison can mix it in the prison-issued lemonade since they deprive the brothas of Cherry-Ade in lock up.

Needless to say, I don't know how long I'll be in business because you know the man will try to bring a brotha down sooner or later. Even though all I'm trying to do is aid in the progression of the black man in today's society.

If you want some of this here, you better jump on it *now*. Brothas, buy it because you want to fuck for three weeks straight. Sistas, buy it for your man so he can fuck you for three weeks straight.

Send $59.99 plus $4.95 shipping and handling to:

Niagra
ATTN: Dr. Ripuoff Formoney
Post Office Box 6969
Washington, DC 52419

Well, they're waving their hands in the air, letting me know my minute is up so peace and remember, if you value your sex drive, buy you some Niagra today and *never, ever, ever, ever, ever* leave home without it.

We now return to the regularly-scheduled program, "Shame On It All," already in progress.

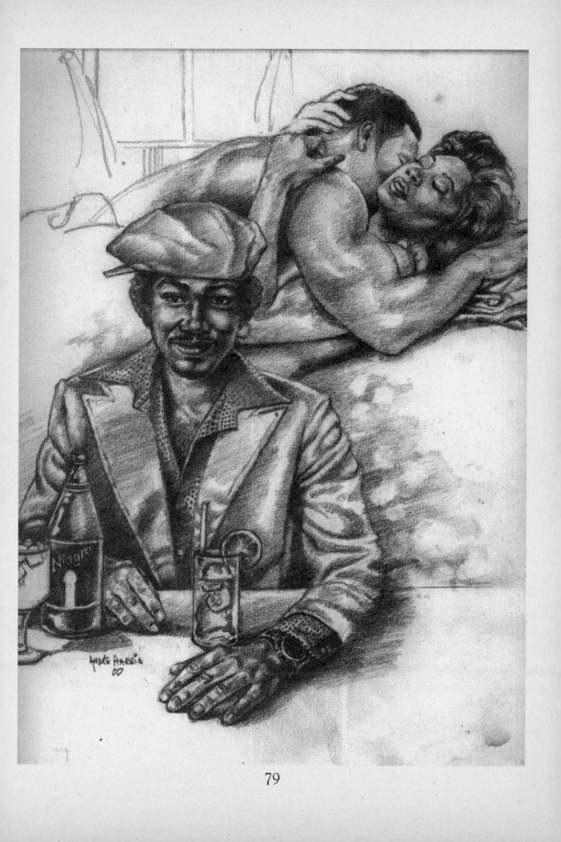

Part Two:
Crazy Ass Nuccas

Chapter Six

Dirty Drawers

Bryce had just plopped down on the couch and kicked up her feet when the phone rang. She was exhausted from working up a storm in the kitchen, preparing a special meal for her man. She couldn't wait to see him. She was past horny and planned to jump his bones the second he walked through their front door.

The cordless was charging on the cradle across the room and Bryce just glared at it for the first three rings. She didn't want to answer it, but George was late and she suspected it might be him.

"Damn!" She got up to get it, stubbed her big toe on the coffee table, and repeated, "Damn!"

"Hello, George?" she asked excitedly.

"Hell, naw, this ain't George!" Colette blared from the other end of the line.

Bryce was highly disappointed and it showed. "Oh, hey, Colette," she said despondently.

"Well, try not to sound so excited."

"No, I didn't mean to sound rude. George should've been home from his business trip hours ago and he hasn't called or anything."

"You still dealing with that trifling ass Negro? All this good ass dick in the D.C. area and you're settling for his bullshit. You're a trip, Gurl!"

"Colette, all of the men in D.C. are playas. Stop the madness. You're just fooling yourself if you think otherwise. Look at the ratio of women to men. Hell, if I was man with those kind of odds, I'd be getting my jimmy waxed day and night, too."

"Kind of like the way you waxed that brotha's dick in Lamar's basement, huh?" Colette asked sarcastically.

"Fuck you, Colette!"

Colette started cackling and Bryce couldn't help but join in.

"George and I are cool now. I know I said I was gonna dump him after he came back from his last trip, but he was so charming and irresistible when he got home." Bryce plopped back down on the couch. "He even bought me a silk teddy and a huge teddy bear. I named it Casanova Brown."

"Oh my, how *black* of you," Colette responded.

"Sheit, you're just jealous because the nuccas you deal with never buy you anything. Oops, my bad. They do buy you those cheap ass drawers from Wal-Mart and then talk you out of them with Cracker Jack toys."

"Fuck ya, Bryce," Colette said jokingly. "Too bad you can't see my middle finger through the phone because it's sticking up to the ceiling."

They both fell out laughing again, but the moment was followed by an uncomfortable silence. Bryce could sense something was troubling Colette.

"Colette, what's wrong with you?"

"What *chuuuuuuu* mean?" was all she got back.

"You're the most talkative sista I know next to Harmony." Bryce giggled. "Most of the time I have to boguard to even get a word in edgewise. Don't try to play me. I know something's up with you, so give me the lowdown."

"Ain't no lowdown." There was a pause. "But, I did lose my job yesterday."

"Damn!" Bryce sat up and put her feet back on the floor. "How in the hell did that happen?"

"It wasn't anything I did. Matter of fact, I was working my ass off for that old crusty ass white man at the warehouse. He wasn't paying me doodley-squat, but he had no problems working my ass like a slave."

"Hmph, I heard that! Sounds like you're better off without that gig anyway then, Sis." Bryce mused it over for a few seconds and interpreted the true reasoning behind Colette's call. "So what are you going to do to make ends meet now?"

"I dunno, Girl," Colette said sullenly. "I'll find something, I suppose."

"Things are tight at the investment firm right now, Sis. I'm lucky they haven't come up with some unjustifiable excuse to kick me out the door. You know how it is. When you're black, you've got to work twice as hard to prove yourself. But when you're a black *woman*, that means you've got to work ten times as hard."

"I can relate."

Bryce hesitated, but felt compelled to add, "I could ask Harmony to hook you up with a temp job just to tide you over. It might not be something extravagant, but it will mean some cash. Besides, I can't imagine anything else being as bad as that warehouse. It sounds like he was treating you like chattel."

"Gurl, he was. As far as Harmony, yeah right! You know your sister ain't gonna give my ass a job. She hates my fuckin' guts."

Bryce wanted to argue the *fuckin' guts* part, but couldn't since it was nothing but the truth. "Harmony can be the queen bitch sometimes. I'll be the first to admit that, but that's only because she's stressed out."

"From where I'm sitting, she must be stressed out twenty-four seven. Every time I see Harmony, she's bitching."

"Colette, I love you, but don't ever diss my sister like that again." Bryce could make disparaging comments about Harmony, but she wouldn't tolerate it from others. Not even from her best friend.

"Sorry, damn!" Colette hissed into the phone, sensing one of Bryce's litanies coming on.

"Harmony has to carry a lot of weight on her shoulders. I'm

basically independent now, but there was a time when I first left home, that I wouldn't have survived if it weren't for her. Similar to the situation with Lucky now."

"I understand."

"As hard as she can be on us at times," Bryce continued, "Harmony only does it because one of her greatest desires is to see Lucky and me succeed."

"Kewl."

Bryce could sense Colette's boredom with her praise of Harmony and contemplated withdrawing her offer to ask Harmony anything. As usual, her gigantic heart got the best of her though.

"Listen, I'll call Harmony in the morning and talk to her about a job for you. I can't promise you anything, but I think she'll do it for me."

"Thanks! I really appreciate that, Bryce."

"No problem. Just make sure you don't screw up if she does help you. I'll *never* hear the end of it if you do. Harmony has a habit of bringing up negative things that happened more than a decade ago."

"I won't mess it up. I swear," Colette said reassuringly.

Bryce turned on her fifty-inch high definition television to get ready for her favorite program. "Colette, let me holla at you later. I'm about to curl up with my *Essence* and check out *BET Tonight*."

"Girl, is that about to come on?" Bryce could hear Colette moving around, probably reaching for the remote. "Tavis is one fine ass brother."

"Yes, he is fine, but he's much more than that. He's educated, compassionate, and driven. Lawd knows, I just love a compassionate man."

"Sho you right!"

"If his ass is half as passionate in the bedroom as he is when it comes to fighting important issues in the media, I'll drink his bath water."

"You go, Gurl! Better you than me because I'm not drinking nobody's skank ass bath water."

Bryce giggled. "Sis, let me run and throw some steaks in the oven. I already have the vegetables and dessert done, but held off on the steaks so they wouldn't get tough. I have them soaking in some bomb ass marinade. I got the recipe off Epicurious.com."

"Dang, you throwing down like that? I might need to stop through there and get my grub on."

"No way, not tonight. George has to come falling up in here sometime and when he does, I'm going to rock his world."

"You better sniff his drawers when he does and make sure they don't smell like crusty ass pussy juice."

"Ew, Colette, you so nasty."

They both laughed.

"Talk to you later, Colette. I'll be sure to let you know what's up with Harmony."

"Thanks, Gurl. Much love."

George didn't show up until damn near four in the morning. Bryce passed the point of being irritated at midnight. By two, she was a maniac, having done three miles on the treadmill in the basement.

"Where the hell have you been?" Bryce asked, launching her attack the second his key hit the lock. She yanked the door open and leered at him before he could even turn the knob.

George threw on his most innocent expression and pushed past her so he could sit his garment bag in the foyer of their townhouse. He could feel the heat coming off of Bryce so he decided to buy himself a couple of minutes by talking trash about her hair.

"Damn, Baby, what happened to your hair?"

George was right. Bryce ran to the wall mirror and worked her fingers diligently through her weave. After she was satisfied that not a single hair was out of place, she glared at George's reflection. "Is that all you can say after falling up in here at this time of night?"

George sucked in some air. He'd expected drama upon arrival, but Bryce appeared to be in rare form. "Bryce, I'm really exhausted. My plane just landed at BWI about an hour ago."

"Bullshit!" Bryce's bottom lip was shaking something fierce. "Your plane was due to land at six and when I offered to pick your ass up, you said you'd just take a cab."

George wrapped his arms around Bryce and kissed her on the cheek. "I was just being thoughtful. I didn't want my baby caught up in all that rush hour traffic."

Bryce pushed him away from her. "Whatever!"

Bryce stomped into the living room with George right on her tail.

"No, really, Bryce. I was just thinking about you. It's a good thing I told you not to come because I had a long layover in Chicago and we had to taxi on the runway for quite some time before we could even take off."

Bryce leered at him. "You really think I'm going to buy this bullshit, don't you?"

Bryce started pacing the floor in the teddy George had given her after his last trip. She was feeling musty after the treadmill so she'd taken a long, hot bath and worked some magic to get all sexy for him. Meanwhile, he had the audacity to pull a no-show.

"I swore to myself that I wouldn't take any more crap off of you, George, so it's over!"

"No, Bryce. Absolutely not. This is not over and it's never going to be over. We love each other and we will work this out."

Bryce felt her heart flutter and realized he was right. She did adore his skank ass. Maybe George's plane was the only one in American History to land eight hours late despite the fact that there wasn't a rain cloud in sight.

George, convinced that he'd managed to calm her down, started grinning before grabbing his bag and heading up the steps.

"Look, Beautiful, I'm going to grab a hot shower. My entire body feels tense."

"Want me to join you?" Bryce eagerly volunteered. Instead of a throbbing headache, now she had a throbbing pussy. "I could give you one of my infamous massages."

"Umm, that sounds fabulous, Baby, but that's okay. I'm kind of smelly and I want to be nice and fresh for you before I get into our nice, comfy bed and knock the bottom out that pussy."

Bryce grinned and bit her bottom lip.

"You can wake me up in the morning with a massage and that other thing you do so well," George said seductively, referring to Bryce's predilection for waking him up with a blow job.

After George disappeared up the steps, Bryce started fondling her nipples, which were rock hard in anticipation of the hellified sex about to get set off.

George hollered back downstairs. "Something smells damn good! What did you cook for dinner?"

"Your favorite, steak."

"Mmmmm, I can't wait to sink my teeth into it, but first I'm going to sink my teeth into you."

Bryce blushed and then ran upstairs to set the right mood in the bedroom. The food could wait. Since it was so late, it would make a better brunch after five or six rounds of sex anyway.

It hit her somewhere between lighting the vanilla-scented pillar candles and spraying Indian Money into the air. Bryce looked down to retrieve George's clothes, which he always left strewn all over the bedroom floor. She searched and searched and there wasn't so much as a sock to be found so she pondered.

He never puts his clothes in the hamper when he comes home in the early evening but he takes the time to do it at four o'clock in the morning? "Hmmm," she said to herself aloud.

The door to the master bathroom was open so she looked on the tile floor to see if he had possibly altered his routine and undressed in there instead. *Nope, nada!*

That only left one place, the hamper. *Why on earth would he put his clothes in the hamper?"*

Bryce heard Colette's sarcastic ass repeating what she'd said earlier on the phone in her mind.

"You better sniff his drawers when he does and make sure they don't smell like crusty pussy juice."

As ridiculous as it sounded at the time, the clothes in the hamper threw her for a loop so Bryce said, "Fuck it!" Then she headed to the walk-in closest to find the drawers.

They were easy to spot because the clothes George had worn home were the only things in his hamper. Bryce had washed his laundry the day before. She picked up the pair of red Calvin Klein briefs and held them in her hand. She started laughing at the absurdity of herself standing there in order to do a drawers inspection. The only thing she expected to find was a possible brown line or two down the back. She knew how nasty men could be when it came to wiping the ass.

Bryce decided either she trusted her man or she didn't and threw them back in the hamper. She had the door to the closet halfway shut when George started singing in the shower. In all of the years she had known him and during the eighteen months they'd been shacking up, she'd never heard his ass sing. Rather less sing in the shower, but there he was, belting out *Always and Forever*.

That shit did it! Bryce flung the closet door back open, snatched up the drawers, and carried them out into the hallway so she could get more light. She almost vomited when she saw them. Not only were the dookie trails there she was counting on, but there was some crusty white stuff in the front.

She put them up to her nose, took a good sniff of the musty odor, and then ran downstairs to the kitchen, taking the steps two at a time.

"Where are you, Beautiful?" George descended the steps dressed in the silk robe Bryce had given him for Christmas with nothing on underneath. "I thought you'd be waiting anxiously naked in the bed for me."

He noticed something brown on the floor leading into the living room. When he picked up a piece of it, he was astonished to discover what it was. *Bryce had ripped the tracks out of her hair weave.*

He wasn't sure whether to run back upstairs, get in the bed, and fake sleep, or go into the living room and ask her why she did it. Before he could make a final decision, Bryce turned the corner with one hand on her head and the other one behind her back.

"What's wrong, Baby?" George took two steps back. "Why'd

you rip out your hair weave?"

Bryce didn't say a word. Just took a few more steps towards him, forcing him to back up until he was pressed up against the door.

"Honey," Bryce said lovingly.

"Yes-s-s-s, Baby?" George stuttered.

"You know I love you, right?"

"Yes-s-s-s, Baby." George tried to keep some composure, but it was hard to do with all the patches of matted hair on Bryce's head.

"You know I would do anything for you, right?"

"Yes-s-s-s, Baby, and you know I would do anything for you, too! *Any-y-y-ything at all!*"

George spotted something shiny out of the corner of his eye and dodged the blade of the ten-inch butcher knife just seconds before Bryce rammed it into the front door.

They were off and running. Bryce chased his ass up the steps. "*Then why the hell did you come home with some other bitch's pussy juice all over your damn drawers?*"

George got the bedroom door shut and locked just in time. Bryce started banging on it. "*Open this fucking door!*"

"Listen to me, Bryce! I can explain!"

"You can explain away a lot of things, but you *sure as shit* can't explain away pussy in your drawers."

George fell silent. After a few seconds, Bryce put her ear up to the bedroom door. She could hear him on the phone whispering to one of his homeboys.

"Charlie, you've got to come over here and help me out, Man!"

Bryce started laughing at his pathetic ass and realized he wasn't even worth it. She could get herself another man. *Fuck him!*

"George, tell Charlie he doesn't need to come rescue your skank ass because I'm leaving. Whoever the bitch is, she can have you because you've outworn your usefulness to me."

"Bryce," she heard George call from somewhere in his hideout. "I know you're upset right now, Baby, but we will work this all out. I'll leave for the night if you want me to. You have to promise not to stab me if I come out, though."

She laughed harder. *His ass was really scared.*

"I'm sure you would leave. Probably run back to that whore whose pussy you just crawled up out of."

"It's not like that, Boo!"

"I got your Boo." Bryce took the knife and rammed it into the bedroom door. It wasn't as sturdy as the front door and it went clear through. Bryce peeked in and could see his ass curled up on the bed like a bitch.

"I'm leaving, George. I'll be back tomorrow after work. Don't be here when I roll through and have *all* your shit gone, or I'll use this knife and do a Lorena Bobbitt on your ass."

Bryce could see George cover his dick with his hands, flinching from the mere thought of it. She started walking down the steps, feeling liberated and victorious at the same time. "While you're making phone calls, you might as well go ahead and call Tyrone, too."

She smirked and started singing her favorite cut by Badu as she got a blazer out the entry closet to cover up the teddy and retrieved her purse. She had the door open when she had an afterthought. She yelled back up the steps. "*By the way, you're not the only one who knows how to get their freak on! I fucked this big dick brotha on the pool table over at Lamar's on Memorial Day!*"

A few seconds later she heard the bedroom door swing open. She knew she had gotten to him. Most men can't handle the truth. They can dish it out, but can't take it. She decided to throw a couple of lies up in the mix for effect.

"*Not only did I fuck him on the pool table, I fucked him in our Jacuzzi the next day and I even fucked him in the back seat of your Lexus!*"

That shit did it! Bryce heard George's footsteps coming down the upstairs hall. *Knife or no knife for protection, he was about to beat her ass.* She ran out the house, slammed the door behind her to give her a few extra seconds to make it to her car, jumped in her Toyota Camry, and started the ignition.

By the time she got the headlights on, George was standing there looking at her with his piercing gray eyes. "*You bitch!*"

He started banging on the hood of her car, making his way over to her side and then tried to yank open the door. She put the car in reverse. He made one last ditch effort, took his fist, and punched out the driver's side window.

Bryce backed out the driveway and yelled out the window she had no need to roll down since the glass was all over her lap and legs. *"Just make sure your ass is gone by the time I come home tomorrow!"*

She made a slicing motion with her left hand, reminding him of her Lorena Bobbitt threat, and then rolled out.

Chapter Seven

What's A Catfight Or Two Between Siblings?

"Bryce, I sincerely hope you're not planning on moving up in here." Harmony was up and bitching over a cup of coffee by 8 A.M.

"Harmony, I've only been here three hours," Bryce snapped back. "How in the hell do you figure I'm moving in?"

"I'm just saying." Harmony rolled her eyes and picked up her *Afro-American* newspaper. "You come busting up in here, using your extra key in the middle of the damn night. What if I had a man up in here getting busy?"

"When cars fly! The only man who might have *possibly* been over here is Zachary and he's used to me." Bryce giggled. "Remember the time I watched you two fucking on the hood of Daddy's car. One thing's for sure. Zachary is not a little dick man like Javon. I know that for a fact."

Harmony debated about slapping the shit out of Bryce, but decided to have mercy on her. She looked ugly enough with the matted weave. A black eye would have only added insult to injury. "Well, you won't be running into him here because we're over," Harmony remarked snidely.

"Whatever! You're just mad at him right now for some reason you probably don't even comprehend your damn self. That's *usually* the case. He'll come groveling back and the next thing you know, your little kitty will start purring for him all over again. That man has had your kitty dick-whipped so long, we might as well nickname him *Fancy Feast*."

"Hmph, you can think that if you want to!"

Bryce got up from the table, on a mission to raid the fridge. "Damn, Harmony. How come you never keep any food in this big ass house?"

"Not that I have to answer to you, but I work most of the time and have business dinners at restaurants three or four nights a week."

Bryce stood behind her, leaning on the counter, and mouthed the words, mocking her. Harmony glanced at her and then pointed at the pantry. "There are some Frosted Cinnamon *Pop Tarts* in there."

"My girl! I knew you would come through."

Harmony sneered. "Don't I always?"

"Speaking of which," Bryce said as she sat back down at the table with the box of *Pop Tarts*. "I was talking to Colette on the phone last night and..."

Harmony cut her off. "Was this before or after you ripped the tracks out of your head over that no good, hedonistic maggot you've been wasting your time on for the past few years?"

Bryce slammed her fist down on the table. "I knew I shouldn't have come here! You're always riding my ass!"

"Then why did you come here?" Harmony put the paper down and stared at Bryce, waiting for an answer.

"Colette lives with her mother and I couldn't go over there at five in the morning. Lucky only has a twin bed at the dorm and she sleeps too damn wild." Bryce got up again to get some juice. "Besides, I need something to wear today. You're the only one with the bomb ass business suits."

"Colette probably wasn't home at five, anyway. She was probably hooking on the corner. As for Lucky, you would have traumatized the poor child if you went over there in the middle of the night looking like Buckwheat with a fade."

"Shut the hell up, Harmony! Colette's not a hooker. Don't even go there."

"Seriously? I could have sworn I saw her ass on that HBO Special *Pimps Up, Hoes Down*."

"Harmony, I won't let Colette say *anything* negative about you. In fact, I jumped on her ass just last night about that."

Harmony sat up in her chair. "What did that trick say about me last night?"

"Never mind. Forget it." Bryce bit into a *Pop Tart*. She waited until Harmony was engrossed in the paper again and then continued, "There's something I need to ask you, though. I need a favor."

"Aw, hell!" Harmony got up, folded the paper under her arm and headed out the kitchen door. "I have to get ready to go to work. I have a long day today. As far as the suit, I wouldn't so much worry about wearing one of my suits as I would doing something to that fuckin' head. You either need to cut that shit off and get you a bumpin' ass cut or get those tracks put back in."

Bryce followed Harmony upstairs to her bedroom. Harmony went into her massive walk-in closet to pick out a suit to wear.

"Harmony." Bryce was about to blurt it out, no matter what the reaction. Her word was her word. "Colette got fired and needs a job. I told her you would hook her up."

Harmony came charging out the closet, braless with tits swinging, while Bryce plopped down on the bed. "Are you out of your damn mind?"

"I'm serious, Sis. I need you to find something for her, *anything*. I would do it myself but I don't have it like that at the firm. At least, not yet."

Harmony just stood there in the middle of the floor, half-naked and pouting. Bryce was shocked to see her sister with some black thong satin panties on. *Maybe she did have some freak potential, after all.*

Bryce gave Harmony a few more moments to stew it over while she got dressed. Bryce turned on the *Donny Simpson Morning Show* on WPGC 95.5, waiting for her to come back out the closet. She didn't want to miss the entertainment report from Huggy Lowdown. He was just too damn hilarious and Bryce tried to catch him every weekday, if possible.

Harmony finally appeared in a double-breasted cream suit and bronze pumps. "Harmony, that suit is smoking."

"Thanks!" Harmony was viewing herself in the full-length mirror, basking in Bryce's compliment when her sister went for it again.

"Harmony, Lucky asks you for a lot of stuff. Mostly because she has to and I know I used to have to depend on you for everything from food to oxygen but, in the past few years, how many times have I asked you for anything?"

Harmony deliberated on it and then replied, "Not often."

"Please do this one thing! Not for Colette, but for me!"

"Bryce, I don't know why you think it is your duty to take care of Colette. She's a grown woman and needs to start acting like one."

"Colette does act like a grown woman. It's not her fault that she got fired. At least she had a job in the first place, unlike a lot of these sistas laying up on the sofa all damn day watching soap operas."

"You see, you automatically assume getting fired wasn't her fault. Did she give you any details or just another sob story?"

"Colette keeps it real, Harmony. Always. Sometimes I think you're straight up hatin' on Colette."

"Straight-up hatin'? She even has you sounding like her now."

Bryce rolled her eyes at Harmony. "There could be worse things, Miss High and Mighty!"

Harmony really didn't feel like getting into it with Bryce, but felt like they needed to get some things straight.

"Bryce, I don't hate Colette. I just don't appreciate the effect that she has on you sometimes."

"I'm my own woman and Colette can't make me do anything I don't want to do any more than you can." Bryce couldn't believe the nerve of Harmony. All she wanted was a simple favor and Harmony had to start going off. "Colette is my friend and she'll continue to be my friend until the day I die."

Harmony could see the fury in Bryce's eyes. She could understand Bryce's loyally to Colette to some extent. When Bryce had first started college at Howard, Colette came to her rescue and helped her out of a sticky situation. Bryce was working part-time at the McDonald's across the street from the main campus. After work one night, some brothers who'd had a tad too much to drink started roughing Bryce up in the parking lot because she refused to give them any play. Colette and a few friends were pulling in to grab a late night snack when they saw the stressful situation unfolding. The rest of the sistas with Colette were willing to pretend like everything was everything, but not Colette.

She jumped out of the vehicle while her friend still had it in motion headed for the drive thru lane, whipped her can of pepper spray out, and started going for their beady eyes without a second's hesitation. Colette instructed Bryce, a total stranger, to hop into the back seat of the car and proceeded to start kicking various sets of balls like she was the punter for the Redskins sweating over the possibility of hanging left on the game-winning field goal.

From that moment on, a friendship was born. Bryce returned to McDonald's just long enough to turn in her uniform. Bryce spotted two of the brothers at the student union while she was there with Harmony and Zachary. Zachary and his frat brothers put the fear of being involuntarily enrolled in How To Get Your Ass Whupped 101 into them and they ended up on their knees begging for Bryce's forgiveness. It was quite a scene and Harmony couldn't help but miss Zachary as she stood there drowning out Bryce's ranting and raving.

"Harmony, are you even listening to me?" Bryce asked, poking Harmony in the shoulder.

That snapped her back into reality. "Hey, watch the suit!"

"Did you hear what I said or not?"

"Kind of, but back to the point I was trying to make. Colette needs to start taking some responsibility for her own actions. I'll tell you exactly where she needs to start, too."

"I bet you will," Bryce lashed out at her.

"Her appearance. Don't get me wrong. You need to do something about your hoochie outfits also, but at least you dress professionally when you head into the office. I don't think I've ever, in life, seen Colette in something that didn't look like it could cut her booty to pieces if she sat down in it the wrong way."

"If Colette is happy and content with her appearance, then what's it to you?"

"It's something to me if you plan on insisting that I hook her up with a job."

"Does that mean you're at least considering it?"

"I'm considering doing *you* a favor. However, Colette can't show up wherever trying to get dicked down by every man in sight."

"Oh, so now you're going there? Harmony, you need to take a chill pill, for real."

"I know how she is, Bryce," Harmony continued. "Colette is always going after men that are way out of her league. She expects a man to possess traits that she doesn't possess herself and she'll never learn. Sure, they'll accept the carte blanche ass, but they'll never consider her as relationship material as long as she carries herself that way."

"Since when did you become the expert on Colette?"

"Since you've been telling me all of her business, just like you tell her all of mine and Lucky's."

Bryce had no comment. There was no sense in trying to deny that she had a big ass mouth. Maybe it was somewhat her fault that Harmony had such a low opinion of Colette. Every single time a man dogged Colette out, Harmony knew about it less than twenty-four hours after Bryce did.

"If you don't want me to say negative things about Colette, don't keep dishing out her dirt to me," Harmony said, confirming Bryce's thoughts. "That's just like a woman bragging on her man's dick at every opportunity and then inviting the town skank to spend the weekend."

"Whatever, Harmony. This is getting us absolutely nowhere. Either you're going to help Colette out or you're not. So which is it?"

Harmony glanced at Bryce and had to admit she was proud of her. In the face of all the shit that happened between her and George the night before, she was still trying to help out a friend. Harmony had to genuinely admire that.

"I'll find her something."

Bryce jumped up off the bed. "*Really?*"

"Really!"

"You're not shitting me, are you?"

"Nope, I'm not shitting you." Harmony starting putting on a

pair of gold earrings. "It won't be anything major. I doubt Colette has *any* marketable skills. I'll stick her in a receptionist position or on a switchboard somewhere."

Bryce ran up behind Harmony and threw her arms around her shoulders. "I knew you would come through for her."

Harmony pushed her arms off and then turned around to face her. "I'm not coming through *for her*. I'm coming through *for you*."

"I love you, Harmony!"

"I love your trifling ass, too!" Harmony reached on her dresser to get her watch. "You're going to be responsible for getting her some decent clothes."

"Done!"

"I really have to run. I have a meeting in thirty minutes." Harmony picked up her purse and keys. "Tell Colette to call me at the office in a couple of hours."

"Okay, I'll call her right now and let her know."

"As for you, you need to take one of those sick days you've been accumulating and do something about your fuckin' hair. My hairdresser, Monique's number is in my Rolodex in my study downstairs. You need to make like the hoochie you are, go down the *skreet*, and get your hair *did*."

Bryce took a good look in the mirror. "You're right! My hair is fucked!"

They both snickered.

"Your hair is fucked and then some," Harmony added. Then she headed down the stairs. "And call AAA about your car window."

Chapter Eight

Just Another Day in the Trenches

Harmony glared at Jerry Morrison, one of her top clients, sitting across from her, and could tell from the expression on his face that he wasn't there to exchange pleasantries. She'd barely been in her office for ten minutes when her secretary announced his unexpected arrival.

They'd taken seats and he'd declined a cup of coffee or tea. Harmony was ready to get the drama over with, whatever it might be.

"So, what can I do for you today?" she asked, feigning a smile.

He shifted in his chair and loosened the knot on his tie. "Ms. Whitfield, this is extremely difficult for me, but I feel like something must be said."

Harmony closed her eyes briefly, hoping that one of her employees hadn't developed a case of sticky fingers. That was always a risk whenever you hired people based on two quick references and a required drug test. While most of them were great people simply down on their luck, some of them had been unable to find permanent employment for a reason.

"Something needs to be said about what?"

"The racial mix-up of your company."

I really don't need this shit today, Harmony thought. "What's wrong with the racial mix-up of my company? For that matter, what makes you an authority on it?" she asked irately, immediately going on the defensive. She didn't like the nature of his statement and wasn't about to pretend otherwise.

He cleared his throat. "We, at the Diamond Chocolate Company, try our best to support minority-owned businesses. However, we are concerned because out of the five temporary employees you've placed with us over the past ten months, only one has been a member of the majority."

"The majority? You mean White?"

"Exactly. You've placed three African-Americans and one Hispanic into our secretarial pool."

"And only one *White?*" Harmony said, emphasizing the last word.

"Yes."

"Jerry, may I call you that?"

"Certainly."

"Jerry, you want to know the reason I started Whitfield and Associates?" She gave him a few seconds to reply. When he didn't, she answered the question anyway. "I started it because when I first moved here from California to go to college, I survived by working temporary jobs. I worked for several temp agencies and there was one thing I noticed the second I walked into every single one of their offices to endure yet another batch of filing and typing tests."

"What was that?" he asked with disinterest.

"All the people conducting interviews, all the people administering tests, and all the people sitting behind the receptionist desks were White." He sighed deeply and straightened his necktie. Harmony continued, "That in itself wouldn't have seemed strange if all the people in the waiting area filling out applications weren't African-American, Asian, and Hispanic." Jerry didn't comment. He just glared at her with disdain. "Now, you might take offense to what I'm about to say. Frankly, I don't care. I'm at the point in my life where I realize I don't have to kiss up to anyone."

He threw his palms up in the air. "Ms. Whitfield, I didn't mean to upset you. Please don't, how do you people say it, *go off* on me."

Harmony rolled her eyes. "Is that how you view me? As some sort of angry minority looking for the space and opportunity to exhibit stereotypical hatred against *the man?*"

"No, I never said that. You're putting words in my mouth. I simply came here, on a friendly basis I might add, to inform you of our concerns."

"As I was about to say, I grew tired of watching *the majority* capitalize off of the minority and while I harbor no fantasies of changing the world, I decided to change my little slice of it." Harmony smirked at him. "I was never cut out to work for other people. I knew that early on when people used to glare down their aquiline noses at me and address me like I was beneath them."

"I see," Jerry said, getting up from his chair.

"Let me finish," Harmony said, directing him with her fingers to sit back down. He did. "I'm not beneath anyone. I see everyone as my equal. I started Whitfield and Associates for several reasons. Mostly, I wanted to make sure that just because someone is humbled down to the point where they have to seek temporary employment to tide them over, they wouldn't have to deal with someone treating them like they were a piece of gum stuck to the bottom of their shoe."

"Like I said before, I didn't come here to offend you," Jerry said defensively, obviously uncomfortable with the direction the conversation had gone in.

"And there was no offense taken. I'm a firm believer that there can be no progress without discussion. I'm glad you took the time out of your busy schedule to come down here and voice your concerns face-to-face. I might have taken offense to a phone call. I prefer to read a person's facial expressions during such conversations." Harmony let her words sink in before continuing. "Now, I have no intention of replacing any of the employees I have placed at your company unless you can show just cause or substantiate below par job performance. You have a contract with me that doesn't expire for another six months. Try to break it and I'll see you in court."

Jerry Morrison was appalled, but had to admire Harmony's

tenacity. "Would you at least guarantee that if and when we place an order for an additional secretary, you will send us someone else?"

"Someone else? You mean a White person?" Harmony chuckled. "Don't beat around the bush. Say what you mean and mean what you say."

"Okay, fine. I would prefer a White woman if another temporary employee is sought through your firm," Jerry said sternly.

"You will get whomever I have available that is skilled enough to perform the duties prescribed in our contract, whether that person is White, African-American, Hispanic, Asian, or Pakistani." Harmony glared at him and asked, "Do you follow me, Jerry?"

"Yes, unfortunately I do," he conceded, wishing that he had never come.

"Good." Harmony stood up, walked around her desk, and opened up the door leading to her outer office. "If you'll excuse me, I have a meeting in a few moments."

"I have to run along, too." Jerry got up and walked to the door. "I'll just see myself out."

Harmony shook his hand. "Have a nice day and enjoy the beautiful weather."

He forced a smile and left. Harmony slammed the door behind him. She wanted to make sure he never came to her with such racist bullshit again.

Harmony collapsed into her desk chair, holding her side, and wretched with pain. She rang for her secretary, who responded over the intercom. "Yes, Ms. Whitfield."

"Could you please call Dr. Dresher's office and see if she has any appointments available today?"

"Yes, Ms. Whitfield. Right away."

Harmony scrambled to dump the contents of her purse on her desk, rifling through them until she located a prescription bottle of pills. She popped the cap off and tossed two pills into her mouth, swallowing them dry.

Bryce didn't get into her office until mid-afternoon. Monique, Harmony's stylist, had whacked away at Bryce's hair after informing her that she'd suffered serious weave damage. Bryce felt about ten pounds lighter but had to admit, after swiveling back and forth in Monique's chair with a handheld mirror to take in all angles, that her hair looked damn good.

The administrative assistant, Jean, handed Bryce a stack of messages from clients and there was one red-flagged message from her boss, Winston Ross. Bryce smacked her lips when she saw that one. He'd been getting on her last nerve lately. A high falutin knee-grow that swore he had it going on, Winston didn't realize that their firm wouldn't hesitate to get rid of either one of their black asses if the mood hit them.

Bryce went to her cubicle in the bullpen, sat down, and hooked up her headset telephone. People all around her glared at her as if to say, "You've got your nerve, coming in so damn late while we're sitting here strung out."

None of them would ever actually say something smart to Bryce, though. One white girl, Jolene, who thought she was the reincarnation of Marilyn Monroe, attempted to step to Bryce one time about a mutual client who was displeased with their recent stock portfolio. Whether it was a valid point or not, Bryce wasn't going to let the bitch talk down to her. She told her ass off good, right in front of everyone, and didn't give a damn who heard it.

Jolene was so embarrassed that she resigned on the spot the following Monday. Bryce and Lucky had shared about two hours of laughter at Jolene's expense after they spotted her waiting tables at the Hooters in Rockville and insisted on being seated in her section. They ran Jolene ragged and, even after she had catered to their every whim to prevent being fired, Bryce still asked to see the manager and insisted that Jolene be reprimanded for providing "shitty ass service and expressing blatant racism."

Word got back to the office so everyone was fully aware that Bryce was ready, willing, and able to summon Ms. Thang if need be.

The only coworker Bryce truly liked was Yvon, who was originally from Hawaii. They got along well and even did lunch a couple of times during the week when they could make a fast getaway. Yvon waved at Bryce from her cubicle across the pen and pointed to her own hair before giving Bryce a thumbs up on the new hairdo. Bryce winked at her and started dialing Colette's number.

Colette yanked the phone up on the first ring. "Who this be?"

"What are you, still sleep?" Bryce whispered into the phone. "It's after two."

"Well, Bryce, it's not like I have any place special to be," Colette said nastily. "I'm ass out of a job, remember?"

"Oops, my bad," Bryce said, having completely forgotten to call Colette earlier about Harmony. "Harmony wants you to give her a call. She said she'd hook you up."

"Are you serious?" Colette said excitedly, not believing her ears.

"Yes, but I won't lie. It wasn't easy to convince her. I had to sit through a tongue-lashing."

"Dang!"

"Listen," Bryce continued, glancing at the clock/calendar on her desk, "Harmony might be out and about by now, so try her cell phone first. You still have the number?"

"Yeah, I have it in my address book."

"Cool." Bryce hesitated briefly while she tried to gauge if one of her coworkers within earshot was trying to be nosy. "Sis, now that I've done you a favor, I need one."

"Sure, you know I'm down with you. What's up?"

"Remember what you said last night about the juice?"

"The juice?" Colette was totally confused.

"Yeah, the juice," Bryce repeated, raising her voice slightly.

"Oh, damn, the juice!" Colette screamed into the phone, recalling her pussy juice comment. "You're not trying to tell me that Negro actually had some in his drawers?"

"That's exactly what I'm telling you."

"Shit, Bryce! That's fucked up!"

"Isn't it?" Bryce said with disdain. "You know it got ugly, right?"

"Gurl, hell yes, I know. Just let me ask one thing. Is George still breathing oxygen or do you have his ass pushing up daisies somewhere?"

"He's still breathing, but he better not be breathing at my crib."

"You kicked him out?"

"I told him not to be there when I got home this evening or it's on for real."

"Damn, Bryce! I wish I could've been there. I would've laid it on him."

"Trust me, I laid it on him enough for both of us."

"So what you need, Gurl?"

"I want you to meet me at my house at six. Just in case he's still there, I might need you around."

"To protect you? I can bring my bat."

"No, to protect him. I'm afraid that if he's still lounging up in there, I'll end up having to shank a few dykes in the women's penitentiary that want to make me their all-day sucker."

An older woman sitting directly beside of Bryce cleared her throat loudly.

"Hold on for a second, Colette." Bryce took the headset off and stood up, looking over the partition. "Can I help you with something?"

"Excuse me?" the woman stated angrily.

Bryce smacked her lips at her. "Sure, I'll excuse you. This time."

Bryce sat back down and put the headset back on. "Sorry about that, Colette. I had to handle something right quick."

"No problem, Gurl. Maybe we should just talk later."

"Yeah, cool. You go ahead and call Harmony and I'll see you at six, right?"

"Guaran-damn-teed!"

"Ooh, I know what I forgot to tell you!" Bryce exclaimed, after a slight breeze from the vent above her head swept across the nape of her bare neck. "I made a drastic change today. Wait till you see me."

"What'd you do? Did you get your tongue pierced, Bryce? You so nasty!"

"No, Colette, but that's my next move," Bryce chided. She had often joked about getting her tongue pierced, but had never exerted an ounce of effort to locate a place to get it done.

"So what then?"

Bryce was anxious to spill the beans, but decided to hold off so she could let Colette be totally shocked.

"Never mind. You'll see in a few."

"Dang, you know I hate it when you do this."

Bryce giggled. "Don't have a hissy fit." Bryce spotted Winston headed in her direction. "I have to run. See you at six."

She yanked the headset off and stood up, preferring to deal with Winston's sarcastic ass face to face.

"Ms. Whitfield," he stated vehemently, "do you realize what time of day it is?"

"Yes, I do," Bryce replied in an equally nasty tone.

"Did you not see the message I left for you?"

"Yes, I saw it, and I was about to head into your office as soon as I returned a pressing business call."

The woman seated in the next cubicle cleared her throat again. Bryce dared the heifer to reveal that her call had been personal. She would feel her wrath.

"According to your voice mail, Ms. Whitfield, you had to get your car window fixed today."

"That's correct."

"Then how come you have a fresh hair style?" Winston asked accusingly. "Did you take the liberty of neglecting your work to go to the salon?"

"Actually, I went to get my hair done last night," Bryce lied. She'd actually had AAA tow her car into a garage and caught a cab over there from the salon to pick it up. "Is there some unwritten rule that I can't get my hair done on my own time?"

Winston smirked at her and Bryce smirked right back at him.

She dug into her purse, retrieved the receipt from the garage, and flashed it in front of his face. "Wha-la! As you can see, I just signed for my car less than thirty minutes ago."

He leered at her and turned his back on her, walking away. "My office, five minutes."

Bryce had to resist the urge to run up behind him and shove her size eight pump up his ass. She spent the next five minutes on the Internet, looking up assassins for hire.

Chapter Nine

Easier Said Than Done

Harmony really didn't feel like doing a power dinner, but she had been after a particular government contract for more than a year and there was no way she was going to miss the opportunity to finally give her sales pitch.

She met Clayton Maxim at Georgia Brown's and he was incredibly handsome in his Lorenzo Latini suit. Harmony found herself attracted to his looks, but his attitude left a lot to be desired. Besides, her heart had always and would always belong to Zachary.

"So, Ms. Whitfield, I'm glad we finally have the opportunity to sit down and discuss the possibility of doing business together."

"Yes, I have looked forward to this for quite some time."

Harmony was about to get her flirt on over filet mignon and red-skinned potatoes, even though she had no romantic interests. She did have an interest in the contract that he held the key to. She never got the chance because Zachary strutted over to the table and sat down uninvited.

"No wonder I haven't heard from you, Harmony," Zachary spat at her vehemently. "You've been busy with your new man."

Harmony was stunned, but not completely surprised. Zachary had a way of jumping to conclusions.

"Is there a problem?" Clayton asked nastily. "Do I need to get security?"

Harmony waved Clayton off. "No, that won't be necessary. Zachary and I have a past."

"And a future," Zachary interjected. "Harmony belongs to me. Now and always."

Harmony tried to laugh off the embarrassing moment. "Zachary, you're blowing things out of proportion. Mr. Maxim is a potential client and we're having a business dinner."

Zachary eyed Clayton suspiciously before his eyes fell on the proposal on the table. "I'm sorry. I just saw you two looking *cozy* and made assumptions."

"That's quite understandable," Clayton said coolly. "If I had a woman in my life as lovely as Ms. Whitfield, I would be overly-protective of her also."

"Harmony is lovely, isn't she?" Zachary eyed Harmony seductively and she almost melted into her chair.

"Yes, she is," Clayton agreed. "Lovely and then some. Not to mention a wonderful businesswoman."

"You two keep this up and I won't be able to squeeze my head through the door," Harmony said jokingly. "A woman can only take so much."

Both of the men laughed and Harmony let out a sigh of relief. They'd managed to avoid major drama.

"Zachary, what are you doing here anyway?" Harmony inquired, hoping he wasn't there to meet a female. She didn't think she could be as tactful about it if he was.

"I'm meeting Rodney and Pete for drinks."

"Oh, that's good." Harmony smiled.

Zachary could tell that she'd been probing and he took it as a positive sign. He still didn't know why they'd broken up in the first place.

"Um—Clayton, is it? Do you mind if I steal Harmony away for a moment? It won't take long."

Clayton, disappointed slightly because he had hoped to get to know Harmony personally as well as professionally, conceded to the obvious choice. "Not a problem. I need to return a couple of important calls on my cell phone anyway."

Zachary took Harmony's hand, stood up, and led her away from the table towards the hallway where the restrooms were located. He paused in front of a bank of pay phones and pressed her back against the wall, immediately sliding his tongue into her mouth.

Harmony tried to resist him, but couldn't. She accepted his gift and let herself feel alive again from his touch. An older lady came out of the restroom and leered at them. Harmony pulled away from Zachary while the woman continued down the hall and out of view.

Zachary tried to resume the kiss, but Harmony pushed him away.

"Harmony, what's wrong?"

"Zachary, you and I broke up. Remember?"

"I remember you breaking up with me, and I still don't have a clue as to why."

"It's complicated," Harmony replied, her eyes dropping to the tile floor.

"Complicated?" Zachary grabbed her by the elbow. "Harmony, you and I have been together for years and while we've had our share of problems, there was always some sort of reasoning behind them. Mostly misunderstanding and immaturity, but there was a reasoning. But we were doing great, making plans, and then all of a sudden you just ended it. I deserve some sort of explanation."

Harmony raised her eyes to his. "You're right, Zachary. You do deserve an explanation, but I can't do this right now. Not with a client waiting and not here."

"So when? Where?"

"I'll call you or come by, okay?"

"When?"

"Soon."

With that, Harmony freed herself from Zachary's grasp and slinked away into the bathroom so she could get out a good cry before returning to her table.

When she came back out to join Clayton, Zachary was nowhere in sight.

"Looking for your friend?" Clayton asked.

"Um—not really," Harmony responded sullenly.

"Oh, because if you were, he left with a couple of male buddies a moment ago. He asked me to give you something though."

Clayton handed Harmony a folded napkin, which she opened. It simply said, "I'll love you forever. Call me."

Chapter Ten

Making Hate Again

When Bryce arrived home to her townhouse that Friday evening after work, Colette was chilling out front as promised. Fortunately, George was gone and so was all of his stuff. Bryce had already called a locksmith to come change the locks the following morning. It was a relief to end the whole ugly situation without having to actually go through with the Lorena Bobbitt threat. She would have though. If George was foolish enough to stay there, she was foolish enough to cut his damn dick off.

"Bryce, I must admit it. Harmony's not all bad. She was mad kewl with me when I hit her up on her cell phone today."

Bryce smiled, still elated about the new haircut Monique had hooked her up with. "I knew she would be. Did she find you a position yet?"

"Yes. I start Monday morning at this phat law firm downtown."

"*Law firm?*" Bryce was shook. "Doing what?"

"Receptionist."

"That's great. We'll have to go shopping this weekend so you'll be well-dressed on Monday. Peeps be styling hard at law firms."

"Speaking of styling, your hair is fly as shit, Gurl!"

"Thanks." Bryce rubbed the back of her slick head.

"So, you still want to go to Republic Gardens tonight or just check out a movie instead?"

"What's playing?"

"I wouldn't mind checking out *Double Take*. Eddie Griffith is in that one."

"Yeah, he's a funny mofo." Bryce giggled. "Whatever, Gurl. The first thing I want to do is grab something to eat cause I'm starvin' like Marvin and I don't mean Lucky's med school dean she fucked the hell out of."

They both fell out laughing. Bryce had held true to form and told all her sister's business the first second the opportunity arose.

The phone rang. Colette reached for it. "Got it. Hello!" There was a momentary pause. "No, this isn't Bryce. Who the hell is this?"

Bryce grabbed the phone out of Colette's hand and pressed it up against her chest. "Don't answer my phone like this is *Joe's Chicken Joint!*"

Colette replied, "It's a *man*."

She sauntered off to the kitchen to get a Coke. When she returned, Bryce was sitting on the couch with her compact mirror out putting on lipstick.

"Since you're getting all hoochied up, I guess we're going club-bing, huh?"

Bryce glanced up at her. Colette noticed that Bryce had put on mascara while she was in the kitchen getting the soda. *Gurlfriend works fast!*

"Actually, Colette, you think we could hang out tomorrow? I kind of have other plans."

"Aww, some dick calls you up and you're just gonna diss me like that? I see how it is now!"

Bryce smiled. "Well, you know the deal. The best way for me to get over George is to replace him."

"True that. So give up the goods. Who are you fucking tonight?"

"None of ya!"

"Aw hell, we're keeping secrets and shit, too? My bad for even asking."

Bryce got up and put her hand on Colette's back, directing her towards the door. "Don't be mad at me, Colette. We'll definitely go shopping tomorrow. Wanna go out to Potomac Mills? My treat!"

Colette instantly forgave Bryce when she heard the words *my treat*. "Aiight, Gurl. I might head on down to the club anyway. Some fine nuccas hang out up in Republic Gardens on Friday nights."

"Yeah, why don't you do that?" Bryce was still pressuring her out the door. "Go have a great time."

"Aiight, Gurl! Much love!"

Bryce waited until Colette had pulled out of the driveway in her 1989 Chevy Impala and then ran back into the living room, grabbed the cordless phone, and pressed *69, hoping like all hell he didn't have his return call blocked.

An hour later, there was a knock at Bryce's front door.

She opened it and let Troy's trick ass in. He turned around to shut the door behind him, noticing the dent in the door caused by the butcher knife the night before.

"Damn, Gurl, what did you do to your door? Was someone trying to get in or did you trap some homie in here and he did that shit trying to get out?"

"I fucking hate you," she hissed.

"The feeling's mutual!"

He threw her up against the wall, forced her legs open, lifted her up in the air so her legs were straddled behind his back, and started tonguing her ass down.

They didn't come up for air for five minutes.

"I was really surprised when you called me tonight," Bryce said.

"Was it a pleasant surprise?" Troy bit on her earlobe. "You look damn delicious. Did you pretty yourself up just for me?"

"Hell, no," she lied. "I had this old thing on all day."

"Hmmm, so you wore a skintight black booty dress to work today, huh?"

She laughed and gave him some more tongue.

"I need to get a job there if honies walk around looking as fine as you. I love your hair cut. Much better than that fake shit you were sporting at Lamar's."

She rolled her eyes. "Fuck you, trick ass!"

"I fully intend for you to fuck me." He bit her neck and she flinched until he had a nice round hickey in place. "I'm like a lion. I like to mark my territory."

"And I like to mark mine." Bryce returned the favor. Troy moaned as she gave him a hickey tit-for-tat.

"You're a rough gurl. I like that in a honie." He started lowering her dress straps. "I still hate your ass, though."

He started sucking on Bryce's left breast, biting gently on the nipple. "If you hate my ass so much, take me upstairs to my bedroom and make hate to me!"

"Thought you'd never ask." Troy dashed up the steps with Bryce bouncing on his hard dick through his pants. He spotted the grapefruit size hole in her bedroom door. "Damn, what have you been doing up in here, Gal?"

"Just shut up and fuck me!"

Troy literally threw Bryce on the bed and then started taking off his clothes faster than Superman changes his clothes in a phone booth.

"Hold up, what's all this shit over here on your night table?"

"Whatever do you mean?" Bryce tried to hold in her laugh. "I have no idea what you're talking about."

"Aww, playing games, huh? You know good and damn well I'm talking about all this sex stuff you have over here on your dresser!"

Troy started picking up the items one by one. The only items he recognized were the vibrator, the handcuffs, and the dildo. He held up a circular item. "What on earth?"

"That's a cock ring." Bryce smirked.

"And this?" he asked, picking up a velvet box from the table.

"Umm, those would be Ben Wa balls."

"What the fuck?" Troy chuckled. "I see why you got homies fighting to get up out of here now."

Bryce sat up on her elbows. "Can I tell you a secret?"

"Please do, Baby." Troy picked up the dildo and looked at the size of it with resentment, wondering if any of his homies had a dick that damn huge.

"I've never used any of these things before."

He gawked at her with disbelief.

"No, I really haven't. I'll admit that I had a man until *very* recently, but his ass was hardly ever here. I never got to experiment with him."

Troy sat down on the bed beside her. "You're a fucking trip, Gurl."

She reached out and ran her fingertips up and down his arm. "Even though I do hate your guts, I was kind of excited when you called. But, I'm still going to kick Lamar's ass for giving up my dig-its. Tell him I'm gunning for his ass."

"Lamar didn't have a fucking choice *but* to give me the digits," Troy boasted.

"And why is that?"

"Because I'm his boss."

"*Get the fuck out of here!*" Bryce exclaimed. "You mean to tell me that you're Lamar's manager at the auto dealership?"

"Actually, I own the joint."

Bryce laughed harder, collapsing back on the pillow. "You mean to tell me that you fucked me on the pool table at one of your employees' houses?"

Troy blushed. "Damn sure did and tore that pussy up at that!"

"Wait till I tell Colette, Lucky, and Harmony this shit!" Bryce had to hold her side. Her laughter was so intense.

"Who are they?"

"I'll tell you later." Bryce stood up and took off her dress, revealing the fact that she was butt naked underneath. "Right now, I just want to experiment on your ass."

She straddled on top of him and pushed his back onto the bed. His dick was rock solid. She knew from last time, he could fuck her for a good hour straight off pure hatred alone.

She started kissing his chest. "So, when did you get into all this weird sex stuff? Don't get me wrong. I'm loving it!"

"I bought this book called *The Sex Chronicles* and got a ton of ideas."

"Oh my!" Troy replied as Bryce moved her mouth further down in search of the dick. He closed his eyes when she took the head of it in, but then she abruptly got up off the bed and went into the bathroom. A minute later, she came back with a bottle of Listerine.

"What the hell is that for?"

"You're about to find out." Bryce screwed the cap off the bottle and then got back on the bed. "Now fuck me like you hate me!"

Harmony went home early that afternoon after her doctor's appointment. She crawled into bed and fell asleep in the fetal position, trying to block the pain out of her mind.

She woke up a little after eight, took a hot shower, and decided eating dinner was out of the question. She didn't have any food in the house and was too sick to go out anywhere. She made a mental note to do as Bryce requested every time she came through and buy some damn food.

She crawled up on her couch, popped her favorite movie, *Imitation of Life*, in the VCR and watched it. Just like the fifty million times she had viewed it previously, Harmony began to cry on the part with Mahalia Jackson singing and the girl throwing herself on her mother's coffin because she never got a chance to say goodbye.

Harmony made another mental note. She'd *definitely* say goodbye.

She reached for the phone and started dialing Zachary's number, but thought better of it. The last thing he needed, the last thing he deserved, was having to deal with her in her current state. Her heart and body yearned for his touch, but it was just not to be.

Harmony thought about Bryce and Lucky. She realized she was too hard on them, particularly as of late, but it was vital that she prepared them to be independent.

She clamped her eyes shut. The tears began to form a stream down both her cheeks until the toss pillow that her head was lying on was drenched and her heart was broken.

Troy was handcuffed to the bed, pussy-whipped, and worn the hell out after being Bryce's guinea pig for the evening. She had done everything from having him fuck her with a dildo and letting him watch her lick her own pussy juice off of it to sucking his dick with Listerine in her mouth.

Never had a woman turned him on so much and he knew, at that very moment, that *Poppi* was home to stay. She told him she had to go downstairs to get something. He figured it was probably some whipped cream or some other kinky shit like that. Whatever it was, he was ready for her ass. She would cry *uncle* first because he wasn't even going out like that.

Bryce appeared back at the doorway with an open book in one of her hands. He raised up on his elbows so he could see the title. It was *The Sex Chronicles*. "Oh damn! What now?"

Bryce pulled her other hand from behind her back, showing off two of the weirdest damn things he had ever seen.

"What the fuck are those?"

"Anal beads and testicle gauntlets."

"Aww, shit! Uncuff me, Bryce! Uncuff me right this damn minute!"

She climbed on top of him with the book still in one hand and the sex toys in the other. "But, Darling, I'm not finished hating you yet!"

He squirmed, trying to get away. She threw her head back and laughed like Jack Nicholson as the Joker in the original *Batman*.

One of her neighbors was almost ready to call 911 when he heard someone screaming, *"UNCLLLEEEE!"*

Chapter Eleven

Lucky Lucks Out

Lucky was working part-time at the med school library during summer break to make a little extra spending cash. Her parents helped out as best they could but they were a couple of little means, having lost most of their valuables when a hurricane tore through their farm in Southern California four years earlier. Chester Whitfield had allowed the insurance payments to lapse briefly while he played catch up on some other bills. Unfortunately, there was nothing any of them could do about the loss but accept it and adapt.

Harmony had quickly stepped up to the plate when things went downhill. She was *literally* carrying most of the family on her shoulders with the profits from her temporary agency. Bryce had earned an MBA and was doing well at her investment firm. Thus, she was no longer a heavy burden on Harmony.

Lucky hated having to always ask Harmony for money. She fully intended to pay her back every last penny once she became a pediatrician. It was difficult to swallow her pride and ask Harmony for money on a weekly basis. That's why she had taken the job at the library.

Around midnight one Friday night, Lucky was bored and

decided to browse through one of the textbooks she would be required to use during the Fall semester. She was transfixed in the book and didn't see anyone approaching her.

"Excuse me, you wouldn't happen to have an extra pencil, would you?"

Lucky looked up from her books and almost creamed in her pants. It was the dark-skinned brother she'd been interested in for months, but too busy with books to approach. She took the pencil she was sucking on out of her mouth, embarrassed about the way she was working her tongue on it, and responded, "No, sorry."

He took a seat across from her, not even asking if it was alright to sit down. "Weren't you in my molecular biology course this past semester?"

Lucky blushed. "Yes, I was."

"Your name's Lucy, right?"

"Actually, it's Lucky," she replied disappointedly. He could have at least gotten her name right.

"Oops, my bad." He shifted in his seat and placed his book bag on top of the study table. "I'm Robbie. Robbie Cruise."

Lucky stared into his deeply-set brown eyes and held back a sigh. "I know who you are."

Robbie chuckled, glad that she remembered him. He'd been checking her out, but could never get her alone to talk. He was elated when he'd spotted her sitting all alone and made up the pencil line. He had at least a dozen in his bag.

"How'd you do in the course?" he asked her. "Professor Martnick really gave me a hard way to go. I'm surprised I escaped with a C."

"I did okay and Professor Martnick's not all that bad. He's just devoted to science and I can't help but admire that."

"If you say so." Lucky looked back down into her book and Robbie felt like he was losing her attention. "So, what courses are you taking in summer school? I'm taking immunology and genetics."

"I'm not in summer school," Lucky replied, glancing up at him.

Robbie was stunned. "If you're not in summer school, what are you doing studying this time of night?"

"Getting a jump start on next semester." Lucky realized how

nerdy that made her sound as soon as the words left her lips, so she added, "I work here part-time, also. Trying to make some spending change, you know."

"I feel you. I do deliveries for Dominos. The hours are lousy and the tips are few and far between, but it helps supplement what my parents dish out to me."

Lucky was impressed. At least he had a job. A job, in medical school, and fine. Nice combination. "Where are you originally from?"

"Minneapolis. You?"

"The San Fernando Valley."

"Cool. California." Robbie chuckled. "You must've had an exciting time growing up."

Lucky rolled her eyes, remembering her strict upbringing. "I wouldn't call my childhood exciting. Far from it. I grew up on a farm with an overprotective father."

"If I ever have a daughter as fine as you, I'll be overprotective of her also."

Lucky grinned from ear-to-ear. "Flattery will get you everywhere."

Robbie decided to lay his cards on the table. "I'm done studying for tonight. If I do any more studying, my brain might explode. I came over here and asked you for a pencil just so I could holler at you for a minute."

"Like I said, flattery will get you everywhere," Lucky repeated, this time seductively.

"You drink?"

Lucky winced at the question. The last time she'd taken a drink, she ended up rolling on waves with Dean Mitchell. "Not as much as I used to. I recently made a bad decision while I was under the influence so I'm extremely cautious about my alcohol consumption."

"Oooh, I won't ask what the bad decision was," Robbie chided.

"Good, because I wouldn't reveal it anyway," Lucky replied snidely.

"I was thinking of heading down to Georgetown to hang out. It's such a pretty night."

"Sounds like a plan. Enjoy yourself."

Robbie was disappointed that Lucky didn't jump at his sugges-tive remark. It was obvious that he wanted her to join him. He decided to make it more obvious. "I'd enjoy myself a hell of a lot more if you were with me."

"Is that a formal invitation?"

"If it is, will your answer be yes?" Robbie asked nervously.

Lucky could tell he was uneasy. She decided to let him off the hook because she wasn't about to turn down an opportunity to spend quality time with Mr. Fine. "Definitely."

"Then, it's a formal invitation."

Lucky got up from the table. "Let me just go grab my purse. It's behind the information desk."

"Aw, so you give out information?"

"That's the general idea."

"Well, I need some information."

Lucky giggled. "Is that right?"

"Yes, I need to know your phone number and address."

"Pushy. Pushy." They both laughed. "Let's head to Georgetown first, get to know each other a little, and at the end of the night, if I feel so inclined, I'll give you all the information you asked for and then some."

Robbie followed her to the information desk. "Sounds good to me."

"Let's go!" Robbie said, motioning Lucky towards the parking lot once they were outside. "My car's right over here. It's the blue Volkswagen Bug."

Lucky starting laughing.

"What's wrong? You don't like the new Bugs?"

"Hell naw, I love them," Lucky replied, pointing over to their left. "Mine is the red one over there by the street lamp." They both guffawed. "See, we have something else in common already."

"Most definitely!" Robbie took Lucky's hand while they made pleasant conversation on their way to his car. They didn't notice anyone watching them. Nor did they notice the black Mercedes trailing them with its headlights off as they pulled out of the library parking lot.

Chapter Twelve

Trapped

Lucky and Robbie became very close in the month that followed. They hung out almost every day when Lucky wasn't working and he wasn't in class. They did have tons of stuff in common, including a love of African art and cultural activities. Summertime in D.C. is the perfect time to get in tune with your Afrocentricity because there are tons of various fairs and music festivals catered towards African-Americans. Even the world's only African-American owned and operated circus rolled through town during the summer. They tried to hit it all.

They held off on becoming intimate though. Robbie wanted to make sure that Lucky was just as attached to him emotionally as she was physically. It was torture to Lucky because she often lay in bed at night next to him willing him to reach for her and fulfill her every fantasy.

One day, Lucky decided that she couldn't fall asleep one more night without Robbie inside of her so she devised a plan. Robbie often shared his love of dogs with Lucky. His eyes lit up whenever he saw a cute one in the park while they were bike riding or whenever one passed them on the street. So when he told her that his birthday was coming up in less than two weeks, Lucky decided to give him her present early.

She looked up local animal shelters on Yahoo that offered pet adoption, since she knew that there was no possible way she could afford a pedigree, and adopted a precious female beagle for him.

Robbie loved the puppy and, in honor of Lucky, named her Lucinda. They made love for the first time that night, after Lucky gave Robbie a full-body massage with heated aloe vera and recited two poems to him that she had written.

The first one was titled *You've Put a Smile on My Face* and the second was titled *Now Can I Put a Smile on Yours*. The first one described how Robbie had come to mean so much to Lucky through his caring, giving nature while the second described, in erotic terms, what Lucky wanted to do with him sexually.

Needless to say, Robbie couldn't keep his hands off of Lucky by the time she got to the last verse and it was on. Clothes started flying in the air, bodies started moving in unison, and they didn't pass out from exhaustion until eight or nine hours later.

"Robbie," Lucky whispered afterwards. "I realize that we haven't been together long, but I want you to know something."

"What's that, Baby?" Robby asked, kissing her gently on the forehead.

"I love you, Robbie. I really do," Lucky confessed on the brink of joyous tears.

Robbie wiped her eyes. "No need for those. I love you, too, Lucky. I'm so glad we finally hooked up because I had my eye on you for quite some time."

"I'm happier than I've ever been, Robbie."

"That's makes two of us and this is only the beginning."

Lucky loved Robbie's level of maturity. Something it had been extremely hard for her to find in a man her own age. She had kept her promise to Harmony by staying away from Dean Marvin Mitchell, avoiding him like the plague. But one day fate intervened and it was also the day all hell broke loose in Lucky's life.

She was in the chemistry building looking for Robbie in one of the labs when Marvin came into the lab behind her and locked the door.

"What are you doing here?" Lucky asked.

"Last time I checked, I could go anywhere on this campus I pleased."

"I didn't mean it like that. Sorry."

Lucky turned so her back was to him, hoping he would just leave. Her heart started palpitating faster. She sensed something was wrong.

"Lucky, why haven't you been by my office or my place to see me lately?" She could feel his eyes taking a survey of her body. "I thought we had a good time that night."

She swung around to look at him. "We had a good time, but…"

"But, what…?"

"We should've never done that. It was wrong and unethical."

"Because I'm the dean, right?"

"Right," she replied, nodding in agreement.

"Well, this might come as a surprise to you." He started walking closer to her. "But you're not the first student from this school I've entertained in my bed. Far from it."

"You fucking bastard!" Lucky tried to slap him, but he caught her arm by the wrist before impact. "I really thought you cared about me."

"Oh, *I do care*. In fact, I care so much that you could say I'm obsessed with you."

Lucky glared at him with fear in her eyes.

"Like I was saying before you so rudely interrupted me. You're not the first student I've had in my bed, but you're definitely the best. I want some more of your sweet, young pussy."

She tried to slap him with her free hand but he got a hold of that wrist also. She was immobilized, pressed against the lab table.

She was repulsed when he took his thick tongue and lapped the side of her face like a dog.

"The way you devoured my dick that morning was such a rush.

I've been waiting for you to come to me, but I see you've been busy with Robbie Cruise."

Lucky tried to fight him off to no avail.

"I don't mind sharing your little pussy with him. You're damn sure going to have to share this dick. I've got a lot of mouths to feed but none are quite as creative as yours."

Lucky spit in his face before he forced her to turn around.

"Now, now. Don't fight this. If you value your future as a medical doctor, you'll do *everything* I say *whenever* the hell I say it!"

Lucky cried as Marvin held her head down on the table, forcing her face onto the linoleum surface. She cried as he lifted her skirt and ripped her panties off. She cried as he took her from behind. She cried because she wished that Robbie would save her. Most of all, she cried because her promise to her sister had been broken.

"Why are you so quiet, Baby?" Robbie kissed Lucky on the forehead as they lay naked together in each other's arms in his apartment.

"Nothing's wrong!"

Silence.

"You've been acting kind of strange for the last couple of weeks."

"Strange how?" Lucky asked as if she didn't know the answer.

"Just different things I've noticed."

"Like?"

"You're not your normal talkative, jolly self. You don't want to go out anywhere. We had tickets for the Budweiser Superfest and you said you were too tired. Yet, you were about to do cartwheels when I first got the tickets. You don't laugh anymore. Shall I go on?"

"Not really." Lucky had heard enough. She only prayed Robbie would never find out the horrid truth.

He went on anyway. "When we make love now, it's like you aren't even here. You're physically here but your mind seems to be in another place."

"That's absurd," Lucky protested. "I love when you make love to me. I love you period."

He kissed her lightly on her lips and then said, "Okay, Baby. Maybe it's me."

No, it's not you, Baby, she wanted to say.

She looked over his chest to the alarm clock on his nightstand and noticed it was ten minutes to midnight. She jumped up off the bed and started getting dressed. "I have to go!"

Robbie sat up. "Lucky, why are you always running out of here in the middle of the night?"

"I told you. I took on another job as a waitress at an all-night diner."

"What's the name of it?"

"You wouldn't know if I told you. Just some hole in the wall."

"Well, you don't have your car over here tonight so I'll get dressed and drive you. That way I can see this *hole in the wall* with my own two eyes. I don't want you working someplace unsafe and you don't need money that bad anyway." He reached on the floor beside the bed to get his jeans. "I can help you out and your sister makes big bank. Does she know you're working two jobs?"

"No!" Lucky snapped. "And there's no reason for Harmony to find out. There's no need for you to drive me either. I'll just catch a cab."

Robbie sighed. "Lucky, I'm not normally the jealous type, but you're setting off alarms left and right."

Lucky finished getting dressed quickly, leaned over the bed to kiss him goodbye, and then grabbed her purse. "I'll call you in the morning."

He pulled her close to him and slipped his tongue into her mouth. She was shaking like she was afraid of him and pulled away. "I love you, Lucky."

"I love you, too, Baby."

No sooner had she walked out the door of his apartment than the puppy started yelping to be walked.

Robbie threw on his jeans and slipped into a pair of Nikes. He was walking Lucinda through the courtyard of his complex when he spotted Lucky standing on the curb.

He was about to yell out to her and tell her he was driving her ass to work whether she liked it or not. Before he could get a word out, a large black Mercedes with tinted windows pulled up and Lucky jumped in. It took off before she could get the door fully closed.

Robbie stood there wondering where he had seen that car before. More importantly, he wondered what the hell was going on with his girlfriend. One thing was for sure. He was damn sure going to find out.

Chapter Thirteen

Chained Souls

"What are you doing?"

Zachary looked up from under the hood of his silver Infiniti and was overwhelmed to find Harmony standing there.

"Just checking my oil and other vital fluids that make this baby go."

Harmony lowered her Ray Bans to look at him. He was covered with grass stains from cutting the grass earlier that morning and there was oil stuck underneath his normally manicured fingernails.

"That's cool," she replied, but he didn't hear it. He was caught up in her eyes. There was something different about them. They were soft and warm and sparkling like they were when he fell in love with her their freshman year in high school.

"I'm surprised to see you here, Harmony."

"I suppose you would be. After the way I've been acting towards you lately, I wouldn't blame you if you hated me."

"I could never hate you. You know that." He wanted to take her in his arms but didn't want to push it. "So, what brings you here?"

"I wanted to see you. We need to talk," she replied as he

slammed his hood down.

"Yes, we do need to talk. Then again, that's all I've been trying to do all along. I'd expected you to call me shortly after I saw you at Georgia Brown's, but the call never came."

"I needed some time." She looked down at his freshly paved driveway. "I see you finally did something about the asphalt. Looks great."

"Not as great as you." He leaned on his hood and wiped his hands with an oilcloth. "Let's go inside where it's nice and cool. The sun is kickin' today."

"I think it's a pretty day. In fact, that's the reason I stopped by. I was wondering if you wanted to take a ride with me?"

Zachary looked at her, happy as hell to finally be given a glimpse of hope. "I would follow you to the ends of the earth."

"Well, I don't think we can get that far on a tank of gas so how about Annapolis instead?"

Zachary blushed. "Sure! Come on inside for ten minutes while I hop in the shower and get cleaned up."

While Zachary was in the shower, Harmony took a quick survey of his house and immediately noticed something extremely bizarre. Everything was exactly the way she had left it the last time she was there months before.

The blazer to her red suit was still hanging on the back of the chair in the kitchen. The *Essence* magazine she was reading was still open to the same page on the coffee table and the coffee cup she had used the last morning she was there was still sitting in the same spot on the counter with her mocha lipstick on the brim.

Tears came to her eyes as she realized that Zachary loved her so much, he couldn't even let the slightest remembrances of her go. She was almost afraid to come over there that morning, expecting to find another woman had taken her place. *What a fool she had been!*

"Ready to go?" Zachary asked as he popped his head in the kitchen, smelling like expensive cologne and dressed in neatly ironed khakis and a crisp, white cotton shirt.

"Ready when you are!"

"Then let's roll. You want me to drive?"

"Sure, but let's take my car. We can leave the top down and I have a surprise for you in the trunk."

"Hmmm, you've peaked my curiosity."

"Have I now?"

"Yup. I just hope it's not the body of Jimmy Hoffa. They never found him, you know?"

Harmony slapped him on the shoulder. "Silly ass." She chuckled.

An hour later, they were sitting on a blanket on the private beach they used to frequent almost every weekend the year they had both moved from California to attend college. They had been inseparable for many years until Harmony had distanced herself from Zachary without an explanation.

Zachary pointed to the pavilion up on the hill that overlooked the ocean. "You remember how we used to talk about getting married in that pavilion?"

"Of course, I remember." Harmony took a nibble off of one of the turkey and Swiss sandwiches she had prepared for them.

Zachary was surprised when he opened up her trunk. Instead of finding Jimmy Hoffa, he found a lovely basket full of all his favorites. Strawberries and cream, turkey and Swiss on croissants, sparkling apple cider, and chocolate cheesecake.

"Baby, I still can't believe you wanted to see me today," he remarked. "I feel like I just won the D.C. Lottery."

Harmony stared at him. "I've been so horrible to you and there's no way to really make it up to you. I realize that but I can try."

"You're wrong about that." Harmony gave him a perplexed look. "There's *one* way you can make it up to me."

"Tell me and I will do it."

"You promise, Harmony?"

"I promise." She took a finger and crossed her heart to validate the statement. "Anything you ask of me, I will do."

Zachary took her delicate hand into his own, kissing her fingers one at a time before holding her palm up to his cheek and feeling her pulse emit her very essence into him.

She closed her eyes for a brief moment, bit her bottom lip, and waited to hear his request. She was so sick of holding back everything from the people who truly loved her. Zachary was the *only* man she had ever loved in return.

"I know that you love me, Harmony," Zachary said. "I never doubted it for a second."

"I do love you." A single tear flowed down her right cheek. "I always have."

"In that case, grant me one wish. Tell me what's wrong."

There was silence while they stared at each other for what seemed like an eternity.

"Please," he added. "For me! For us!"

Harmony got up off the blanket, kicked off her sandals, and pulled the bottom of her red sundress up around her waist. "I'll race you to the water!"

Harmony ran into the ocean fully-clothed with Zachary right behind her. It was there that she told him the truth.

Five minutes later, he came back ashore, fell down on his knees, and screamed, *"NOOOOOOOOO!"*

Harmony sat down behind him and cradled him in her arms while he cried. They stayed there on the beach, in that position, until sundown.

They went back to Harmony's house that night instead of Zachary's. He prepared them a light pasta dish while Harmony took a long, hot bath.

Zachary brought the tray of food upstairs so he could feed her in bed. All Harmony could think was *the pity has already begun*.

He was brushing her thick brown hair when he asked, "Why haven't you told your family and Fatima?"

She didn't hesitate to answer. "Because they'll only treat me like an invalid. Just like you're doing right now. Besides, I haven't talked to Fatima in awhile now. She's all caught up in her divorce proceedings."

"I'm not treating you like an invalid!" Zachary protested. "I'm

simply taking care of the woman I love."

"You really want to take care of me, Zachary?"

"Do you even need to ask that?"

She got up from her vanity bench, untied her robe, and let it tumble to the floor. "Make love to me!"

Zachary wanted and needed Harmony so bad but he didn't want to cause her any physical harm. The firmness of her breasts and the roundness of her ass made him flashback to all the times they had made love and crave the times they would never get to make love.

"Are you sure it's okay to do that, Harmony?"

"I'm sick. Not contagious." She ran into the bathroom and slammed the door. "I knew this would happen."

Zachary pushed the door open, unable to control his need for her any longer. She was looking in the wall-length mirror over the double-sink when he walked up behind her and started caressing her nipples.

She surrendered to him and turned around to offer her tongue to him. They made love on the bathroom counter and then he laid her down gently on the bed so they could do all the things both of them had been dreaming about during the months they were apart.

"You know, the resemblance between you and Bryce is uncanny," Zachary remarked as they lay in bed afterwards. "You two look so much alike, it's almost scary. If not for the different hairstyles and a couple of other things, you could pass for twins."

Harmony leaned up on one elbow, her caramel skin glistening in the moonlight emitting from the skylight above her bed. "I know what you're thinking, Zachary. I could never ask her for such a sacrifice."

"Even if it means saving your life?"

"Yes, even if it means that!"

Harmony turned over on her side, facing away from him. Zachary kissed her on the shoulder and then watched her fall asleep in his arms, hoping that in due time she would reconsider.

A Word From Our Sponsors

Weave Central

I KNOW YOU'RE ALL CAUGHT up in the drama but can I steal a minute to tell you about my new hair shop, Weave Central? My name is Conchita Dina Alonzo Morales and I'm all into this book, too, so I'll make this fast. Speaking of the book, is this shit wild or what?

That fucking Bryce has issues! What in the hell is a testicle gauntlet? Her chica, Colette, is not much better. Sheesh! Couple of hoochies if you ask me.

I feel sorry for that Lucky gurl though. She's going to med school, making good grades, got a good man, and now some older brotha who loves the way she sucks a dick wants to fuck everything up for her. I have a feeling he's going to get his though. I feel that way and so do all of my customers at the shop.

What do you think is wrong with Harmony? Gurlfriend is breaking my heart. This book has everything. Love, drama, tramps, and hoes. Just like a fucking Ghetto soap opera.

Sorry, I didn't mean to get off track. I'm just so caught up in this shit and dying to see what happens next but I must move on. Half my time is up already so here it goes:

Weave Central, located at the corner of Extension Avenue and Tracks Lane in Fakehair, MD. We have everything you need and we even got a restaurant where we sell everything from Jamaican bean pies to tofu burgers to pig's feet.

Come on down and check us out. Mention this ad and I'll give you a huge discount. I mean *HUGE*, at least 5% off your total bill.

For you sistas, pimps, and transvestites who are strapped for cash, we even have a layaway program so you can have them bad boys paid for and be sporting them by Christmas.

If you have a job making at least $1000 a week and a major credit card, you can go on our deferred payment plan. Wear your weave home today and you won't have to make a payment until next year. The finance charges are only 37.9%. Cheap, huh?

Well, my time is up so let's get back to the drama. One last thing, we also have a colorful collection of contact lenses for you sistas who want *everything* to be fake and a manicurist who can hook your nails up. You can come into our shop looking like Jimmy Walker on crack and leave out with the total package: fake hair, fake nails, fake eyes, the whole nine yards.

Come on down to Weave Central. Once again, we're located at the corner of Extension Avenue and Tracks Lane in Fakehair, MD, conveniently off the Capital Beltway.

My name is Conchita Dina Alonzo Morales and I would be more than happy to work on your weave personally. My prices start at $199.99.

Harmony, keep your head up chica!

We now return to our regularly-scheduled program, "Shame On It All," already in progress.

Part Three:

The Shit Hits The Fan

❧

Chapter Fourteen

Hell Naw, You Can't Come Home

Javon stormed into the living room, after waiting more than five minutes for the maid to answer the door. He'd been standing out front banging so hard on the cherrywood that his knuckles were practically bleeding.

His eyes narrowed with malice when he saw Fatima and Harmony lounging on the expensive furniture he'd paid for, drinking cocktails and eating gouda cheese and club crackers. The seventy-inch high definition television was blaring as *Waiting to Exhale* played in the DVD player. It was at the part where Angela Bassett was putting her husband's clothes in his car about to set it ablaze. Fatima and Harmony were laughing hysterically at the scene, refusing to even acknowledge Javon's presence in the room.

Javon walked over to the television and cut it off. "Fatima, don't you think you're taking this entire situation to the extreme? A man shouldn't have to knock to get into his own castle."

Fatima reached for the remote on the coffee table and clicked the television back on. "And a woman shouldn't have to lie down with a mangy, dishonest pitbull every night either."

"I already explained this. Harmony threw herself at me." Javon pointed an accusing finger at Harmony. She rolled her eyes at him and bit into another cracker. "I felt sorry for her. You're the one that kept saying she was depressed over her break-up with Zachary."

Fatima and Harmony glanced at each other and cackled.

"What the fuck are you doing here, anyway?" Javon asked, leering at Harmony. He turned his attention to Fatima. "Fatima, what is this?"

"What does it look like?" Fatima replied sarcastically, taking another sip of her Blue Hawaiian. "Harmony and I are having a girls night in."

"So I get kicked out of the house and she gets to lounge all over my furniture and eat my food?"

"Yes, she does." Fatima held up her palm so Harmony could slap her a high five. "As a matter of fact, we're both exhausted from spending the entire afternoon packing up your things. Will you be arranging to have them picked up or shall I have them delivered someplace?"

"This is insane!" Javon blared, turning the television back off.

Fatima stood up and walked over to him, poking her index finger into his chest. "No, you're insane to think I would continue to be your wife after all of your dirt."

"Harmony, you bitch!"

Harmony glared at Javon and clucked her tongue. "Javon, don't make me get up off this couch and hurt you."

"I'd like to see you try."

"You have one more time to call me the 'B' word and it's on," Harmony spewed at him.

Fatima slapped Javon on the forearm to draw his attention back to her. "Javon, this isn't even about Harmony. This is about you. I looked the other way for years while you were out gallivanting with skank hoe after skank hoe. Not anymore. It's over. I'm taking my life back. I'm going to…" Fatima waved her hand in Harmony's direction, like she was trying to recall something important. "What was that word you used earlier, Harmony?"

"Reinvent," Harmony giggled.

"Yes, that's it." Fatima turned the television back on and gave Javon a look that let him know he better not even consider turning it off again. "I'm going to reinvent myself and find me a *real man*."

"I am a real man, Fatima," Javon said, trying to sound convincing. "I never cheated on you before that night with Harmony. I swear."

"Save it!" Fatima sat back down next to Harmony on the sofa. "I was a fool, but not one moment longer. I knew you were cheating on me years ago. At least, I knew you had the trait. I tried to convince myself that I could change you. That my love was so strong, you wouldn't dare stray from home, from the comfort zone, because you would be afraid of losing me. What a crock!"

"I am afraid of losing you. I'm terrified."

Harmony tapped Fatima on the hand and shook her head. "He's full of shit!"

Fatima grinned. "Well, you better learn to get over your fear because you and I have reached the end of the road."

"What about the kids?" Javon asked nastily.

"What about them?" Fatima replied just as nastily. "You destroyed this marriage; not me. You put our future in jeopardy, but now my future is bright because it doesn't include you."

"I have a right to see my children."

"Yes, you do have rights, and I'll be very agreeable to visitation rights in divorce court."

"Divorce court!" Javon looked like his knees were about to give out on him. He sat down on the arm of his favorite recliner.

"Hell yes, divorce court. Haven't you gotten it through your thick head that I am moving on?"

"I won't let you do this me. I'll fight you tooth and nail."

"And I'll fight back. I'll be in court with my little videotape in my purse for safe-keeping in case I need to break it out and pop it in the VCR for the judge."

Javon pondered over Fatima's comment, imagining the horror his life would become if the tape ever surfaced in court and how much money he'd have to dish out in a divorce settlement. "You wouldn't!"

"Yes, I would," Fatima stated without a second's hesitation.

"Fatima, now I know you're the one full of shit! Even if you wanted to embarrass me, you wouldn't do that to Harmony in public."

"Actually, it wouldn't exactly be public," Harmony interjected. "This isn't something worthy of Court TV or anything like that, Javon. Besides, I told Fatima she could use the tape if she had to. I messed up and I'm willing to do whatever it takes to make it up to her."

Harmony winked at Fatima and she winked back. They still had Javon fooled about the events of that night. Things were working out perfectly.

"Does Zachary know about this? Does he, Harmony?" Javon cracked a wicked grin, realizing he did have some bargaining power after all. Harmony worshiped the ground Zachary walked on. He'd been witnessing that for years, ever since college. "I'm sure he doesn't, but I'd be more than happy to tell him."

"Utter one word of this to Zachary and I'll cut your little dick off!" Harmony lashed out at him. "If I can even find it!"

Fatima started laughing so hard, tears began to fall. Harmony joined her.

"Fatima, why are you laughing? This isn't funny."

"Javon, you know what?" Fatima giggled, wiping her damp eyes with her sleeve. "You do have a little dick and, after flipping through some magazines Harmony brought over to cheer me up, I realize I've missed out on a lot over the years." She gave Harmony a slap on the thigh. "A *whole* lot! Now that I've seen what real dicks look like, I'm amazed you even managed to impregnate me twice."

Javon jumped up from the arm of the chair and placed his hands on his hips angrily. "I'm not going to stand around here while the two of you insult me."

"Good!" Fatima squealed, still laughing hard.

"So leave already!" Harmony giggled.

Javon glanced at the television, where one set of women was acting similar to the pair in his living room. "Fatima, we'll talk about this later. Sometime when we can talk in private."

Fatima finally stopped laughing. She wanted to drive her next point home with a tone of seriousness. "I have nothing further to say to you. You'll be hearing from my attorney."

"I'm not going to make this easy for you."

"I'm ready for whatever you throw at me."

Javon headed for the foyer, but turned around. "Where are my kids? I'd like to see them before I leave."

"They're in the swimming pool."

"Alone?" he asked accusingly.

"No, they're not alone." Fatima got back up and walked over to him, staring him dead in the eyes. "Don't even insinuate that I'm a bad mother. Don't even try it."

Javon diverted his eyes from Fatima long enough to throw Harmony an I-better-not-ever-catch-your-ass-in-a-dark-alley look. "I'm going to spend some quality time with them while you sit up in here and giggle with your fellow loony bird."

"Whatever, Javon!" Fatima pointed to the rear of the house, moving out of Javon's way so he could get by her. "I want you gone by nine though. The kids need to be in bed by then."

"I'll leave when I'm good and ready."

"You'll leave whenever the hell I say, or I'll have you thrown out."

Javon stopped in his tracks and swung around to face her. "Please! By whom?"

"Don't worry about it. Just be gone by nine." Javon stormed towards the back patio. Fatima yelled after him. "I want your things out of here by next weekend, or I'm donating them to charity!"

"You tell him, Sis!" Harmony exclaimed, applauding from her eagle's eye view on the couch.

"How'd you like that?" Fatima asked, plopping back down beside of her.

"It was awesome!"

"You proud of me? I finally learned to stand up to his ass."

"I'm extremely proud of you."

Fatima grinned and crossed her arms over her chest. "Yeah, I'm proud of me too."

Chapter Fifteen

The Strap-On Story

"I don't know why you need to hang out with Colette tonight anyway," Troy said sarcastically as he paced around Bryce's living room. "She's nothing but a *straight up* hoe and you got a man now. You can't be hanging out at all hours of the night with skimpy ass outfits on and shit."

"Troy, I never complain when you hang out with your friends and at least you know where I'm going." Bryce was checking herself out in the mirror and had to admit she looked damn good in the hunter green sheath with three-inch leather pumps to match. "Half the time when you fall up in here at 3 AM, I have no clue where you've been. Probably out at tits and ass bars with your freaky ass."

"Freaky? Sheit, all the kinky ass shit you make me submit to up in here. Make a brotha want to call for backup."

"You love every minute of it." Bryce walked up behind the couch and leaned over it to give him a big, fat kiss. "If you want, I can get Colette to pick you up a jar of Niagra. They sell it around her way. I hear your dick stays hard for three weeks on that shit."

"Hell naw, I don't want none of that shit. I heard it's some kind of hallucinogen mixed with Cherry-Ade."

Bryce laughed, sat down on his lap, and looked at her watch. "Damn, ole gurl is always late."

"So, where'd you say you're going again?"

"Well, *Poppi*, we're going to a house party. One of the gurls Colette used to work with at the warehouse is having it."

"And the house is located where?"

"Hmmm, I'm not quite sure. The gurl lives in Northwest, but the party is at her cousin's girlfriend's fiancée's uncle's daughter's house."

"Shit," Troy replied. "In other words, you don't know where the hell you're going your damn self?"

Bryce giggled. "Colette's driving. I just told her I would go along with her for the ride. Plus, she doesn't know these people that well. Colette's just trying to be kind because the gurl called her a dozen times sweating her to roll through."

"Whatever!"

"Hey now, don't go stealing my word!" Bryce tapped him on the shoulder. "*Whatever* is my word and *Marvelous* is Harmony's word."

"And what's Lucky's word?"

"Hmmm, Lucky doesn't really have a word." Bryce sat there, deep in thought. "Speaking of Lucky, I need to call and check up on her. She hasn't called in a couple of weeks and that's unusual."

"Didn't you say she has a new homie in her life?"

"Yeah but still, my sisters and I always keep in contact."

"Your baby sister is probably too busy getting her groove on to call. You and I fuck *every* damn night. Maybe she's doing the same."

"First of all, you and I don't fuck *every* night. Secondly, blood before dick."

"Name one night we didn't fuck?"

Bryce rolled her eyes. "We didn't fuck on Monday night. The night we went over Harmony's for dinner."

"Point made. Your sister's a sweetheart."

Bryce giggled. "Sometimes. Don't piss her off though cause she will get in that ass."

"By the way, leave her number so I can get in touch with Zachary."

"Aiight." Bryce decided to be nosy and make sure the men weren't scheming behind her and Harmony's backs. "What do you want to talk to Zachary about?"

"The brotha is mad cool and he invited me to play golf with him tomorrow. I just want to call to accept."

Bryce looked at Troy with astonishment. "Don't get me wrong. I'm glad the two of you are bonding because Harmony and I plan on keeping you around until hell freezes over or impotency sets in, whichever comes first, but..."

Troy gave Bryce a *love-slap* on her ass. "Impotency? Gurl, I might have to tear that ass up before Colette shows up, you keep talking like that." He grabbed his dick and moved his sack over. "You know this is the joint."

"Whatever!" They shared a brief kiss. "Anyway, like I was saying, I'm glad the two of you are bonding, but what does a ghettoized nucca like you know about playing golf?"

"Shit, you have a versatile man. In fact, I'm *THE MAN* just like my vanity plate says. Better get used to it." He started pinching her nipple, seriously contemplating taking her to bed and refusing to let Colette in the door. "I might act Ghetto a lot, but you know that shit's not true. Besides, I know how to play golf because some of the auto brokers I do business with at the dealership play once a week and sometimes I join them."

Bryce blushed, happy that she had *finally* found herself a good man. One that was responsible, loving, successful, and most importantly, one that mirrored her freakiness. "I hate you, Baby!"

"I hate you, too!" They started tonguing. By the time Colette showed up, Troy was eating a snack and she had to wait outside until he got done.

"Damn!" Colette exclaimed after Bryce got into her Impala. "You smell like fucking! No wonder it took your ass so long to come outside!"

"It's your fault," Bryce replied. "You were so late, Troy said fuck it and got his groove on before I left. I'll spray on some cologne."

"Please do because I don't want you falling up in my gurl's house with crusty semen between your thighs and dick breath." Bryce punched her in the shoulder. "I got some Tic Tacs if you need one."

"Naw, I didn't have time to suck his dick. If I had started on the dick, you would've been rolling by yourself tonight because I'm *damn addicted* to the dick." Bryce sprayed on some CK cologne. "Besides, where's this party anyway? Troy asked me and I looked like an idiot cause I didn't know."

"Southeast."

"Southeast as in by the waterfront, by Capitol Hill, or *Southeast* as in Gangsta's Paradise?"

"Bryce, you're always such a smart ass," Colette complained. "You've totally ignored me since you hooked up with Troy. I should've known it was his ass that called you up that night."

"I haven't ignored you. I've just been busy. Besides, you've been working at that law firm and keeping busy yourself." Bryce noticed Colette was *too* quiet. "Aiight, what now?"

"Whatcha mean?"

"You know what the hell I mean, heifer. I mentioned the law firm and your ass clammed up so what's going on?"

Silence and then Colette tried to play that *turn-the-radio-up game*, but Bryce was the master so she reached over and turned it completely off. She kept pressing. "Are those people Harmony hooked you up with mistreating you because, if so, she can get you another hook-up?"

"Naw, everything's cool!"

"Hmm, okay, but just let me know because there's one thing Harmony doesn't fuck around with and that's clients trying to mess over her temps."

"I know, Gurl. Harmony's real nice to me now. I'm shocked. Every time I go by the agency to pick up my weekly paycheck, she makes a sincere effort to tell me how well I'm doing and how proud she is of me."

"Say what? My sister does that?" Bryce was shocked. "Well, I must have been wrong."

"Wrong about what?"

"At first, I thought what was bothering her months ago was something major, something I couldn't put my finger on, but it must have been all about Zachary." She added as an afterthought, "I'm glad Zachary is back, though. She's a different person now and even likes Troy."

"Word?"

"Yeah, she even invited us over for dinner this week and you know Harmony usually refuses to let me bring nuccas over to her house."

"I heard that."

They were quiet for a couple of minutes and then Colette said, "I did go out with this junior partner at the firm. He's the only brotha there."

"Hmph! And?" Bryce didn't like this shit from jump and she knew Harmony better not ever get wind of it because she believed in professionalism at all times.

"And..." Colette glanced over at Bryce while they were stopped at a red light and saw the *you-might-get-pimped-slapped-if-this-is-bad* look in her eyes. "I fucked him with a ten-inch strap-on."

"Excuse me while I yawn to clear out my ear canals. Did you just say that you fucked a partner at the law firm with a ten-inch strap-on?"

"Yeah," Colette said casually. "Bryce, don't look at me that way. He asked me to."

"Whatever!"

"Really! We ended up at his place after dinner and he told me he had this fantasy he'd always wanted to play out. I was tore the hell up drunk so I said fuck it and strapped the shit on."

As pissed as Bryce was, she couldn't help but laugh. Especially, since she and Troy were doing mad freaky-deaky shit out of her favorite book, *The Sex Chronicles*. The thought of Colette with a strap-on dick on, pumping it in and out a nucca's ass, was funny as shit.

"First, he told me he wanted to know what it felt like to give a blow job, but didn't want to do it with a man since he was *only* bi-curious and not sure he went that way. So, I stood there and let him suck the fake dick while I was wearing it."

"You have got to be making this shit up." Bryce chuckled. "No fucking way!"

"Yes, way." Colette cackled. "I even gyrated my hips and moaned like he was really sucking me off. He waxed that jimmy, too! I think that brotha might be able to suck a dick better than me and you know that's saying sumptin'."

"Then what happened?" Bryce was all into the shit by that point and trying to picture every move.

"Then he told me to put it in his ass slowly. At first, I only put the tip in but he kept asking for more and more until I had the whole thing rammed up his ass."

"What did you use? KY-jelly?"

"Hell naw, that Negro took that shit raw dog."

"*Eww!*" Bryce flinched. "He took the whole thing?"

"Hell yeah and then he kept telling me to fuck him harder and harder."

"Shit," was all Bryce could say in response. "I hope you didn't see his ass again after that?"

"Nope, he never asked me out again after that. Thank goodness!"

"Amen to that." Bryce seconded the notion.

"In fact, I can't say this shit for sure but I think he may be dating another junior partner from the firm now. This white dude. They seem *mighty* close. Giggling and shit like gurlfriends all the time."

"Well, I guess he's *more* than bi-curious then, but he better get him a Mandingo dick brotha if he took ten inches up the ass raw dog."

They were both still laughing and holding their sides when they finally pulled up to the house where the party was. Two seconds after they pulled up, they were stuffing their cash in their bras and pushing their purses underneath the car seats.

Chapter Sixteen

Limp Dick Leprechaun Midgets

"*Gurl!*" Bryce plopped down on Harmony's living room sofa. "Wait till you hear the shit Colette and I did last night!"

Harmony laughed as she sat a pot of warm tea and a plate of cinnamon bran muffins on trivets on the coffee table. "That bad, huh?"

"Hell, yeah!"

"Great. I could sure use a good laugh. I'm glad you decided to come over today to keep me company while our men go make asses of themselves on the golf course."

"Zachary can't play good?" Bryce asked.

"I'll put it this way. My baby tries hard but he'll *never* be as good as Tiger Woods. Troy knows how to play?"

"He claims he plays with some of his clients but my baby will probably never be good enough to even be Tiger's caddie."

They both laughed hysterically.

"Damn, Sis." Harmony plopped down beside Bryce, tucking one of her legs underneath her. "You sure are hard on a brotha."

"Yeah, that's my baby though." Bryce blushed.

"You really love the man, don't you? I don't think I've ever seen you glow as much as you do now."

"I love his ass to death, *but* I would never admit it. He and I always tell each other we hate each other when we're getting busy."

"Silly ass." Harmony slapped Bryce on the hand. "Are you taking him to the family reunion in North Carolina this year? Momma's been ringing my phone off the hook, making sure we're all coming."

"Yeah, she's been working my phone lines, too. I'm taking Troy. I want Daddy to go ahead and meet him so I can get all the objections out of the way. Daddy can't stand the men any of us date."

"That's because they're men, Bryce. Daddy doesn't like the idea of us having sex no matter how old we get," Harmony replied.

"Ain't that the truth! Yet, he and Momma spit us out like they were breeding rabbits." Bryce giggled. "You taking Zachary?"

"Gurl, please, you know Zachary goes every year. He's afraid I might go down there, get me some countrified dick, and never come back."

"I wonder if Lucky's taking Robbie. I still haven't had a chance to meet him, but he sounds like he has it going on."

"I haven't met him either. They're getting real tight so I suspect she will take him." Harmony reached for the kettle. "Let me pour us some tea while you tell me about the wild adventure you and Colette had last night."

"Well, you remember when we were little and still living in Cali and you used to talk trash about all the boys because they were so much shorter than us before puberty settled in? Before they shot up like trees?"

"I remember it well. I always called them *limp-dick-leprechaun-midgets*. I used to have nightmares."

"Well, Colette and I lived out your nightmares last night because we fell up into a house full of them bad boys!"

"Oh, shit!" Harmony exclaimed as they both guffawed. "I'm all ears. I wish Lucky was here to hear it."

"Me, too." Bryce nodded, starting to relate her tale of the *limp-dick-leprechaun-midgets*.

Across town at that very moment, Lucky was banging on Robbie's door and begging him to let her in. "Robbie, please just let me come in and explain!"

"There's nothing to explain!" he screamed from the other side of the door. "I saw you with him with my own two eyes!"

"*Please!*" Lucky scratched at his door like a kitten trying to get in. "If you just let me talk to you, I'll tell you everything!"

"Get away from my door, you fucking whore!" Lucky started wailing when he called her that. It was like being stabbed through the heart with a knife. "You're nothing but a fucking tramp! I can't believe I wasted my time on you!"

Lucky backed away from the door until the small of her back touched the railing. She turned around and looked down into the courtyard. For a brief second, she contemplated jumping. That's when she heard Robbie's door swing open.

Lucky turned around and smiled, thinking he was finally willing to listen to her. Instead, he started throwing the little bit of clothing she kept over his place at her. "Take all of your shit and get the hell away from me!"

He slammed the door. She was sniffling and picking up her clothes when he swung the door open again and gently sat the puppy down outside. He glared at her. "And take the damn dog, too!"

She got into her car, wrapped her arms around the steering wheel, laid her forehead on the top edge of it, and started screaming. The frightened puppy sitting in the passenger seat beside her wanted to scream, too, but all she could do was yap.

"*Gurl*, we pulled up to this house party last night and it looked like a scene from *Boyz N The Hood*!" Bryce exclaimed. "Except it was the Tom Thumb version!"

Harmony started laughing so hard, some of her tea flew out her mouth onto her white T-shirt. "Get out of town!"

"Shit, I ain't lying! We stuffed the cash we had on us in our bras and our purses under the seat. You know the routine?"

"Yeah, I definitely know the routine." Harmony nodded. "Whose party was it?"

"This gurl Colette used to work with at the warehouse. When I met her, I didn't know whether to shake her hand or shield my eyes from the glare."

"What glare?"

"The glare coming from the fifty million gold teeth in her damn mouth."

"Oh, shit!" Harmony managed to say through tear-drenched eyes. "Then what happened?"

"Hold up! First, let me set the scene for you!"

"Aiight!" Harmony jumped up and walked over to the shelf stereo system and cut the volume down. "I don't want to miss a word."

"Okay, picture this." Bryce held her hands up with her fingers spread like she was directing a movie. "Picture a row house full of *pleather* furniture covered up with heavy plastic."

"Damn, not *pleather?*" Harmony giggled as she sat back down.

"Now picture it full of men shorter than the Oompa Loompas in *Willy Wonka and the Chocolate Factory.*"

They both laughed hysterically.

"This one brotha, looking like Gary Coleman with a Jherri Curl, had the audacity to ask me to dance."

"Oh shit, not a curl?"

"A mofo curl! That's why the furniture was covered with plastic. Every mofo in there had a curl." Bryce shifted in her seat. "And check this out. The song that was playing was *The Breaks* by Kurtis Blow."

"Get the fuck out of here!" Harmony exclaimed. "Bryce, your ass has got to be exaggerating!"

"Sheeeeeeeeeeeeeit, I ain't lying!" Bryce slapped Harmony on the arm to emphasis the point.

"So what did you say?"

"I told him he better take his little midget ass on before I slapped him in the head with my knee!"

"HAHAHAHAHAHAHA!!!" Tears started guzzling down Harmony's face. "This is too fucking funny!"

"Wait, here comes the good part." Bryce picked up a bran muffin to nibble on. "He says to me, *I know what it is, Gurl. You think I'm a playa cause I'm so damn fine.* Then, he ran his stubs down the back of his head and some of his curl juice fell in the sista's drink behind him."

"Oh, hell naw!"

"So I told him, *Yeah, you're a playa. I can tell*, hoping that agreeing with him would make him get the fuck on."

"And did he?"

"Hell naw! He comes back with this lame ass line. He said, *I'm not a playa. I just fuck a lot.*"

"Now I know you're shitting me, Bryce. You've got to be making this shit up."

"I'll call Colette *right now* if you don't believe me." Bryce pointed to the phone. "It was the wildest shit I've ever seen in my entire life."

"Damn, damn, damn! A house full of midgets. Why didn't you just roll out?"

"Oh we did, we sure as hell did, but not before this other *limp-dick-leprechaun-midget* asked Colette if she wanted to go upstairs with him and suck his dick."

They started laughing hysterically again.

"Colette set his ass straight with a quickness."

"I bet she did." Harmony giggled. "What did she tell him?"

"She told him a woman couldn't find his dick with tweezers and a magnifying glass and that he couldn't butt fuck a rat."

"Oh, shit!"

"Then, then," Bryce said, laughing so hard she could barely get the words out. "Then, he tells her he'll eat her out so good, he'll suck her ovaries out."

"What did she say then?"

"Not a *damn* thing. She poured her Corona on his head and didn't even have to lift her hand up past her ribcage to do it. His ass was so short."

Bryce and Harmony were pouncing all over the couch, laughing and holding their sides, when they heard the door slam.

"Zachary." Harmony chuckled. "You and Troy played eighteen holes that fast?"

Bryce interjected, "That's because neither one of their asses can play."

They gave each other a high five.

Harmony realized there was no response and grew concerned. "Zachary?"

They heard yapping just as a puppy came running in the living room and jumped up on the fireplace hearth.

That's when Harmony and Bryce knew something was wrong. That's when they turned around and saw Lucky standing there with a sundress on that was ripped on the shoulder. That's when they saw the hurt and disappointment in her bloodshot eyes and that's when they forgot all about *limp-dick-leprechaun-midgets* and the smiles disappeared from their faces.

Chapter Seventeen

Time For A Beatdown

Bryce started around the couch but Harmony took a short cut, jumped over the cushions and the back of the couch, and got to Lucky first. She grabbed her by the shoulders. "Listen to me, Lucky. Whatever this is, we can fix it."

Lucky looked at Harmony and shook her head. "No, you can't fix this. No one can."

Bryce started rubbing the small of Lucky's back. "Wanna talk about it?"

Harmony lifted up the shredded material of the sundress off Lucky's shoulder. "Did someone hurt you? What happened to your dress?"

Lucky shook her head. "The only thing hurt is my pride."

Bryce felt something warm on the back of her ankle, looked down, and the puppy was peeing on her. "Oh, shit!"

Lucky and Harmony giggled, but it still didn't enhance the mood. Normally, Bryce would've gotten dramatic and talked shit about the puppy for a good fifteen minutes and Harmony would have had a fit and a half about her cream carpet. Instead they just turned their attention back to Lucky, wondering whether or not they could fix whatever was wrong.

"Is this the puppy you bought Robbie?" Bryce asked, beginning to put two and two together.

"Yes," Lucky replied, still trembling. "I couldn't take it back to my dorm. They don't allow pets so I had to bring Lucinda here. I'm so sorry, Harmony. I'll find a home for her on Monday."

Harmony directed Lucky over to the couch. "That's the last thing I'm worried about. Besides, Zachary loves dogs and probably won't let you take her up out of here anyway."

After they were seated on the couch, with Lucky on Harmony's left and Bryce on the coffee table in front of them with her legs spread like a sailor since etiquette went out the window once they saw Lucky's face, Bryce inquired, "You and Robbie broke up, huh?"

"Robbie hates me!" Lucky was hysterical. She jumped up and starting running up the stairs. "Once you find out what I did, you'll both hate me, too!"

They heard the door of the guest bedroom slam. Harmony glanced over at Bryce and wished she would close her fucking legs but didn't stress the point. "Well, it's obvious this isn't going to be easy."

"Quite obvious," Bryce replied. "I wonder what happened between Lucky and Robbie."

"I don't know. I never met the brotha, although he seemed on the up and up from what I heard."

"Me either. We've both been too caught up in our own relationships to keep an eye on Little Sis."

Harmony nodded. "Yeah, we've both been real selfish."

After a few moments of drowning in guilt, Harmony added, "Okay, this is what we're going to do. I'll go upstairs and run Lucky a hot bubble bath and wash her back just like I used to when we were kids and you..."

"Me what?"

"Well, I was going to tell your ass to go in the kitchen and cook, but you can't cook worth shit so order a pizza to be delivered instead." Bryce rolled her eyes. Harmony ignored it. "Her favorite.

A deep dish with Italian sausage and mushrooms."

Harmony went upstairs while Bryce went into the kitchen to find the Ledos Pizza magnet on the fridge, muttering to herself. "I can cook. Not like you have any food up in this bitch anyway."

By the time the pizza arrived, Harmony had bathed Lucky. Bryce had fed the puppy and then taken a quick shower herself to get the urine off and threw on some of Harmony's jeans and a tee.

No one really had an appetite so the pizza lay basically untouched on the middle of the black down comforter on Harmony's bed. Lucky laid her head down in Harmony's lap while she sat propped up on a pillow and ran her fingers through Lucky's soft, short neatly-cut Afro. Bryce gently rubbed Lucky's back through the white terry cloth robe.

No one said a word for what seemed like an eternity.

"You're going to hate me," Lucky whispered. "Especially Harmony. I fucked up big time."

"Look at me." Harmony held Lucky's face up so she could look into her eyes. "I could never hate you. Not in a million years."

"Me either." Bryce nodded in agreement. Lucky laid her head back down in the comfort of her big sister's lap.

"I've been too hard on you, Baby Sis," Harmony continued. "I should've seen this coming. Med school is pressure enough on you as it is. The last thing you needed was me pressuring you even more. Insisting you ace everything."

"That's not it Harmony," Lucky protested. "If it weren't for you and Bryce keeping me in line, I would've given up on medical school a long time ago."

"You're a Whitfield and Whitfields never quit," Bryce said out of habit more than anything else.

"Harmony, I broke my promise to you," Lucky blurted out while she could find the words. "I slept with Dean Mitchell again."

Bryce glared at Harmony, begging her with her eyes not to go off on Lucky. "And Robbie found out about it?" Bryce asked.

Lucky nodded. "I didn't want to sleep with him. I swear. He made me."

Bryce forgot all about being calm, cool, and collected, jumped up off the bed, and went off herself. "Hold the fuck up! What do you mean, *he made you?*"

"Harmony, I know that look in your eyes," Bryce said less than thirty minutes later after Lucky had told them everything before falling asleep upstairs.

Harmony stood by the large picture window in the living room while Bryce resumed her seat on the coffee table. "He fucking abused her," Harmony hissed. "Used his power at the med school to have his way with her."

"Yeah and from what she said, she wasn't the only one," Bryce added. "So what now?"

Silence.

"Harmony?"

"Bryce, do you remember when Momma and Daddy drove us down to Tijuana, Mexico that time in high school, when Lucky was in about the seventh grade?" Harmony asked the question in too placid a manner for Bryce's liking. She could always recognize the calm before the storm.

"Yeah, I remember."

"They went to hang out in bars and left us back in that half ass motel with the brown water and roaches all over the walls. And after Lucky fell asleep, you and I stayed up and watched this wild ass movie?"

"Yeah." Bryce chuckled, vividly remembering the movie. "It was called *Biker Bitches From Mars.*"

Harmony swung around and looked Bryce square in the face, her eyes speaking everything that needed to be said. It took Bryce a moment to let it sink in.

"Aw hell naw, Harmony! Hellllllllzzzz naw! You can't be serious?"

"I'm *dead* serious!" Harmony walked towards the kitchen. "You call Colette and get my laptop out my study while I go out to the garage to get the rope and duct tape."

"Harmony, we can't do no shit like that," Bryce said excitedly.

"Don't get me wrong. I'm pissed and I say we beat his fucking ass at the very least but *Biker Bitches From Mars?* We'll all end up in the slammer!"

"Not if we don't get caught and we won't." Harmony continued her path to the side door in teh kitchen. Bryce was right on her tail.

"Why do you want me to call Colette?" Bryce was shocked that Harmony would bring up Colette.

"Because she's a roughneck and we need a roughneck in on this operation."

"Aiight." Bryce watched Harmony go out into the garage. "But what's the deal with the laptop?"

Harmony ignored the question. Bryce headed to the study to find the laptop. "Shame on it all!"

"Bryce, what did Colette say?" Harmony asked, returning into the house with one of Zachary's Dallas Cowboys duffel bags, filled to the brim with stuff to do their *dirt.*

Bryce replaced the phone back on the cradle. "Colette has *beeeeeeeeeeeen* on her way. She left her house in a flash. She's pissed."

"Then who was that on the phone?"

"Troy. He *claims* that he and Zachary are going to check out a movie this afternoon after they leave the golf course and then go out for a few drinks."

Harmony and Bryce looked at each other, knowing good and damn well their nuccas were lying. "In other words, they're going to a booty club down in the District and don't want us to know?"

"Word up," Bryce agreed, nodding her head.

"Good, I didn't feel like explaining my whereabouts tonight anyway." Harmony picked up the phone. "Go get Lucky up and dressed. I want her to see what we do to that mofo."

"Who are you calling?" Bryce wondered.

"Fatima." Harmony dialed the digits.

"Damn, how many biker bitches do we need?"

"Trust me, Sis," Harmony answered while the phone was ringing on the other end. "Fatima loves Lucky to death and she's more scandalous than all of us put together."

Bryce began to doubt Harmony would go through with the whole thing. Surely, she would become rational at some point. "Harmony, are you really serious about all this?"

"Fatima!" Harmony yelled into the phone. "Is Javon's gun collection still at the main house?"

"Oh, shit!" Bryce exclaimed. Harmony went out on the deck to finish her conversation and fill Fatima in. *She's damn serious*, Bryce thought to herself, and then headed upstairs to get Lucky.

Chapter Eighteen

The Avengers

"I'm coming! Hold your horses!" Fatima swung open the heavy wooden door of her eight-bedroom mansion and couldn't believe her eyes. "Damnnnnnn! You sistas look like a cross between *The Witches of Eastwick* and *The Women of Brewster Place!*"

"Hmph! You've got some nerve," Bryce hissed, barging past Fatima into the foyer. "Your hair looks like you lost a fight with the freakin' lawnmower."

"Speaking of hair," Fatima came back at her. "Thank goodness you finally got rid of that fucked up hair weave you were sporting all of those years."

"Sheit! Your hair is *toooooooo* through! You need to go down to Weave Central and get Conchita to hook your ass up," Bryce snapped.

"Excuse um moi, idiots," Harmony interrupted. "I realize the two of you are as happy as a teenage boy in a whorehouse to see each other but can you shut the hell up!"

They gave each other the *Harmony-is-about-to-pimp-slap-us-look* and complied.

"We're here for one reason. To fuck ole boy up."

"Damn right." Colette nodded, starting to look around Fatima's house and walking into the living room with twenty-foot cathedral ceilings. "Good gracious! I thought Harmony had a big ass house!"

"Lucky, are you all right, Baby?" Fatima hugged Lucky and led her into the living room. "You know you're my heart and soul, Gurl."

"I know, Fatima. Thanks." Lucky kissed her on the cheek and followed everyone else into the living room.

"I say we kick his ass from here to Somalia and back," Colette suggested.

"No, that's much too peaceful," Harmony said. "I have something ten times better in mind. Dean Marvin Mitchell is about to meet his worst nightmare and he'll never do this shit to a sista again."

They all stared at each other, hoping Harmony wouldn't take shit to the extreme. Lucky was severely concerned. While she wanted Marvin to get his more than anyone, she sensed Harmony was about to go off the deep end.

"Fatima, did you manage to get everything I asked for?" Harmony inquired.

"Yes, I got the blueprints." Fatima paused before adding, "And the guns."

"Good. Let's go into the drawing room so none of your staff will overhear us scheming."

"No need." Fatima placed her hands on her hips. "I told them all to take the evening off and the kids are doing a sleepover."

"And Javon?"

"*Fuck a Javon!* He's staying at the Hyatt and refuses to get a place or move his things. That fool still thinks there's a chance for us after his dirt."

Bryce thought to herself, *Fuck a Javon, huh? Harmony already did that.*

"Well, Fatima, it's your fault," Harmony stated.

"How do you figure?" Fatima was obviously offended by the remark.

"I tried to tell you about that voodoo shit."

"What voodoo shit, Harmony?" Lucky's interest was piqued in spite of the ugly situation.

"We don't have time for this," Harmony said. "We have a schedule to keep."

"Aw, come off it. You can't mention voodoo and then leave us hanging," Bryce insisted. "What does voodoo have to do with Javon's little dick ass not wanting a divorce?"

Fatima looked at Harmony with astonishment. Harmony shrugged her shoulders. "Maybe I *mentioned* the fact that he had a little dick. My bad!"

Colette grew impatient. "I wanna know about this voodoo madness," she said as she laid across the expensive chaise lounge, a piece of furniture she had only seen before in old Bette Davis movies.

"Okay, damn," Harmony hissed, wishing she had never brought the topic up, but realizing trying to change the subject was a lost cause. "Our freshman year at Howard, there was this gurl from New Orleans who lived in the same dorm. Fatima and Javon were dating heavy but Fatima wanted the ring so the gurl, I don't recall her name, convinced Fatima that there was only one way to ensure Javon would love her and only her forever."

"Which was?" Bryce asked, sitting on the edge of her seat and hoping the shit wasn't too outrageous so she could do some voodoo on Troy's ass.

"Well, Fatima invited Javon over to our dorm for dinner one night. Zachary and I went to the movies so they could be alone." Harmony glanced at Fatima. Fatima's eyes were rolling around in her head like Linda Blair from *The Exorcist*. "We had a hot plate in the room and Fatima made Javon some spaghetti with one *special* added ingredient."

Harmony paused for a long moment and the suspense was killing them.

"You coming up off the special damn ingredient sometime tonight or not?" Bryce smacked her lips. "Sheesh! Harmony always takes ten freakin' years to tell a story!"

"She put some of her menstrual cycle in it," Harmony blurted out and then started chuckling.

"Fuck ya!" Fatima yelled, giving her the finger but giggling just the same.

The rest of them shouted, "Eww!" and "Ugh!" in unison.

"Damn, Fatima, you's a nasty ass," Bryce proclaimed. "I'll be the first one to admit I've done some trifling shit in the pursuit of hel-lified dick action, but that takes the mofo cake!"

"That's so damn foul." Colette added her two cents. Even she had her limits but, then again, there was the time one nucca had slipped and went down on her before she knew Aunt Flo was vis-iting.

Lucky laughed hysterically, finding something worth smiling about for the first time since Robbie went ballistic on her ass.

Harmony was ecstatic to see Lucky laughing, but time was of the essence. She wasn't about to let some sick ass pervert take advantage of her baby sister and get away with it.

Within minutes, they were all seated around the cherrywood table in the formal dining room. The blueprints to one of the ware-houses Javon owned down on the waterfront were sprawled across the table.

"Okay, that about does it, ladies," Harmony said. "Everyone knows what they're supposed to do, right?"

"Yeah," Colette said, "but how in the hell do you expect us to find all this shit on the list within the next three hours?"

"Where there's a will, there's a way."

"Whatever," Bryce hissed, still hoping Harmony would give up on the elaborate scheme and just beat the nucca's ass.

Fatima asked, "How are you going to make sure his dick stays hard long enough for us to do all of this crap?"

Bryce glanced over the table at Colette. "Did you make that stop I asked you to?"

"Yeah." Colette pulled a grape jelly jar out the left pocket of her lightweight jacket. "Here it is."

"You sure this shit works?" Bryce took it out Colette's hands. "Looks like plain old Cherry-Ade to me."

"Shit! That stuff works and then some," Colette proclaimed. "When I went by there, Ripuoff answered the door with a dick that looked like it could split bricks. He had mad hoochies up in there waiting to get fucked *every* which way!"

"Word?" Bryce grinned with delight. "Aiight, I was just making sure because..."

"What in the world is that?" Fatima interrupted Bryce in mid-sentence.

"Niagra," Harmony answered before anyone else. "You'll see what it does tonight. I heard some pimps talking about it when I was in the liquor store playing Powerball. They swear it's the bomb. They can drink as much Mad Dog 20/20 as they can handle and still fuck the living daylights out every hoe in their stable in one night."

Fatima made no further comment, but picked up the jar to get a closer look at the contents. *Looks like Cherry-Ade*, she thought.

"Time to roll up on out of here," Harmony announced. "Fatima, Lucky and I will take the items we already have and head over to set up the warehouse. We'll stop by the costume shop on the way."

"Aiight, Sis." Bryce decided consenting to getting jiggy with it was the best plan.

"Bryce, you and Colette take care of the entertainment for tonight's festivities. See if you can get a hold of some chloroform while you're at it."

Bryce had to sustain the urge to slap Harmony upside the head. "Now, I know you've lost your damn mind. It's bad enough you've got Colette and I cruising street corners, but *chloroform too?*"

"Okay, forget the chloroform. We'll just cold clock his ass."

They all gave each other high fives, except for Lucky who had an unsettled look on her face.

"Well, I guess that does it," Harmony stated. "Except for synchronizing our watches."

"Whew, we really into some *Mission Impossible* type shit here,"

Colette said excitedly and started humming the theme song for the TV series while she did the Butterfly in her chair.

Bryce took her fingernails and dug them into Colette's arm. "Quit, dufus!"

Harmony, Fatima, and Lucky got up and headed to the garage. "See you when you get there."

Once they were out of earshot, Colette reached in her other jacket pocket to retrieve the second jar of Niagra. "You're not really going to give Troy this concoction on the sly, are you?"

"Wanna bet?" Bryce replied, putting it in her purse for safekeeping. They both fell out laughing on their way out the front door to start searching street corners.

Chapter Nineteen

Black Biker Bitches From Mars

Marvin Mitchell had just poured an E & J Brandy with Coke when the phone rang. He cleared his throat before he answered, figuring it was one of his sweet young thangs calling to beg for some dick. So what if he applied a little pressure in order to get the nana? Such is life! It was all a means to an end and bottom line, he had more pussy at his beck and call than brothas half his age.

"Hello," he said in his deepest, sexiest voice.

"Hellllllllllllllloooooo," a female voice squealed into the phone. "Is this Mr. Mitchell in Apartment 10-D?"

"Yes," he replied with disappointment in his voice, realizing it wasn't a booty call after all. "Who is this?"

"This is Penelope Wyatt Lawrence Bainbridge, your neighbor in 8-H. I've run into you a few times in the elevator. Do you recall?"

"Yes sure, I remember you now," Marvin lied, trying to hold in his laugh because the woman caller sounded like something was crammed up her nostrils. "What can I do for you, Miss Bramidge?"

"That's Bainbridge!"

"Sorry, Miss Bainbridge." Marvin was getting impatient and didn't want to be bothered with any phone calls that didn't pertain to pussy.

"The reason I'm *callllllllllllling*, Mr. Mitchell, is because when I pulled into the underground garage this *e-ve-ning*, it looked like someone had tampered with your car."

"Really?" Marvin jumped up off the couch, looking for his keys.

"Yes, some sort of auto vandalism," Penelope replied. "Pity that vandals would hit a neighborhood such as ours."

"Yes, yes, it is. Thanks for calling and letting me know," Marvin said with gratitude. "I'm going to go check it out right now!"

He hung up the phone before either party could say goodbye, grabbed his keys, and headed to the elevator.

Fatima clicked the power off button on her cell phone. She couldn't hold in the laughter any longer. Harmony was sitting beside her in the driver's seat of Javon's Expedition glued to a pair of binoculars.

Less than three minutes later, Marvin came flying off the elevator worried sick that someone had fucked with his prize possession. When he got to his assigned parking space, a whimper was all that he could manage to get out once he saw the words *Rapist*, *Pervert*, and *Bastard* spray painted all over the hood and doors.

He walked around to see if anything was on the trunk of the car, which is what they were all counting on. He was too busy trying to make out the word on the trunk, which was intentionally misspelled and nothing more than gibberish, when Bryce hopped up from behind the Jeep Cherokee parked beside it and cold clocked his ass with a tire iron.

Colette grabbed the keys out his comatose hand and unlocked the trunk. They struggled to lift him into the trunk of his car. When they dropped him in, a foul odor emitted from the plush velvety trunk.

"Di-zammmmmmmmmm!" Colette held her nose. "What the hell is that smell?"

"He farted." Bryce giggled. "Punk ass!"

They slammed the trunk and jumped in the front seat. Bryce had trouble starting the engine with the surgical gloves she was wearing. They were both wearing them to guard against fingerprints. She finally got it started and they pulled out the garage, taking the dark, back streets Harmony had mapped out with the rest of the crew following close behind in the Expedition.

"Damn, Bryce, why'd you have to hit him so hard?" Colette asked. "Now we can't even wake his ass up."

"No names!" Harmony kicked Colette in the shin.

"Aiight, damn!" Colette bent down to rub her leg. "He didn't hear me, anyway. He's ass out."

Harmony glanced at Lucky, who was dressed in a yellow duck costume, and then pointed to a far corner of the warehouse. "You go over there and keep the camcorder rolling. Make sure you don't say a word, Sis. He'll recognize your voice."

Lucky nodded and then made her way over to the corner slowly, having some trouble walking in the webbed feet.

Harmony handed Fatima the instant camera. "Make sure you get some good shots from different angles."

"I'm on it," Fatima said through the mask of her panda bear costume. "This shit is fun!"

Harmony looked at Bryce, who had on a fluffy dog costume and Colette, who had on a Chiquita Banana costume with a gorilla mask covering her head. They were still trying to get Marvin's ass to wake up.

"Move out the way," Harmony instructed. "I'll wake his ass up!"

They moved and Colette went to take her place for the next part while Bryce stayed there. With a swift kick to the groin, Harmony did as she promised and woke his ass up.

Marvin opened his eyes, in horrible pain, and was petrified to find a dog and a green frog standing over him holding guns with laser beams pointed at his temple.

"Okay, Dean Mitchell." The frog talked to him while he squirmed around holding his dick. "We're about to play a little game."

"Who the fuck are you sick people?" he asked through blurry eyes, never imagining any shit so bizarre would ever happen to him.

Bryce quickly replied, "We're The Black Biker Bitches From Mars!"

The two costumed figures standing over him started laughing. He also heard other laughs coming from somewhere in the darkness of the place they had taken him.

"Where am I?"

"*Hell*," the frog replied. "So, you like to take advantage of young coeds, huh?"

"I don't know what the hell you're talking about, you afflicted bitch!" He knew what she was talking about, but dreaded the fact that his actions had finally caught up to him. He didn't recognize any of their voices, which meant it could be anyone.

The frog kicked him in the balls, causing excruciating pain. "Sit his ass up in the chair," the frog instructed.

The dog grabbed him by the arm and then a panda bear stepped into the light with a camera and helped the dog lift him up onto a steel chair.

"Your reign of terror is up, Dean Mitchell," the frog continued. "Time to pay for all your sins."

"I didn't do jack shit to anybody!" he yelled, professing his innocence, which only fell on deaf ears.

"Drink this!" the frog ordered, pulling some sort of liquid in a jar from behind her back.

"What the hell is that?" He panicked. *Looks like Cherry-Ade*, he thought to himself. "Whatever it is, I'm not drinking it! No way!"

He heard the guns click and decided protesting was out of the question.

"Drink it or I'll blow your fucking brains out," the frog repeated her demand.

He took the jar and drank it reluctantly. *It is Cherry-Ade!*

Twenty seconds later, he realized something was awfully wrong. His dick sprouted up and felt ten pounds heavier than normal. "What the hell did you do to me?"

"He's ready!" the frog yelled out, looking over her shoulder. "Take off all your clothes!"

"Hell no, I'm not taking off my damn clothes!" The frog put the gun on the head of his dick.

"Take off your fucking clothes, *Now!*"

Marvin Mitchell was a fallen man. His pride was gone and his only hope was that they wouldn't kill him. He complied and took off his clothes.

"I'm going to be nice and give you a choice," the frog said after sharing a laugh with her costumed friends at the hardness of his dick, which looked like it could lay concrete.

She pointed to three doors in the back of the warehouse. "You can have the punishment behind door number one, door number two, or door number three. You have ten seconds to make up your mind."

"You sick bitch! Fuck you! I don't know who the hell you are, but I'll track all of you down and kick your fucking asses!"

"Wrong answer," the frog hissed. "I was trying to be nice but now you're going to get all three!"

With that, all three doors swung open and Marvin Mitchell lost his bladder control. Behind door one was a person dressed in a Chiquita banana costume and gorilla mask wearing a strap-on dick. Behind door number two was a 400 lb. transvestite dressed in woman's lingerie and behind door number three was a fuckin' goat.

Marvin Mitchell started to scream but the laughter of his abductors drowned him out. It didn't matter anyway because Marvin Mitchell was on a deserted waterfront with no one around for miles. He was simply *ass out!*

A Word From Our Sponsors

Raoul's Midget Breeding Farm

THE NERVE OF THEM CHICKS, talking about some *limp-dick-lep-rechaun-midgets*! Don't they realize that midgets got it going on?

As a matter of fact, here at Raoul's Midget Breeding Farm, we have the finest specimens of big dick midgets on the East Coast. I'm Raoul, just in case your dumb ass didn't figure it out yet. You have my personal guarantee that any midget acquired from my farm will turn *your* ass out.

All of our midgets are scientifically bred to have Herculean, gigantesque, elephantine, mastodonic, mammoth dicks and come with a full twenty-minute money back guarantee.

Hold up! Give me a moment to scale up onto the porch, aiight? Where's my damn grappling hook when I need it?

(Ten minutes later, after using the grappling hook with shoe laces attached to climb up onto the front porch)

Whew! I finally made it! Give me a second to catch my breath over here on the lounge chair I bought from Ken at a yard sale. You know Ken? That blonde chick's boyfriend; trick ass.

Anyway, like I was saying about oh, thirty minutes ago, come on down to Raoul's Midget Breeding Farm and get you some *real* dick.

I'm about to use my G.I. Joe parachute over here to get back down to ground zero so I can hop in my radio-controlled hooptie and go take advantage of the clearance sale at the Baby Gap.

I guess you all want to get back to them trifling ass Whitfield sisters and their silly ass gurlfriends anyway. Damn shame they tortured that Marvin dude like that; sick huzzies.

As for you, Bryce, talking all that shit! I'd like to show you a thing or two or even three. I'll give you some hellified dick action, aiight? If I whipped my dick out right now, you would think it was a full eclipse out in this mofo. I'd have you screaming out my name in forty-two different languages. Speaking in tongues and shit.

Aw hell, here comes that daschund from down the street again. I hate it when that damn dog chases me. I gotta roll, aiight? The mall is ten miles away so it will take me about five hours to get there in my ride if I get this baby up to two miles per hour. If you need directions to the farm, give me a holla at 1-900-MIDGETS. Peace!

Calls are $9.99 for the first minute and $29.99 for each additional minute.

We now return to the regularly-scheduled program, "Shame On It All," already in progress.

Part Four
Love, Whitfield Style

Chapter Twenty

The Aftermath

"Ladies, what can I possibly say?" Harmony raised her flute of champagne to propose a toast. "We pulled off the teach-a-trifling-mofo-a-lesson crime of the century and didn't even have to load a single gun or break out the duct tape."

All of the women clicked glasses and passed high fives around Fatima's screened-in porch.

Bryce decided to get in on the celebratory remarks. "I'm proud of each and every one of you Black Bitches from Mars."

"Hell yeah, I'll drink to that!" Fatima exclaimed, reaching out her glass to click it against Bryce's. "I must admit that I was skeptical about this entire thing at first. But I'll tell you what, I had much fun. I haven't had this much fun since Harmony and I hid in two of the lockers at Howard after a football game. We got our peep on that night."

Harmony giggled. "That was something. Remember Reginald Field? He was hung like no tomorrow."

"Yes, I remember Reginald. I gave him some."

"Gave him some what?" Harmony asked.

"Ass! What do you think?" Bryce interjected. "She gave him some puddy, some coochie, some booty."

Harmony rolled her eyes at Bryce. "I get your point." She turned to Fatima. "You fucked Reginald? You go, Gurl! Let's toast to that."

They all did and took some seats.

"That damn Niagra!" Fatima squealed. "Gurl, that was too much for me! I say we keep the costumes and do a repeat performance next weekend on Javon's ass. Instead of a rapist tattoo like you gave ole boy tonight, we can give Javon a little dick one. That'll serve his ass right."

"Fatima, you're too much," Lucky giggled, shaking her head. "On the serious tip, I would like to thank you sistas, both blood and honorary, for coming to my rescue like you did. Much love."

Lucky got up to distribute individual hugs and kisses. For a brief moment, the mood turned emotional.

"Damn, a Kodak moment," Colette chided.

Everyone laughed except for Bryce. She elbowed Colette, darting her eyes towards the rest of the group.

"By the way," Colette began on Bryce's cue. "Bryce and I were discussing this in the car on the way back and…"

"And?" Harmony prodded, thinking *I bet she's about to say something totally ridiculous.*

"We decided that we were so smooth tonight, maybe we should take a bank."

Colette and Bryce gave each other high fives and giggled. Harmony clamped her eyes shut to regain some composure before picking up a toss pillow off the wicker love seat and getting both of them in one shot. "Stupid asses!"

"Fa real, Sis!" Bryce wiped the champagne off her shirt with a cocktail napkin. "We can be like Jada, Queen Latifah, and them in *Set It Off!*"

"N-E-Way." Harmony smacked her lips and rolled her eyes. "Dean Marvin Mitchell won't be a dean much longer. I can guaran-damn-tee that. After the officials at the medical school get a peek at the videotape, it's all over for him."

"Are you seriously going to send them the tape?" Lucky asked, finding it hard to digest.

"Hell yes! After I edit our voices out with some theme music. They only get one copy though. I'm definitely storing the original for safekeeping. We could make a killing selling that bad boy on the Internet. We might even outsell that *Jerry Springer Too Hot For TV Tape*."

"Speaking of Internet," Fatima cackled. "My favorite part was when you pretended to use that digital camera and send out photos over the web with your laptop."

"Who was pretending?" Harmony asked sarcastically. "There are pictures of him and the transvestite getting busy in the sixty-nine position *everywhere*. Not to mention, the ones of him and the goat."

Colette eyed Bryce. "Shame on it all! Damn! Remind me never to get on your sister's bad side."

Bryce giggled at Colette, wondering how she didn't recognize the fact that she was already on Harmony's bad side. "Don't forget the pics of Colette tearing up his ripe, virgin booty with that strap-on! That shit was off the hizzy!"

Harmony had a perplexed look on her face. "Colette, that reminds me. I wanted to ask you something. Have you ever used a strap-on before? You looked like an expert!"

Bryce answered before Colette could even open her mouth. "Hell, yeah, she's done it before! Let me tell you the story."

Colette slapped Bryce on the knee. "Chill out, Oprah!"

"Sheit, you could put Long Dong Silver to shame. As a matter of fact, I might get daring one night and let you come over to the crib and fuck me in front of Troy with it."

"Eww!" the rest of them yelled out in unison.

"Naw, the big punisher is going into retirement after tonight." Colette grabbed her crotch, pretending to adjust an imaginary ball sack. "No more ass fucking for me. Although, I wouldn't mind finding out how a thick, juicy dang-a-lang would feel up the old Hershey Highway. That Marvin dude was enjoying the hell out of that shit!"

Harmony leered at Colette and Bryce. "Ya'll are truly demented!"

"We're demented? Aiight, Queen Conspirator and President of

the Fuck A Nucca The Hell Up Club," Bryce hissed, glancing down at her watch. "It's getting rather late. I better get back to the crib before Troy sends 5-0 out searching for me."

Harmony giggled. "Not a chance. I phoned home from the car and Zachary said Troy is calling the hogs on our couch."

"Too many drinks at the booty club, huh?"

"My thoughts exactly." Harmony took another sip of her champagne.

"You let your men go to tits and ass joints?" Colette asked.

"They don't think we know about it," Bryce replied. "It's all good though. Two can play that. We need to check out that dicks and balls club I keep hearing all the sistas praising. I think it's called The Black Screw."

"Yeah, I've heard of it," Fatima proclaimed.

"You've heard of it?" Harmony asked, shaking her head incredulously. "I must be seriously out of the mix if Fatima's opera-going, socialite ass has even heard of it."

"I wanna go see some dicks and balls." Colette cackled. "Maybe we can go there for my birthday. It's in a few weeks."

"Sounds like a winner," Harmony said, while everyone else nodded in agreement. She eyed Lucky, who still seemed extremely depressed. "It's late. Bryce, why don't you take Lucky and Colette and head back to my house. Everyone might as well spend the night, what's left of it."

"What about you?" Lucky asked. "Aren't you coming with us?"

"No, I'm going to chill here for a few and play catch-up with Fatima. I'll drive one of her cars home."

"At three in the morning, you're playing catch-up?" Bryce asked suspiciously.

"Yes, Momma." Harmony rolled her eyes at Bryce. "Besides, I'm too hyped up to sleep. Tell Zachary I'll be home in about an hour."

"Whatever." Bryce wasn't buying into it for a second. She started giggling. "You think Marvin's still where we left him?"

"Yeah, I'm pretty sure he is. Who'd want to be discovered handcuffed to the toilet in the men's room at the fifth precinct with rapist tattooed across their chest? Not to mention his jacked up car out front with the same thing all over it," Harmony replied. "They'll find him eventually and what can he possibly say? 'I was abducted and tortured by residents of Old McDonald's Farm.' "

Everyone started crying laughing.

Once the other three were gone, Fatima cut straight to the chase. "Why'd you really stay? I'm interesting, but I'm not that damn interesting."

"I need to make a stop on the way home."

"At this time of the morning?"

"Yes. We fixed one wrong tonight. Now it's time for me to fix another one." Harmony got up and headed into the house. "Give me the keys to your Porsche."

"Who the fuck is it?" Robbie yelled, making his way into the living room from his bedroom. He couldn't believe someone was banging on his door at three-thirty. Then he had a revelation. "Lucky, I told you that it's over! I have nothing else to say to you!"

Robbie swung his door open and his jaw almost hit the floor. He was shocked to discover an older, more distinguished version of Lucky standing there. While not identical, the large sepia eyes, smooth caramel skin, and full sensual lips were a dead giveaway.

"Do you know who I am?" Harmony asked, already knowing the answer.

"You're Lucky's sister, Harmony. I've seen your picture before in Lucky's dorm room."

"Great! Then we can dispense with the formal introductions, along with the bullshit!"

"Listen, I know why you're here and I'm telling you right now, it won't do any good. Your sister fucked up big time. It's as simple as that."

Harmony wondered if Robbie was even worthy of Lucky. She decided he was justifiably upset because he didn't know all of the circumstances.

"Why wouldn't you listen to Lucky earlier?"

"There was nothing left to be said. I saw her with his hands all over her. They were in his car on campus." Robbie's tone of voice was irate. "I even caught him picking Lucky up here one night in his big fancy car. Your sister was sneaking out of here in the middle of the night to go crawl up in his bed."

"I see," Harmony stated with disdain. "You think you have it all figured out, huh?"

"Pretty much." Robbie stood in his doorway so she couldn't get past him, not that she attempted to. "It's rather simple, actually. Lucky's been sexing down our dean. Why, I have no idea, but she has been. I've never loved anyone the way I love Lucky and she *claimed* to have the same feelings for me. That's the truly fucked up part. I really loved her. I still do."

Harmony was about to turn around and head back to her car, but found his words touching and genuine. "Robbie, you didn't listen to Lucky, but you're damn sure going to listen to me."

"I admire your persistence, Harmony. I really do. But there's nothing you can say that will change anything."

"Are you aware that Dean Mitchell was forcing Lucky to have sex with him so she wouldn't get kicked out of med school?"

"Are you serious?" Robbie asked, taking a few steps back because he felt faint.

"Do I look like I'm kidding?" Harmony came into his living room and sat down on his sofa. Robbie sat across from her in an armchair. "Lucky wasn't the only one, either. He had himself a little harem of scared young girls that felt trapped."

"This is unbelievable."

"Yes, it is. What's even more unbelievable is your doubt about Lucky's feelings for you. She loves you and one of the main reasons she gave into his demands was his constant threats of kicking you out of school because of your grades."

"Are you saying she did this for me?" Robbie felt like someone had just gutted him with a paring knife.

"I'm saying she did this to protect both of you from a lunatic that believes in preying on innocent women."

Tears started cascading down Robbie's right cheek. "He has to be stopped."

Harmony smirked. "Don't worry. I have a feeling that he'll get paid back for his dirt in spades."

"I sure hope so."

"The question is are you going to make Lucky pay for Dean Mitchell's dementia or are you going to be a real man, come home with me, and make amends with your woman?"

It was after five by the time Harmony arrived home. Bryce was lying on top of Troy's chest on the couch, drooling all over it. Harmony covered them up with a throw and headed up the stairs.

She checked in on Lucky in one guest bedroom, delivering a package while she was at it. Then she checked on Colette, who was fast asleep in the other guest bedroom. She went into the master bathroom and took her medication before crawling up in the bed beside Zachary and passing out in his loving, warm arms that reflexively wrapped around her.

"Harmony, is that you?" Lucky sat up and rubbed her eyelids, after hearing Lucinda yapping at the foot of the bed. She thought she saw the outline of a figure by the door. "Harmony?"

"No, it's not Harmony."

Lucky heard a voice that was music to her ears. She thought she was dreaming until Robbie reached out to her in the darkness and grasped her hand.

"I'm so sorry, Baby," Robbie whispered. "I could kill him for what he did to you."

Lucky didn't answer. She just flung herself into Robbie's arms. They both began to weep.

"So you guys went to the movies last night, huh?" Harmony asked, pouring herself a cup of Java. She glanced over at Bryce, who was shocking everyone by being domestic. She was making pancakes on the electric griddle and had bacon broiling in the oven. Bryce glanced back at Harmony and winked.

"Yeah." Troy was the first one to set himself up. "We went to check out *Traffic.*"

"Excellent movie," Zachary added, sitting across from Troy at the dinette table. "Extremely entertaining. I'd give it a four out of five."

"Where did you go see it?" Bryce inquired, not turning around from the counter.

Troy started coughing while Zachary cleared his throat. Bryce and Harmony just smirked at each other. The men were saved by the bell for a few moments when Robbie and Lucky descended the stairs with Colette in tow. Everyone took the time to officially welcome Robbie to the clan.

Lucky gave Harmony a kiss on the cheek and whispered, "Thank you, Sis. You always come through for me."

"Don't mention it. Maybe one day you can return the favor."

"Just name it and I'm there for you."

Harmony giggled and told Lucky to, "Watch this." She walked over to Zachary and started rubbing his shoulders. "Which theater did you say again?"

Zachary and Troy, who'd both assumed they were off the hook, stared at each other. They wanted to make sure they didn't yell out different theaters. Troy nodded his head, letting Zachary know he was deferring the question to him.

"We went to Greenbelt," Zachary answered.

"That's funny," Bryce interjected. "I was just in Greenbelt the other day and I don't recall seeing *Traffic* listed on the marquee."

"Really?" Harmony asked suspiciously. She sat down at the table next to Zachary and leered at him. "That is strange."

"It just started there the day before yesterday," Troy stated, wishing like all hell that they would just drop it.

"Oh, aiight." Bryce said. "No wonder."

Harmony picked up the round of twenty questions where Bryce left off. "Isn't that the movie with Samuel Jackson? The brother from *Pulp Fiction?*"

Robbie was about to correct her, but Lucky tapped him on the leg underneath the table and mouthed the word *no*.

"Yeah, that's the one," Troy lied. "Brotha man turned the movie out, too."

"He sure did," Zachary added.

Harmony couldn't hold in her laugh any longer. "I only have one thing to say to you two. You are cold busted."

"B-U-S-T-E-D," Bryce agreed, spelling the word out in case they were missing the point.

Troy sank down in his chair. Zachary tried to bury his face in the newspaper.

Colette made a suggestion. "I say you sistahgurls withhold pussy privileges for a few weeks."

"Naw," Harmony giggled. "They'd only go get their jollies off at the booty club where they were hanging out last night."

Everyone settled down to eat Bryce's dry ass pancakes and burnt bacon, having a good morning laugh at Zachary's and Troy's expense.

Less than an hour later, they all had to take turns using the three bathrooms. Bryce's meal gave them the runs.

Twenty-One

Let's Make A Love Scene

Bryce was eyeing her coworker Yvon's hairstyle, wondering what the hell was up with it because she couldn't tell if it was supposed to be straight or curly. They were off in a corner of the conference room picking through a platter of cookies while eight other people sat at the conference table making chit-chat about boring topics. They were all waiting patiently for Winston, their boss, to return from yet another trip to the bathroom.

"Have you noticed that Winston's been in and out of the restroom a lot today?" Yvon asked Bryce, stirring a cube of sugar into her coffee.

"How could I not notice it? This meeting is taking *forever*," Bryce replied sarcastically.

"He must have an upset stomach."

"Could be." Bryce held in a laugh and almost choked on the oatmeal raisin cookie she'd just taken a bite of. Winston had spoken nastily to Bryce yet again the week before, so she'd taken the liberty of sneaking into his office. She'd mixed a container of powdered laxative into the muscle building shake he fixed first thing every morning. She was the only one that knew why he was making mad dashes to the bathroom. "All I know is I won't be shaking his hand anytime soon."

"Bryce, you're so crazy!"

Bryce wasn't offended since the statement was true. "You still seeing Joshua, also known as R. Kelly, Jr.?"

"Yeah, Girl! Joshua and I are going strong." Yvon was seeing a musician that Bryce nicknamed R. Kelly Jr. since he tried to emulate him in clothing, body language, and of course music. "How about you and George?"

Bryce rolled her eyes. "Hmph, George is history. I found myself a new man."

"I'm shocked. I thought you'd walk down the aisle with George."

"I thought that, too, until he decided to cheat."

"Aw, Bryce! I'm so sorry, Girl."

Bryce giggled. "Don't be sorry. George's fuck-up was the best thing that ever happened to me. Troy's ten times the man George will ever be."

"Troy, huh? How'd you meet him?"

"Long story."

"Judging by how long it's taking Winston to come back from the restroom, I have time for a book," Yvon said loud enough for everyone else to hear. She wanted it known that she was irritated by the delays.

Bryce smirked, wondering why Yvon thought she had some sort of clout when she was dead last on the seniority pole. "We met at a Memorial Day cookout over a mutual friend's house."

"Is he fine?"

"Can you picture me dating a man who isn't fine?" Bryce asked incredulously.

Yvon chuckled. "No, I guess not."

"I know not. I want to wake up in the middle of the night and see a pretty face; not an extra from *The Night of the Living Dead*."

"You are such a fool."

"Just keeping it real."

"You want to hang out someplace tonight? Joshua's going to a bachelor party."

"I can't. Troy and I are going to get busy tonight," Bryce replied, winking at Yvon.

"Oh yeah? What's up?" Yvon asked excitedly. She knew how Bryce liked to get down.

"I'll never tell." Bryce could see Yvon was practically salivating to get into her business, but decided to leave her hanging. "Matter-of-fact, Troy doesn't even know what's up."

"Sounds like you have something kinky in store for him," Yvon prodded.

Bryce laughed and rubbed the crumbs left over from the cookie off the corners of her mouth with a napkin. "I'm not sure kinky describes it, but he'll have a good time."

Winston came walking into the room holding his stomach. Everyone was shaking their heads at him.

"Here comes Winston," Yvon whispered to Bryce. "Promise me you'll give me some details later."

"I don't know about all that, Yvon. You tend to have a big mouth sometimes."

"And you don't?"

Bryce smirked. "Whatever, heifer. I just hope Winston doesn't start lighting up the room with his farts."

"Damn, Bryce, take it easy on my poor dick," Troy said, flinching. "You've been sucking my dick for hours now."

She popped it out for a quick second. "Well, they say practice makes perfect so I'm practicing."

"Practicing for what? The Suck-a-Dick-a-Thon? The Dick Sucking Olympics?" He tried to push her off of him.

"You're so silly," she said as she licked around the head. "I saw this transvestite suck a dick one time. I was envious as all hell so I figure anything a shemale can do, I can do better."

"A transvestite sucking dick! Bryce, I just don't know about your crazy ass sometimes."

She glanced up for a brief moment, looked him in the eyes, and then suckled on the head of his dick, drawing out some precum.

Troy flinched, more so out of pleasure than pain. "I used to pray every night to my Black Buddha doll with the Afro and joint in his mouth to send me a freaky woman but he over did it with your sexually deviant ass."

Bryce almost choked on his dick when she fell out laughing.

He started caressing the back of her neck. After all, the blow job she was giving him was the bomb diggity. "You know, this here is most men's greatest fantasy. Having a woman suck his dick for hours and hours. With the exception of a threesome. Speaking of which, what about..."

Bryce reached underneath his dick, pinching his balls before he could finish his sentence.

"Ouch!" Troy hissed. "I've schooled your ass about this violence shit before!"

Bryce took his dick out her mouth, jumped up, and plopped down beside him on the couch. "I'm full."

"Just like that?" Troy held his hands out and sighed with confusion.

"Yeah, you brought up a threesome and that spoiled the mood." She picked up her *Jet* magazine and started flipping through the Photos of the Week.

"Hold up! Two seconds ago you were going to town on my dick and now you're reading *Jet?*"

"Yep," she replied. "On second thought, I'm too tired to read. I'm just going to call it a night."

She flung the issue of *Jet* onto his lap and got up from the couch, leaving him there looking dumbfounded. "I can't believe this shit!"

Bryce decided to really drive home her point to never bring up the threesome topic again. Even freaky ass women like her draw the line at sharing the dick. "Why don't you just go home tonight? You do have a place, *remember?*"

Troy glowered, trying to figure out his next move. There was no way he was going home and sleeping alone after getting used to being with Bryce every night. Then he remembered he had one more trick up his sleeve. He went into the kitchen to find his briefcase.

Bryce was halfway up the steps by the time he caught up to her. "Just lock the door on your way out," she demanded without even turning around.

"Oh well." He sighed. "I guess we won't be able to microwave some popcorn and watch the bootleg copy of *Jerry Springer Too Hot For TV* I got off this dude down at Haines Point last week."

Bryce swung around, gleaming like a kid in a candy store. "You got the tape?"

Troy waved it around in the air like it was a winning Pick-4 lottery ticket. "I sure did! Anything for my baby!"

Bryce ran back down the steps, flung her arms around him, and kissed him all over his face. "I love you *sooooooo* much!"

"What did you say?" Troy was shocked and so was Bryce once she realized her slip of the tongue.

"I said I hate you *sooooooo* much." She tried to cover it up.

"Naw, naw, *nawwwwwwww* the hell you didn't," he insisted. "You said you *loooooovvvve* me!"

Bryce blushed, diverting her eyes to his chest. "So what if I did say it? What would your response be?"

Bryce nibbled on her bottom lip with nervous anticipation.

"*Well*, if you did say it and that's a big ass if according to you, then I would probably say..." He paused, rubbing his fingers over his chin as if he was pondering the notion.

"Probably?" Bryce rolled her eyes and put her hands on her hips.

Troy looked at her, beautiful even though she was pouting, and couldn't resist the urge to confess his true feelings any longer. He took her smooth, delicate hands into his. "I love you, Bryce! I always have! Ever since the moment I first laid eyes on you!"

She started blushing harder and giggled. "The feeling's mutual!"

She turned around and started running up the steps again. "Last one in the bed is a rotten egg!"

"Cheater!" Troy tried to catch up. "I still can't believe it took a Jerry Springer tape to get you to say *I Love You!* All this good ass dick I've been breaking your ass off with for months? Shame on it all!"

"Ouch!" Lucky screamed, startling both Robbie and Lucinda.

Robbie came running in the kitchen of his apartment with the puppy in close pursuit, only to discover Lucky standing over the stove sucking on her index finger.

"What happened?"

"I got burned by the boiling water." He took her finger out of her mouth and placed it in his own, trying to soothe the pain. "I wanted to cook you a special, romantic dinner and now it's turning into a disaster."

Robbie took the pot handles and moved the steaming pot of noodles to a cool burner. "Spaghetti, huh?"

"Yes, spaghetti with garlic bread and tossed salad."

"Oh, I tell-l-l-l-l-l-l you-you-you what," Robbie stuttered. "Don't worry your pretty little self over it. Let's just order some Chinese and have it delivered."

Lucky wondered why he didn't want her to finish cooking. The sauce was fine and it was just a little finger burn. Then she started giggling. "Umm, Robbie, doesn't your grandma on your father's side live in New Orleans?"

"Yes." He was searching through a kitchen drawer for the take-out menu. "Why do you ask? You wanna go check out the Mardi Gras next year?"

"Yeah, we can." Lucky chuckled. "But I just thought you should know that my period's not due for at least another week."

He looked at her like a little boy caught with his hand in the cookie jar. They both burst out laughing.

After eating three servings of Lucky's *delicious* spaghetti, Robbie got up to clear the dishes while Lucky turned on the stereo. She turned the dial on the receiver to her favorite station, WPGC 95.5, just in time to catch the beginning of *Love Talk and Slow Jams.*

They sat there listening to the callers, both male and female, openly discussing issues related to relationships and sex. A couple of debates ensued between Lucky and Robbie, especially the one about how men always lie on their dick size.

One sista called in and broached the issue. Of course, men got mad offended. Robbie being one of them.

"Listen, Baby," Lucky said. "I don't mean you no harm but men *do* lie on the dick."

"Well, not this man!" he proclaimed. You know better than anyone that I have no reason to lie."

"You're right, Baby," she confessed, knowing that no other answer was acceptable. "You're packing your fair share and then some."

"Damn straight!"

They both giggled.

"Yet and still," she continued. "I was over this gurl Rhonda's dorm room late one night and she was in this black chat room on America Online."

"Yeah, and?" Robbie inquired.

"Nuccas were in there bragging about how they had ten or eleven inches and could knock the bottom out a pussy."

Robbie laughed hysterically. "Sorry asses! On the Internet, trying to get laid. That's pathetic!"

"Oh, you haven't heard the half of it. They were sending out pics, too. Naked ones."

"Get out of here!" Robbie wondered if any of the sistas were sending out nude pics as well but wasn't about to ask.

"Yup, they sure were. Fake pics at that," Lucky said avidly. "Half of them were pics of gay porn stars and the other half were doctored."

"Damn shame, but how do you know they were gay porn stars?"

"My gurl Rhonda is freaky like that!"

"Oh!" They both fell out laughing again.

"Those men were lying. Rhonda and I figured out a formula to come up with the real dick size."

"Which is?"

"Take the Internet chat room dick size and divide it by three to get the actual and factual."

"That's mad funny." Robbie poured them another glass of sparkling apple cider.

"Those men remind me of Bryce's old boyfriend, George. Back in the days when she was sporting that weave."

"Your sister used to have a weave?"

"Not just any ole weave cause some of them look damn good. Bryce had a *fucked-da-hell-up* weave some chica put in her hair over at this place Weave Central. It looks more like a taco joint than a hair salon. They sell bean pies and tofu burgers up in there."

"Eww, damn, the smell of bean pies mixed with burning hair. Makes my stomach turn just thinking about it."

"Speaking of the web," Lucky said hesitantly. "There are some pics of Dean Mitchell fucking a goat all over the place."

"Damn." Robbie chuckled. Then his mood changed at the mere mention of the dean's name. Even though the dean had been fired after some videotape of him doing some vulgar, far out shit was sent to the administration, they still avoided discussing the situation most of the time. "That was wild how he got found out. I wonder who fucked him so bad. One of the homies on campus was passing out flyers of him sucking some shemale's dick. Did you see it?"

"No, I missed that one," Lucky lied, knowing good and damn well she had a ring-side seat for the whole thing. "I'm just glad he left town for good."

"You and I both." Robbie grabbed a hold of her trembling hand. "Enough of all that! It's just you and me now, *forever!*"

They began to kiss feverishly.

"Lucky, just so you know, my love for you *will* last forever so when your period comes on, let's eat out all that week."

She gave him a *love-slap* on his knee and they both started giggling. Ten minutes later, they made love on the balcony underneath the stars.

Harmony arrived home after a sixteen-hour day at the temp agency, ready to grab a sandwich and then pass out. Zachary told her that he had a late meeting himself so she didn't see any reason to plan anything fancy for dinner.

To her astonishment, when she opened the front door and

entered, the house was completely lit up with twelve-inch pillar vanilla-scented candles. There were red roses everywhere. Zachary came out of the kitchen and greeted her with a huge kiss.

"Hey, Baby, let me take your coat." He removed the blazer of her black business suit but didn't stop there. He undressed her completely and then led her into the dining room where he had the table set with a white linen tablecloth and elegant fine china.

"What's all this?" she asked with a big grin on her face. "I thought you had a meeting?"

"I decided some things are more important than business. One thing in particular is more precious than anything on the face of this earth. Our love for one another."

He undressed also and then hand-fed her strawberries dipped in warm chocolate, lobster tails in butter sauce, and asparagus tips. He did it slowly, making sure to lap up any evidence of juice that trickled out of her mouth with his thick tongue.

After dinner, he carried her upstairs and bathed her in their large garden tub, carefully making sure every inch of her was pampered. He laid her gently down on a bed of rose petals and made love to her, licking every part of her from head to toe.

Afterwards, she started to weep while they lay there in each other's arms.

"What's wrong?" Zachary asked, pulling back the hair from her brow and kissing her on the forehead.

"Nothing. It's just that I'm going to miss this so much when I have to go away."

Tears immediately started to flow down Zachary's cheek. "You don't have to go anyplace, Harmony. There is a solution. You're just afraid to seek it out."

Harmony looked up at him and kissed him on the lips. "I can't do that to Bryce, or Lucky either for that matter. I'm on a list. Something will come through."

"Let's hope so!"

"I feel so bad about the fact that I'm sitting around waiting for someone else to die so that I might live."

"That's the worse case scenario, but it doesn't have to be like that. As far as harming Bryce and Lucky, what in heaven's name do you think your death is going to do to them? I can't imagine living in a world without you and I know they can't either. You're the backbone of your whole family and the first one your sisters come running to when something goes wrong."

Harmony ran into the master bathroom and shut the door. She crouched over in pain and rambled through the medicine cabinet to find her pills. Zachary came in after her and drew her a glass of water from the spigot. He handed it to her. "I never thought I would be worried about such a thing, but I would give anything to have been born with another blood type. Your blood type."

"Even if you were, it wouldn't make the slightest difference." Harmony laid her head on his chest. "You probably wouldn't match anyway and I definitely wouldn't let you do it."

"Bryce would match," he blurted out. "Please save yourself before this goes too far. I'm begging you."

"I can't. I could never do that." Harmony's pain began to subside under the effect of the medication. "I'm tired. Can you just hold me while I'm sleeping?"

"Do you even really need to ask?" Zachary carried her back to bed.

Twenty-Two

The Black Screw

"**B**ryce and Colette, we're over here!" Lucky was standing near the front of the long line with Fatima and Harmony. She waved for them so they could spot her easily.

When Bryce and Colette *boguarded* their way into the line, some sistas who were further back started mumbling objections. Bryce turned around to give them her infamous *you-must-be-asking-for-a-beatdown-look* and all objections ceased.

"Wow, this place is jam-de-da-damn-packed!" Colette blurted out. "You would think they were giving out free tickets to a Prince concert up in here."

"That's The Artist Formerly Known As Prince," the sista directly in front of them turned around and interjected.

"He was Prince when I first started feenin' for his sexy ass way back in junior high school and he's Prince now," Colette stated, smacking her lips.

The woman rolled her eyes and then turned back around.

"What time are they going to open up the doors?" Harmony asked impatiently. "We've been standing out here in this heat for damn near an hour!"

"In about five more minutes," Fatima replied. "From what I hear, this show is well worth the wait and then some."

"It better be." Bryce tapped her foot. "If I just want to see some dick, I can see that at home."

"Mmmmm, smells like fried chicken," Colette commented, sniffing the air. "Making me hungry!"

"That's the group of women all the way at the head of the line," Lucky informed her. "They have buckets of KFC, potato salad, and collard greens."

"For a damn dick and balls club?" Bryce asked with astonishment. "This is going to be a wild ass night. I can tell that already."

Exactly five minutes later, just like Fatima said, the doors swung open and they entered *The Black Screw*.

"Di-zammmmm, I felt like OJ running through an airport trying to get up in this mofo!" Colette took a seat at their table, completely out of breath.

"Who are you telling?" Bryce interjected. "I felt like a linebacker for the Dallas Cowboys. That one gurl with the fuschia and black extensions almost got an ass whupping for real."

"Ya'll stop complaining," Harmony insisted, knowing good and well she was better at lodging complaints than anyone. "At least we got pretty good seats. Some sistas are all the way in the back."

"True that," Lucky agreed. "I can't wait for the show to start. I hear it's the bomb!"

"Uh-oh, the lights are going down," Fatima said. "Time for the dicks and balls show to begin."

"Bring them on!" Colette yelled, taking a long sip of her Long Island Iced Tea. "I'm ready to see some big ass dicks!"

The Black Screw was huge. It was a warehouse turned into a virtual fuck palace and the men who were walking around serving the drinks all had enormous dicks. Bryce's eyes almost popped out of her head. She was in love and all, but she avidly believed a sista had a right to look.

She was sitting there eyeing a brother with nothing but a black g-string on and cowboy boots, who was bent over a table across the aisle from them taking the drink orders of some women, when LL Cool J's *Doin' It Well* blared out over the sound system.

They all exchanged high fives and giggles when a fine brotha about 5' 11" with cinnamon skin and a buff ass body came out and introduced himself as the master of ceremony. His stage name was Black Raw Silk and the name was fitting because his skin looked as soft as silk.

One man after another took the stage and did his thing. There was no way any woman, who even remotely loves herself some dick, would not be drowning in her own pussy juice up in *The Black Screw.* There was a stage right smack in the middle of the club, like a boxing ring in the middle of an arena, with tables surrounding all four sides of it so all the women could get a little look-see. In addition, there were circular risers in the four corners of the club with male dancers, who had already performed and taken it all off, on them getting mad freaky. *The shit was all that!* They were so naked the only place they could put the dollars women tipped them was in their boots. Harmony noticed they were all wearing some sort of boots, mostly cowboy style ones. Cash and carry, she supposed.

The gurls got tore up by the third round of drinks and by the fifth round, they were all horny. Bryce was sitting there wishing she could get her hands on Troy's ass right then and there because she would have fucked him like she hated him.

Harmony wasn't quite sure who was wilder, the male dancers or the female patrons. There was some truly freaky shit going on up in that piece.

Men had women bent over tables grinding their dicks up against their asses, they were palming tits, sucking toes, fingering pussy even. As for the women, they were even worst. The women were pulling their shit off too, jacking dicks, riding dicks with their clothes on, everything except actual fucking but then again, no one did a panty check or anything.

There were four wild things that happened that night that freaked everyone the hell out. The first one was when a fine ass brotha came over to their table and almost sucked the skin off Colette's toes for a measly dollar.

"Damn, Baby!" Bryce hollered out over the loud thumping of the music. "I would've just given your ass a dollar. How in the hell could you suck those nasty ass, crusty toes of hers for *any* type of money?"

They all busted out laughing but the brotha kept sucking on Colette's toes like they were baby back ribs.

"That's mad nasty," Fatima added. "When you get done, you can suck my ass out while you're at it. There's five bucks in it for you!"

They all cackled but the brotha looked up like he was contemplating the deal.

Colette threw her head back and ignored them all. She had dreamt of having her corns sucked on many a night and she was basking in every single second of the ecstasy.

"I can't take this shit." Bryce got up from the table. "I'm about to go find the little girl's room. Maybe this nucca will be through eating the crust from between her toes by the time I come back."

While brotha man kept sucking, another fine ass nucca took the stage named Loverboy. One of the women up front lost her fuckin' mind and leapt up on the stage to attack his ass. Bryce shook her head while she made her way past the crowd to the ladies room, laughing at the woman who outweighed Loverboy three to one. She bent over and assumed the position for him to hit it from the back.

He lifted her skirt and started grinding his dick onto her ass from the rear but promptly moved away and held his nose. All the women fell silent, feeling a bit embarrassed for the sista since it was apparent her coochie was less than kosher. That is, until they noticed that her white bloomers were stained from front to back with something brown.

"Damn." Harmony chuckled. "Hasn't she ever heard of wiping her ass?"

The woman got up from the stage and resumed her seat, hiding her face from the room of people who fell out laughing at her stank ass.

Bryce got turned around on her way back from the ladies room and ended up going down a hallway that had a bunch of neon signs hanging outside of various doors. There was a room called *The Red Light District*. Bryce heard some slow jams coming from it and decided to be nosy, which was nothing new.

She peeked through the curtains and didn't know whether to run away or try to join in. There were four couches, one on each wall, and male strippers were getting their freak on with female patrons. They were doing more than freaking. They were straight up doing the nasty and Bryce became voyeuristic. She watched one sista deep throat this brotha's dick and decided the woman could put that transvestite from the warehouse to shame. Another couple was doing the sixty-nine and yet another one was fucking like a pair of wild beasts.

Bryce watched until she was at her breaking point. Five more seconds and she would have knocked one of the bitches to the curb to get her some. She went back out to the main room of the club, panties soaking in pussy juice and all. She knew right then and there, Troy's ass was in for it that night. Not even crying *"Uncle"* would save his ass.

By the time Bryce returned to the table, the nasty ass toe sucker had moved on from sucking Colette's toes to sucking some sista's breasts who was sporting at least a 40DDD.

"Thank goodness that mofo quit sucking those nasty ass toes of yours," she said to Colette. "That shit was making me sick to my stomach. That's worse than eating chitterlings."

"Fuck you, Bryce." Colette giggled. "Your ass is just jealous!"

"Whatever!"

Bryce looked at Harmony and Lucky and they both had that *I'm-ready-to-go-home-and-fuck-the-shit-out-of-my-man* expression on their faces.

"Colette, you about ready to roll? It's late."

"Hell, naw," she replied. "They have a brotha getting ready to come out called Mandingo. I've always wanted a Mandingo-looking brotha to turn my ass out!"

"What the hell is a Mandingo?" Fatima asked, yawning from

the effect of alcohol and looking like she would fall asleep five seconds after her head hit the pillow.

"A Mandingo is a brotha with a big ass dick," Lucky stated. They all laughed. "And I do mean a big ass dick!"

"Well, we shall see," Harmony countered. "If it's too big, I wouldn't fuck his ass anyway."

"Shit!" Bryce yelled. "As far as I'm concerned, the bigger the better."

Black Raw Silk announced Mandingo and he came strutting out on the stage seductively to *You Are Not Alone* by Michael Jackson.

Once he dropped his pants, Bryce recanted her words. "On second thought, no fucking way! That mofo's dick is *tooooooo* damn big!"

All the rest of them were speechless. None of them had ever seen a man with a dick that big anywhere. Not in porno movies, *not any damn where.*

The DJ cut the music off and silence befell the room like Mandingo was Houdini about to do his infamous escape from a sealed water tank trick. Apparently, all of the other women in the club who were regulars knew what to expect but not the Whitfield sisters and their crew.

None of them could believe their eyes when Mandingo, whose dick had to be at least two feet long, sat down on a steel folding chair, lowered his head, and started sucking his own dick.

Fatima was half asleep and drunk as all hell. Harmony was mesmerized. Bryce was trying to figure out whether or not Troy was that flexible, Lucky was sick to her stomach, and Colette was turned the fuck on. No one said a damn word until he had sucked himself off and came in his own mouth.

"Damn, I've heard of men jacking off but shit," Bryce said with disgust. "Time to roll!"

"I agree." Harmony nodded. "Let's get the hell out of here. This is too damn wild!" Harmony grabbed Fatima's arm and yanked her up off the chair. "Let's go, Sistahgurl!"

Lucky sipped down the last of her rum and Coke and got up to follow them out.

Bryce stood up and looked over at Colette. It was obvious she didn't plan on budging. "Come on, Colette, damn! I have to get home to my baby!"

"You all go ahead. I'm going to stay a while longer," Colette replied.

"You sure about this?" Bryce felt guilty about leaving her there alone. "I rode here with you and I should probably ride back with you."

"No, it's cool." Colette smiled up at her. "I'm straight. Harmony, can you give Bryce a ride home?"

"Sure thing." Harmony glanced at her watch and was anxious to get home so she could get some before Zachary fell into a deep sleep.

Bryce headed for the door. "Aiight, Colette. I'll holla at you tomorrow."

Chapter Twenty-Three

Mandingo Dick

Bryce reached over Troy's chest to grab the phone. He was snoring like all hell, as usual. Bryce made a mental note to get some earplugs like peeps wear to motor speedways. She loved her some him but his snores sounded like something out of the twilight zone.

"Hello," Bryce said sheepishly, still exhausted from hanging out at *The Black Screw* half the night and fucking Troy the other half.

"Bryce." She heard a woman's faint voice on the other end, but it was too hard to make it out at first. "Bryce, I need your help, Gurl."

She finally recognized Colette's voice and then glanced at the digital alarm clock. "Colette, it's five in the damn morning. Why are you calling me so late?"

"I need your help," she repeated in a raspy voice.

It reminded Bryce of how her own voice got distorted when she would talk to Troy through the bathroom door while she was taking a shit. So she asked, "Colette, are you taking a shit? You better not be calling my house at five o'clock in the morning while you're sitting on the damn toilet."

"Not exactly," Colette replied. "It's something like that though."

Troy's snoring hit a plateau and Bryce couldn't hear. She knocked Troy's leg off of hers so she could get up out of the bed.

After she hit the carpeted hallway, she held the receiver back up to her ear. Colette was moaning. "What do you mean by not exactly? You're either taking a dump or you aren't!"

"Mmmmmmmmmm, you remember..." Colette blurted out and then paused like she was straining to get a turd out.

"Colette, I may not be an expert on your bathroom etiquette, but you sound like you're taking a shit to me. A constipated shit at that." Bryce's patience was wearing thin. "Look, I'm taking my ass back to bed. Give me a holla when you finally get that elephantine bomb to drop."

"*Nooooooo*, don't hang up!" Colette pleaded.

"Colette, my pussy is sore, my lips are sore, and now you're making my ass sore with all these shitting sound effects." Bryce smacked her lips and rolled her eyes, for her own benefit alone. "What's wrong? Are you drunk or something?"

"Not anymore, mmmmmmmm." Colette moaned. "You remember that stripper from the club, Mandingo?"

"How in the hell could I forget him? He sucked his own mofo dick in front of a room full of women."

"After you guys left, I started kicking it with him and we ended up leaving the club together. Mmmmmmmmm, damn!"

"Gurl, you must be crazy, fucking around with him. He could fuck a mule and have five or six inches left over."

"Trust me, I've learned my freakin' lesson." Colette's moans started again, growing in intensity. "Gurl, you've gotta come get this nucca off me."

"What do you mean, off you?"

"He was drinking a lot and he, mmmmmm, passed out cold with his dick in my ass."

"Holy Mother of Ex-Lax! You let him ram that two by four up your ass?"

"Yes, you've got to come get it out."

Bryce fell out laughing. "I love you like a sister, but you're on your own with this one."

"Bryce, don't laugh. This is some serious shit."

"HAHAHAHAHAHA! You can say that again!" Bryce couldn't help but laugh at the irony of the statement.

"See, your ass is dead wrong for this!" Colette yelled into the phone. "I can't lay here like this forever!"

"Aiight, aiight, where are you?" Bryce bounced up against the hallway walls, trying to keep herself from bursting out laughing again.

"I'm at Raoul's Starlight Motel. Mmmmmmmm, please hurry!"

"Where in the hell is that? Sounds like some seedy shit to me. No pun intended." She giggled.

"It's on Route 69, right across the street from Raoul's Midget Breeding Farm and right around the corner from Raoul's Hamburger Heaven, Home of the Famous Quarter Ouncer Burger."

"Get the fuck out of here!"

"I'm serious! Hurry up, Bryce! We're in Room 12 - *The Snow White and the Seven Dwarfs Suite*."

Bryce couldn't hold in her laughter another second. "Aiight, Gurl, I'm on my way!"

"You coming for real? Mmmm, dammmmmnnn!"

"Yeah, I'm coming but you're going to owe me big time for this. I sincerely hope you didn't eat any corn for dinner cause this could get messy!"

Bryce hit the reset button on the cordless and immediately dialed Harmony's house.

Once Harmony answered, she cut straight to the abbreviated version.

"Listen up! Colette got that Mandingo nucca's plywood dick stuck up her ass out by some midget farm so go get Lucky and meet me in the parking lot of the IHOP on New Hampshire Avenue in Takoma Park!"

"Holy Mother of Ex-Lax!" Harmony yelled in the phone.

"My thoughts exactly! Now hurry up and get your ass moving!"

No sooner had Bryce pressed the off button on the phone and headed in the bedroom to get dressed when it started ringing again.

"Colette! I'm coming, damn!" Bryce listened for a brief moment. "No Harmony, I don't have any film in my camera so you can take pictures to sell on the Internet. Sick ass!"

After driving around in circles for almost an hour, they finally spotted some midgets sitting in a sandbox and drinking Thunderbird outside a shady looking motel. The sun was almost up.

"Damn, look at the pygmies!" Lucky exclaimed. "Where did all these midgets come from? You sure this isn't Willy Wonka's crib?"

While they were getting out of their car, Bryce pointed to one of them. "Hey, that one over there in the Fisher Price jumper is the same one I almost slapped with my knee at that house party."

They all busted out laughing while they found the motel office and went inside.

Harmony started pressing down on the call bell repetitively. She was already impatient for two reasons. One, because Bryce made her get up so early and two, because she wanted to hurry up and see that Mandingo nucca's dick up someone's ass. His dick was like the eighth wonder of the world and she was anxious to witness such a feat with her own two eyes.

Lucky became immediately enthralled in a Godzilla movie that was on the raggedy ass black and white television with a hanger in the place where the antenna used to be. She giggled at the movie, which was made in Japan, because the people's lips were moving at a different speed than the voice-overs. She loved those kinds of movies but had no idea they still came on since the invention of premium cable channels.

Bryce was too busy checking out the furniture. Everything was small-scale. "What is this place? A motel or a day care center?"

Harmony laughed. "Hell if I know, Sis, but they need to hurry up."

She started banging on the bell harder.

"Hold your horses! I'm coming!"

"Who said that?" Bryce asked. They all started looking around.

"I said it," a male voice with a Puerto Rican accent replied snidely.

They looked down at the counter and saw some stubby little fingers appear over the edge. The *thing*, because they had no idea what to call him, climbed up on the counter. They all fell out laughing again.

"Damn, who are you?" Harmony asked.

"I'm Raoul, dammit, and I already know who you trifling ass Whitfield sisters are!"

"Is that right?" Bryce rolled her eyes, not taking kindly to the *trifling* comment.

"Yes, that's right. As for you, *Miss Bryce*, I'd like to break my dick off in you and teach you a lesson. All that shit you keep talking about *limp-dick-leprechaun-midgets*. You need to try one from my midget farm on for size."

"Look, we don't have time for your scrawny ass," Bryce replied. "Give us the key to Room 12 - *The Snow White and the Seven Dwarfs Suite*." Bryce held out her hand and rubbed her fingers together, waiting for the key.

"There's already someone in Room 12 and they asked not to be disturbed!"

"We know there's someone in there, dufus," Lucky lashed out at him. "Just hurry up and give us the damn key. It's an emergency."

"Naw, we don't allow any orgies or freak shows here at this fine establishment." Raoul sat down on top of the hand bell. "Unless, of course, I can join in."

"That's it!" Harmony had finally heard enough. She pounded the bell again, with him sitting on top of it, and it made his eardrums explode. "Give us the key before I let Bryce slap you with her knee!"

"Arrrrrrrgh, what are you trying to do? Make me deaf?" He got up from the bell and tethered over to the edge of the counter. "Give me a few to get back down to ground level so I can get the key."

"This is bullshit," Bryce said, crossing her hands in front of her. "Colette is laid up in there with a three-foot dick in her ass and we're out here arguing with a nucca who buys his clothes at the Baby Gap."

"Dick in ass?" Raoul asked excitedly. "Damn, you want me to call the bamalance?"

"No," Harmony said. "I just want you to beat it. I'll get the key myself!"

"You can't come behind my counter without permission but if you ask me nicely, I'll let you come behind here and then I'll make you CUM behind here, too."

Bryce hauled off and plucked him with the tip of her thumb. He went down for the count. "When you wake up, call the bamalance for yourself!"

Harmony got the key. They were headed out the door when they noticed Lucky was not coming.

"Lucky!" Harmony hollered. "Forget that damn monster movie and come on. We have to go battle a monster ourselves. A drunk mofo with a leviathan dick who won't take his telephone pole out Colette's ass."

When they got to Room 12, Bryce stopped dead in her tracks. "Maybe I should go in alone. This could get pretty ugly. She sounded like she was shitting on the phone."

"What could be uglier than the things we did to Marvin in Javon's warehouse?" Lucky asked.

"Good point." Bryce nodded in agreement.

"Get out of my way!" Harmony pushed by them both and slipped the card key with a nude picture of Raoul imprinted on one side into the lock. "I'm not missing this shit for nothing!"

"I don't think any of us are going to miss the shit." Lucky chuckled.

"Ya'll are truly sick." Bryce giggled.

When they entered the room, it was pitch black and the alcohol stench was nauseating.

Bryce reached around for the light switch, turned it on, took one look, and then turned it back off. "This is too much for me! I can't even deal!"

"Let me see!" Lucky demanded. She went in, turned on the light, and then turned it back off. "Hell, I can't get down like that either!"

Harmony decided to be the brave one. She cut on the light and left it on. "Colette, you okay?"

"Damn, she's passed out cold." Bryce entered the room and walked towards the bed to try to revive her. Colette had finally passed out cold from the one trillion-milligram suppository Mandingo had laid on her.

Lucky looked at the bed. "Damn, is that a crib mattress they fucking on?"

"Looks like it," Harmony replied. "Okay, this is more serious than I thought. We've got to get him off before her anal muscles are completely destroyed."

"Eww," Lucky said. "Destroyed as in she won't be able to go to work without shit falling out her ass at her desk?"

Bryce and Harmony both glanced at Lucky and yelled, "Shut the hell up!"

"Well, excuse the hell out of me. I'm just trying to be helpful."

"Since the mattress is so small, their feet are already hanging over the edge so I suggest we stand them upright and then pull Colette off of him that way," Bryce proposed.

Harmony rolled her eyes. "That's your big plan, huh?"

"It's not like you have one," Bryce hissed.

"Aiight, let's do this," Lucky said.

It was a big ass struggle, *literally*, but they managed to get them upright and lean Mandingo up against the Barbie Dream Playhouse dresser long enough to jimmy his dick out Colette's ass with a comb out of Lucky's pocket book. They slid the comb in and then used it as leverage to get the dick out.

"This is no nasty. Shit is everywhere and they're still knocked out," Bryce commented.

"I'm going to wash the skin off my hands," Harmony said and then headed towards the bathroom. The other two followed suit. "Oh, and Lucky, don't forget your comb!"

"Sick ass." Lucky giggled and they all fell out laughing.

"I've been trying to wake her ass up for ten minutes now," Bryce said a little while later. "And no Harmony, you can't kick her in the coochie so get that perverted look off your face."

"Maybe the fresh air will wake her up," Lucky suggested.

"Good idea," Harmony said and then added, "Let's wrap her up in this crib sheet and put her in the back seat of my car."

"Cool," Bryce said, "but you might want to cover your back seat with this baby blanket first just in case. Shit happens, you know."

"Holy Mother of Ex-Lax!" Harmony exclaimed. "Good thinking, Batman!"

"Ya'll are so fucking silly." Lucky chuckled, shaking her head. They all cackled.

Once they had Colette, crib sheet and all, in the car, Bryce was about to get in the back seat with her against her better judgment when she felt someone kick her in the ankle. She looked down and it was the midget from the leprechaun house party.

"What do you want, you Lilliputian?"

"Aw, I remember you! You're that honie that was sweating all over me at Tony's mother's cousin's husband's mistress' house."

Bryce rolled her eyes. "You want me to slap you in the face with my knee?"

"Step up off me, tramp," he said.

"Step up off you?" Bryce giggled. "More like step on you, you sorry excuse for a pygmy."

He kicked her in the ankle again.

"That's it!" Bryce yelled and then kicked some dirt up into his face.

"You bitch." He coughed. "You're in for it now. First, you beat up Raoul and now you're molesting me. You're sexually repressed, aren't you? I'll be glad to give you some."

"Bryce, get in the car so we can go!" Harmony demanded. "Leave his ass here for a skunk to fart in his face!"

"Hold on a second." Bryce held up her hand like a crossing guard. She squatted down, looking him in the eye. "First of all, I didn't beat Raoul up. I plucked him with my thumb. Secondly, I'm not molesting you but if you kick me again, I'm going to pick you up by the seat of your size toddler four pants and dump you in the motel ice chest. Beat it."

"I see how you're trying to play me now," he said, crossing his arms and stomping his size two and a half Stride Rite shoe. "You think just because there's only one of me, you can talk big shit!"

"Actually, there's only one-fourth of you." Bryce chuckled, getting in the car. "Let's roll, Harmony!"

"Oh shit!" Lucky pointed in the direction of the midget farm across the street. "Look!"

Bryce and Harmony looked in the direction of Lucky's finger. There were dozens of midgets running towards them with plastic swords, super soakers, and bows and arrows with suction cups at the ends.

Bryce chuckled. "Oh wow, it's the Night of the Killer Lilliputians."

"Time to haul ass up out of here," Harmony said and screeched out the parking lot just in the nick of time with a plastic arrow stuck to the left tail light.

A Word From Our Sponsors

Niagra No More

RIPUOFF FORMONEY HERE. I only have a second. They're about to slap the shackles on me and ship me off to Lorton.

Just like I suspected, they couldn't deal with a black man trying to become successful. They busted down my door with a battering ram right while I was in the middle of banging the hell out this honie with a big ole fat, juicy pussy.

They convicted me without the benefit of a fair trial. Kind of like Marion Barry. The jury had six nuns, three monks, and three homie-sexuals on it that were mad at me because I wouldn't fuck them in the ass when they rolled past the crib.

Good thing I've been fucking twenty-four seven because the judge gave me two hundred years to life within the amount of time it takes most people to get out a good fart. Looks like my dick is going to have to go into hibernation for a couple of centuries cause I'm not fucking no homie. I don't care if he looks like Halle Berry and tosses my salad with fat-free blue cheese dressing. Not the kid.

Damn, here comes the paddy wagon pulling up now. Maybe I should make a run for it. Naw, they'll just practice their police brutality techniques they learned at the academy on me. I hear they use a Rodney King life-size doll for the demonstrations.

My boy Alonzo, *he's a Sagittarius in case you're wondering,* is supposed to take over manufacturing Niagra. However, just in case he needs to flee the country because of some trumped up charges the FBI is trying to pin on him, I suggest that those of you who have any Niagra in your possession ration the hell out of it.

Well, here they come up the steps so I guess this is all she wrote for me. Damn, I'm going to miss fucking day and night.

Listen, for those of you who believe in my innocence, you can send all monetary donations to:

Ripuoff Formoney's Legal Defense Fund
2289 Take Your Ass To The Cleaners Boulevard
Fraudulent, NJ 58211

They also accept food stamps and cartons of cigarettes. Help a brotha out, aiight? Peace!

We now return to our regularly scheduled program, "Shame On It All," already in progress.

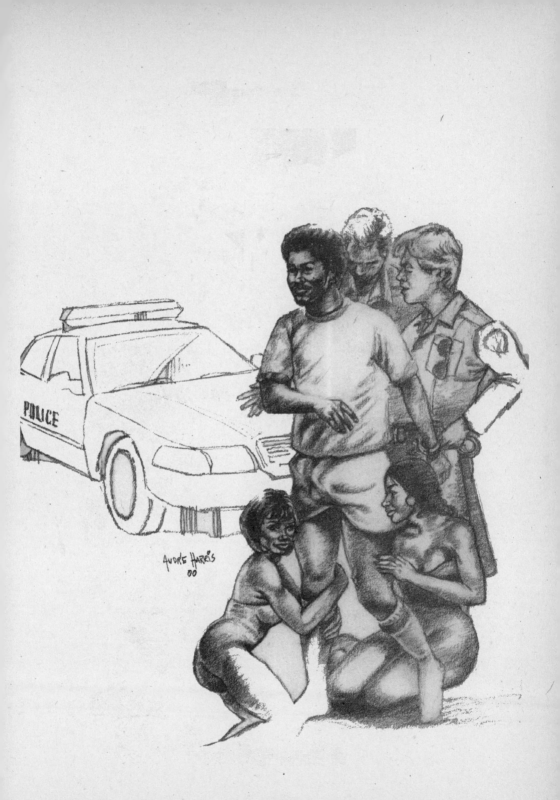

Part Five

Drama, Drama Everywhere

Chapter Twenty-Four

If I Could Stay, I Would

"**M**s. Whitfield, your mother is on line one."
Harmony had her head lying on her desk and was holding her stomach, willing the pain to stop, when her secretary's voice blared over the intercom.

She managed to sit straight up and press down on the talk button. "Thank you."

She took a tissue out of the Kente-cloth covered dispenser on her desk and dried up the few tears that were rolling down her cheeks. Then, she cleared her throat and pressed the speakerphone button. "Hello, Momma!"

"Hey, Dear," Rachelle Whitfield stated from the other end of the line. "Are you on a speakerphone?"

"Yes, Momma." Harmony reached for her mug of Earl Gray tea and took a sip but it was hard for her to swallow. She hoped her mother would not talk long because she didn't know how long she would be able to carry on a conversation without giving herself away.

"Harmony, what on earth is wrong with you?" Rachelle's voice took on a tone of urgency and Harmony knew it was too late already. "Are you sick? Pregnant? Do you have the flu?"

Her mother must have been psychic or something. "No, Momma. I'm just fine. Really!"

"Hmm, you girls may be clear across the country but I can always tell when something is wrong with one of my babies." There was a pause. "Are you sure you're okay? If you need me to come take care of you, just say the word and I'm on the next plane out of Cali!"

Harmony cleared her throat again. The last thing she needed was her mother in town. As much as she missed her parents, she dreaded the thought of them treating her like a paraplegic and confining her to bed. Being terminally ill was bad enough, but dealing with the pity of others was something Harmony feared more than dying itself. She had always been an independent black woman who took care of others. They never took care of her and that's just the way it was.

"Momma, everything's just marvelous! Really!"

"Marvelous, huh?" Rachelle was not buying Harmony's act at all. She knew better than anyone that Harmony only said *marvelous* when something was wrong. She decided to let well enough alone, figuring Harmony was probably just dealing with some business-related stress and would refuse to discuss it anyway. "What day are you and your sisters coming to the reunion in North Carolina?"

"The Friday before Labor Day. I haven't nailed down a time with Bryce and Lucky yet, but I'll make sure I do it this week."

"Oh," Rachelle said, obviously irritated. "You make sure you do because last year, you girls almost missed the whole reunion because of that crazy boyfriend of Bryce's and his *so-called* business trips."

"Actually, Momma, Bryce broke up with George a few months ago. She has a new man."

"*New man?*" Harmony braced herself for the drama. She knew what time it was. "Why is Bryce always switching men like she switches weaves?"

"Momma, that's not even true," Harmony stated in Bryce's defense. She started to tell her that Bryce no longer had a hair weave but decided the looks on her parents' faces when they saw Bryce without one would be priceless. "Bryce was with George for at least two years, maybe longer."

"Maybe so, but it seems like she's too fast for her britches to me."

Harmony couldn't help but giggle at her mother's old-fashioned expression. "Well, I might as well tell you that Lucky has a new man, too."

Silence.

"Momma?"

"I'm still here." Harmony could hear her taking deep breaths and pictured her rolling her eyes while she pondered the thought of Lucky with a man, *any man.* "I hope he's not a hoodlum. I already know the one Bryce has is a hoodlum because that's all she dates. Hoodlums and playas."

Harmony laughed out loud. "Momma, what do you know about playas?"

"I know enough. We had dogs back in the day. Your daddy *thought* he was one until I threatened to kick him to the curb." Rachelle started giggling and they both shared a good chuckle. "Just remember, I have more wisdom than all you girls put together."

"First of all, we're not little girls anymore. We're all grown women. I'm very proud of the way Bryce and Lucky have flourished over the past few years." Harmony began to realize how Lucky felt when she called her part of the younger generation because she dreaded their mother using the term *girls.* "Secondly, Lucky's boyfriend, Robbie, attends the same medical school. I personally think they make a great couple. You've got to let her grow up some time, Momma."

"And what about this new beau of Bryce's?"

"His name is Troy and I think Bryce may have finally met her soul mate. I even invited him over to the house for dinner and he's been playing golf with Zachary a lot."

Rachelle sighed. "Does he have a job?"

"Yes, he does, believe it or not. He owns his own auto dealership and makes a very good living."

Rachelle had to give up the battle on that one and reserve final judgment for a later date. "They bringing those boys to the reunion so we can all get a look at them?"

"They're bringing the MEN to the reunion and don't worry. You and Daddy will have plenty of chances to interrogate them both."

Rachelle chuckled. "Harmony, *you are a mess!*"

"How's Daddy?" Harmony thought about her dad and how he spent so much time toiling a farm that let him down on so many occasions.

"Chester is Chester and you know how Chester is," was her mother's only reply.

"Yes, I know how he is. I also know you love every minute with him."

"What can I say? You got me on that one. I love my man. I just hope you all end up in happy marriages like the one your daddy and I have."

"We will, Momma." Harmony's attitude began to get somber again. She knew she would never have the opportunity to get married or watch either one of her younger sister's walk down the aisle. "We will."

"How's my baby boy, Zachary?" Rachelle took another deep breath. Harmony pictured her getting up off the hunter green recliner in their living room and moving around the house, keeping herself busy as she talked. "You know he's my heart!"

"Zachary's wonderful, as always!" The pain started to kick in again. "Momma, I have a meeting in a few minutes so I really have to go. I'll call you later this week when I know the exact time we should arrive."

"Okay, but make sure you do."

"I will. I promise."

Rachelle hesitated, then added, "Now you know your Daddy isn't going to let you and those boys sleep together at your Grandma's house? Separate bedrooms until you all get the rings on your fingers."

Harmony rolled her eyes and sighed. They always had this same conversation. "Momma, all of us will be staying at The Holiday Inn down on Route 20 so don't worry about that."

"Can't even go without sex for a couple of days, huh? Shame on it all!"

Harmony gawked at that one. "Let me run, Momma."

"One more thing." Harmony wondered what could possibly be next. "Don't you think I've forgotten that my precious baby is turning thirty in November. Your daddy and I want to throw you a big birthday bash here on the farm so make sure you clear your calendar for it, as well as your sisters."

A tear fell. Harmony knew there were hundreds more to come. She would never have a thirtieth birthday. She only prayed she made it until the family reunion in early September.

"That sounds great!" Harmony hesitated, trying to pull herself together. "Thanks, Momma. Thanks for everything you and Daddy have ever done for me."

"You're more than welcome, Precious."

"Goodbye, Momma."

"Bye, Baby."

"One last thing, Sweetie," Rachelle interjected before Harmony could hit the speaker button and cut her off.

"Yes?" Harmony hoped she would get off some time that day because she did have a lot of work to do. She also had an appointment with her attorney.

"Make sure you and Bryce are ready to get your tails whipped in some Bid Whist."

Harmony smirked. "Hmm, I don't know about all that! Bryce and I have a track record to defend."

"You mean, a *cheating* track record," Rachelle snapped back. "Don't think you two are fooling Lucky and I for one minute. We're going to put a hurting on you this year, though."

Harmony smiled and it felt good. She didn't have a comment about the cheating because it was all true. She and Bryce had been cheating people at Bid Whist and Spades since their pre-puberty years.

"Darn!" Rachelle smacked her lips. Harmony could hear her shuffling around.

"What's wrong, Momma?"

"Nothing. I just spilled my jar full of iced tea."

"Jar? Momma, you're getting more countrified by the day. You sound like Grandma. I guess a rocker on the porch and dentures are next."

"Well, one day soon I *am* going to be a doting Grandma. Hint, hint!"

They both laughed.

"Let me let you go, Baby. I know you're a busy businesswoman now. All I have to do is watch *Jenny Jones* and *Jerry Springer* and keep up with my soaps and your daddy."

Harmony giggled. "Good luck on keeping up with Daddy."

"Hmm, that's easy. He can't get but so far on that tractor of his and I make it a point to hold the keys to his truck. None of these Southern California hoochies are getting their hands on my man."

Harmony fell out laughing. "Hoochies and playas? You've been learning a lot from watching talk shows, haven't you? You go, Gurl!"

"You're a mess, Harmony!"

Harmony glanced down at her watch.

"Momma, I hate to cut you off, but I really do have to run."

"Okay, Baby. I understand." There was a brief pause. Rachelle always hated to let her babies off the phone. "Take care and always remember that we love you."

"I love you, Momma. Please give Daddy a hug for me."

"Bye."

"Bye, Momma."

Harmony hit the disconnect button and then swiveled around to face the skyline. It was time for her to make some final decisions and preparations because soon, she was really going home. *Her permanent home.*

"You're not hungry, Harmony?" Zachary put his fork down on his plate and intertwined his fingers. "I thought chicken with cashew nuts was one of your favorites?"

"It is." Harmony moved the food around her plate with a fork. "Thanks for stopping by Hunan's on your way home. It's just that I had a long day and I also ate a heavy lunch."

"Business lunch or lunch with Fatima?"

"Business related, sort of." Harmony looked down at the table because she couldn't bear to face Zachary. "I met with my attorney today."

Zachary picked his fork back up and then took a bite, waiting for Harmony to tell him why she met with her attorney but all he got was silence.

"What did you discuss with your attorney?"

"My will." Harmony took a sip of her Coke and gulped hard, having trouble getting it to go down.

"That's just great," Zachary stated sarcastically, dropping his fork back down on his plate. "So, we're just supposed to sit around here and wait for you to die?"

"Everyone dies, Zachary!"

Silence.

"Zachary, I need to discuss some things with you because I don't think I have much time left."

He stared at her with his bottom lip trembling, obviously trying to hold back the tears. "It's like you've given up, Harmony! We can fight this!"

She stared at him, searching for a way to make him understand that it was the way things had to be.

"Baby, pretending that this isn't happening won't make it go away," she pleaded with him.

He banged his fist down on the table, causing the dishes to clatter and his glass to tumble over.

"I understand that, but don't you realize that watching you die is killing me, too?"

Harmony got up and went in the kitchen to get a rag to wipe off the table. When she came back into the dining room, Zachary was gone. She heard his car door slam.

She debated about going after him but decided against it. This was exactly the type of situation she was trying to avoid. Maybe she was wrong for intruding back into his life. It may have been better for them to stay apart and for him to never know about her illness until after her death.

She wiped off the table and cleared away the dishes. As she stood by the sink, rinsing the dishes and putting them in the dishwasher, she made a promise to herself. She wouldn't subject her parents, Bryce, Lucky, or Fatima to her illness. She couldn't. Look at what her honesty had done to Zachary.

She would just make the best of the precious time she had remaining. Live life to the fullest while she still had a life to live.

A couple of hours later, Zachary came home and startled Harmony by climbing into the shower with her, fully-clothed.

For a few seconds, time stood still and they looked at each other in silence.

"Harmony, I love you. I promise to never walk out on you again."

"I never should've told you. I should've just..."

He put his forefinger up to her mouth. "No, listen to me. I'm glad that you told me. I want to be here for you. Scratch that, *I will be here for you.* Always."

"I love you so much, Zachary."

"I love you, too, and you can talk to me about anything and everything. Always remember that."

They embraced and then they both wept, letting it all out and coming to terms with Harmony's illness for once and for all.

Chapter Twenty-Five

Reunited

Zachary watched Harmony rush around the bedroom, trying to remember everything she wanted to pack.

"Harmony, we're only going to North Carolina for the weekend. All you need to do is throw a few pairs of shorts and some tees into a duffel bag so we can roll out."

Harmony giggled, pulling open the top drawer of her dresser and selecting some bras to pack. "Zachary, do you mind if I take some underwear with me? Stop rushing me. Men are always so impatient when it comes to certain things."

Zachary sat on the bed and propped his back up on a pillow. He used the remote to turn on *Divorce Court*. Some trifling man was on there trying to get his wife to pay for a car that his ass was driving. She came back at him by exposing how he'd tried to bed one of her bridesmaids on their wedding day. The stupid fool didn't deny it either. "There's no way he's going to win," Zachary said.

Harmony came out of the bathroom with an armload of toiletries. "No way who's going to win what?"

"Oh, just some idiot on *Divorce Court*."

"You love those court shows, don't you?"

"Some of them. They're popping up right and left now and I'm not feeling all of them."

"The only one I watch faithfully is *Judge Judy*."

"Yeah, I love that one." Zachary saw that Harmony was struggling to get the zipper closed on her bag and got up to assist her. "Let me do that."

"Thanks."

"So whose ingenious idea was it for us to all travel together in one minivan?" Zachary asked, not trying to mask the fact that he didn't like the idea.

"It makes sense," Harmony responded. "Since Troy owns a dealership, it was simple for him to get a Mazda van, so why take two or three cars for no reason?"

"Still, seven hours in a confined space with Bryce might be too much for me to handle."

Harmony laughed at him. "Imagine how I feel? I grew up with her."

"Good point," Zachary said, grabbing Harmony around her waist from the rear and kissing the nape of her neck. "Poor baby."

"Bryce will probably be on her best behavior around Troy."

"Please! Troy can't control Bryce any more than you can."

"Well, maybe Bryce will go to sleep or something. Better yet, you can just go to sleep and by the time you wake up, we'll be there. Did your parents ever use that line on you when you were a kid? Daddy wore it out on us."

"Yeah, they did," Zachary admitted. "I guess I do sound like a little kid, complaining about a trip before we even pull out the driveway."

Harmony turned around and kissed him lovingly. "Remember that you pointed that out and I didn't." A horn blared from outside. "They're here. Do you mind running downstairs and telling them I need five minutes?"

"Okay, Baby." Zachary walked out the room, carrying both of their bags.

Harmony yelled after him, "Can you check all the doors and make sure everything is turned off?"

It was a long ride to North Carolina. Despite Harmony's hopes, Lucky and Bryce got into it no less than ten times about something trivial. Troy, Robbie, and Zachary all sat there with deadpan expressions on their faces while Harmony took on the role of referee.

They were all glad when they finally arrived, getting out of the van at their grandmother's circa 1900 brick house and stretching their arms and legs.

Bryce had to say something stupid, as usual. "That was a tight ride. Thank goodness Colette didn't come with us. Imagine if she'd taken off her shoes up in there. We would have all passed out from the fumes."

Everyone laughed except Harmony. "See, you talk trash about Colette but the moment I say something about her, you have a problem."

"Whatever!"

Bryce rolled her eyes at Harmony and they were about to get into it for the first time that day when Chester Whitfield tore out of the screen door, grinning profusely at the sight of his daughters.

"Aw Lawd, it's the Supremes!" Chester yelled, running down the front steps.

"Hey, Daddy!" Harmony squealed, just as elated to see him. She ran up to him and threw her arms around his shoulders.

"Harmony, my girl!" Chester gave Harmony a huge bear hug before letting her go to shake Zachary's hand. "Zachary, my boy!"

"Mr. Whitfield, nice to see you," Zachary said.

"Of course, it's nice to see me. Look at how fine I am."

Chester spun around for everyone to see his physique. Bryce smacked her lips and said, "Daddy, please!"

Chester's eyes practically popped out of his head when he took a good look at Bryce. "Bryce! Oh my goodness! The rug is gone off your head! Wait till your Momma sees you!"

Bryce hugged him and then pulled Troy towards them by the hand. "Daddy, this is Troy."

"Does Troy have a last name?" Chester asked sarcastically.

Troy reached out to shake his hand. "Troy Stanley. Nice to meet you, Sir."

"Well, at least you're polite. Handshakes a little weak though."

Bryce slapped Chester lightly on the arm. "Daddy, quit!"

"I hear you own a car dealership."

"Yes, Sir."

"What kind?" Chester asked, squinting to see the make of the van they had pulled up in.

"Mazda," Troy responded, clearing his throat because he felt uncomfortable already.

"Mazda. Hmm, what kind of flat-bed trucks do they make? I need a new one and since you're laying up with my daughter, I reckon I should be getting one damn near free."

"Daddy!" Bryce exclaimed.

Chester chortled. "All right. All right. I was just kiddin'."

"Whatever," Bryce said with disdain. She walked towards the front porch with Troy in tow.

After Bryce and Troy moved away, that gave Chester a clear path to his baby girl. "Aw, there she is. Come here, Malcolmenia X!"

"Malcolmenia X?" Robbie whispered in Lucky's ear as they made their way to her father.

"Just a nickname. I'll explain later." Lucky hugged her father. "Hey, Daddy."

"Girl, look at you. Just as cute as ever." Chester picked Lucky up off the ground and swung her around in the air, her legs flailing like a rag doll's. He put her down and eyed Robbie. "And who might this be?"

"Daddy, this is Robbie. My boyfriend."

Chester grabbed Robbie's hand but refused to let it go. "Boyfriend? Does that mean you're having sex with my daughter?"

"I—uh, uh," Robbie uttered, frozen in place.

Lucky pried her father's fingers off of Robbie.

"Daddy, stop embarrassing people," Bryce said from a rocking chair on the porch.

"Bryce, I haven't even started embarrassing you yet." Chester walked up on the porch and asked, "Troy, have you ever seen any of Bryce's baby pictures?"

"No, Sir," Troy replied, happy as hell that Chester hadn't asked him about his sexual relations with Bryce.

"Well, you're in for a treat. Girl was nothing but forehead and ears when she was born. Looked like two open car doors on a basketball."

"Very funny, Daddy," Bryce hissed.

"I'll make sure you get a good laugh before you leave," Chester said, patting Troy on the shoulder.

"Daddy, where is everybody?" Harmony asked, standing on the steps.

"Your Uncle Dawson went to go get a hair cut. For what, I don't know. It's not like any woman would give him the time of day anyway."

Bryce, Harmony, and Lucky all snickered, thinking about their Uncle Dawson. He was Chester's older brother and swore he was a ladies' man. One night he'd gotten drunk and started bragging about how he could take his dentures out and gum a woman's pussy to death.

"What about Momma and Grandma?" Harmony inquired, concerned that Chester was the only one that ran out to greet them upon arrival. That was unusual, to say the least.

"They went shopping at Big Lots."

"That rinky-dink store is still open?" Lucky asked.

"Unfortunately, yes. Your momma's probably buying a bunch of stuff she'll never be able to carry back on the plane. She still has stuff stored in the spare bedroom from two years ago that never made it back to Cali."

Harmony's medication that she snuck into the ladies room of a gas station to take an hour before started to kick in and she was getting drowsy. "Well, I guess we'll all go get checked into the hotel."

Chester folded his arms in front of him and sternly said, "Now you know how I feel about that nonsense."

"Yes, Daddy, but we're all grown," Bryce reminded him.

We'll just see about that, Chester thought to himself. "You girls go get checked in. The boys are hanging out with me."

"Hanging out with you doing what?" Bryce asked, disliking the thought of leaving them alone with their daddy for a second.

"I'm taking these boys hunting!" Chester exclaimed and then chuckled.

"Hunting!" Lucky rang out.

"Hunting!" Troy repeated.

"Hunting!" Robbie yelled.

"Is there a damn echo out here? Yes, I said hunting." Chester eyed each one of the men individually. "Ya'll not a bunch of punks, are you? I know Zachary's not, but the verdict is still out on you other two."

"I'm not a punk, Sir," Troy boasted. He'd never been hunting, but he was THE MAN and wasn't about to back down from anything.

"Good. We'll just see about that." Chester went down the steps and started around the house. "Let's go out back to the shed and dig out the rifles."

"Robbie, you don't have to go. Daddy's just acting silly," Lucky said.

"No, I'm fine." Robbie headed down the steps to follow Zachary and Troy. "To be honest, I used to beg my father to take me hunting when I was a child and he never would. This should be fun."

"If you say so," Lucky said hesitantly.

"Relax. Everything will be fine."

Chapter Twenty-Six

Not A Good Day For Hunting

They were out in the middle of nowhere and couldn't find their way back to civilization if their lives depended on it. Chester had given them all hunting gear and rifles, but didn't load them. He didn't want anyone clipping one off accidentally on the way there and shooting off a toe or putting a hole in his brother's truck.

"Zachary, when are you and Harmony tying the knot?" Chester asked jokingly. "You know I plan on being as sexy as I am right now when I become a grandfather."

"I'm working on it, Mr. Whitfield," Zachary replied, hoping Harmony would do something about her health problems and stay alive long enough for him to do just that.

Chester slapped him on the back, almost knocking the wind out of him. "After all these years, you know good and well you can call me Chester."

Zachary smiled. "Thanks, Chester."

"So Chester, you go hunting often?" Robbie asked, sitting on a rock and loading his rifle.

"I never said you could call me Chester. You can call me Mr. Whitfield," Chester nastily replied.

"I—uh, okay," Robbie uttered, diverting his eyes back to the task at hand.

Chester stared a hole through him and finally let him off the hook by saying, "Lighten up, Son. I'm only kidding."

Robbie looked up at him and smiled, relieved.

Chester glanced over at Troy, who was leaning up against a tree shaking like a leaf and trying to load his rifle to no avail.

"Troy, you have absolutely no idea what you're doing. Do you?" Chester asked, walking towards him.

"No, Sir," he readily admitted.

"Give me that." Chester yanked the rifle and ammunition away from him. "With your fingers trembling like that, you'll never get the damn thing loaded." He loaded the rifle and startled Troy when he swung it upward, directly in line with Troy's chest. "So, what *exactly* are your intentions with my daughter."

"I—uh, what do you mean, Sir?" Troy stuttered, taking two steps back.

Chester lowered the rifle and guffawed. He looked from Troy to Robbie and back again. "For supposedly successful men, you two sure do a lot of stuttering."

"I just don't know what you mean, Sir. Plus, I thought you were pointing that thing at me," Troy replied, realizing that Bryce's father was trying to test his manhood.

"I thought I saw a raccoon," Chester lied. He hadn't seen a damn thing but underbrush. "I *mean*, are you planning on marrying Bryce or just continue dipping your fingers in the treat jar for free?"

"I'd like to marry Bryce. I do love her, Sir."

"You do?" Chester asked suspiciously.

"Yes, and she loves me."

"Are you responsible for her getting rid of that ugly ass hair weave?"

"Not directly, but…"

"But what?"

"She did get rid of it shortly after we met."

Chester grinned. "Then I want to shake your hand." He almost tore Troy's hand off his body. "Whatever you do, don't let her put that shit back on her head ever, *ever* again."

"Yes, Sir," Troy responded, flexing his wrist back and forth to try to regain some feeling in his hand.

Chester walked back over to Robbie. "You go to medical school with Lucky?"

Robbie jumped up off the rock and stood up straight, determined to face him man-to-man after witnessing what Chester had just pulled with Troy. "Yes, Sir."

"What kind of doctor are you going to be?"

"A cardiologist."

"Fixing hearts, huh?"

"Yes, Sir."

"I hope you don't intend on breaking any hearts along the way. Namely, Malcolmenia X's."

"No, not at all, Sir," Robbie replied loudly like he was in the Marines.

"Gonna marry her?"

"When the time is right, Sir. I feel like Lucky and I need to finish school first and get settled into our careers before we consider that type of commitment. When I do it, I want to do it right."

"Good answer." Chester was impressed and wanted Robbie to know it so he repeated, "Damn good answer."

"Thank you, Sir."

Chester stood there, debating about which one of them he could bother next with more questions when he heard something in the distance. "Shh! I think I hear something."

"I don't hear anything," Troy said.

"Be quiet, dammit!" Chester whispered angrily, pointing to their right. "Look, over there."

"Is it a deer?" Robbie asked, not seeing what he was talking about but anxious to finally be doing some hunting.

"If it is, it's a big one. It must be an elk," Zachary commented, seeing a shadow but not the actual animal.

"I have one question for you boys," Chester said coolly.

"Yes, Sir," Robbie said.

"Did you ever climb trees when you were younger?"

"I did," Zachary answered.

"Me, too," Robbie replied.

"Me, three," Troy responded.

"Then I suggest you high tail it up the nearest one now!" Chester yelled out, already pulling himself up to the first branch of the tree right beside of him. "That's not a deer."

"Then what is it?" Robbie asked, still totally confused.

"Something that begins with a B and ends with an R and would just love to have you for dinner," Chester said, looking down at them and wondering what was taking them so long to move.

"Oh, shit!" Troy screamed out. He looked around and realized he was the only one with his feet still on the ground and started climbing.

Chapter Twenty-Seven

Catfish and Cat Fighting

"Here's another load of fish to clean," Rachelle Whitfield said, plopping an aluminum pan of catfish down on the dining room table.

"Wonderful. Just great!" Lucky said, faking excitement.

They'd been cleaning fish for more than two hours for the family reunion's traditional Friday night fish fry. Her grandmother fried it outside in a giant black pot over a fire. People came from near and far to get a fish sandwich.

Rachelle fingered Bryce's hair. "Bryce, I can't get over how nice your hair looks. Please keep it that way."

"Yes, *please* keep it that way," Harmony said sarcastically, picking up another fish and going at it with vengeance. She was ready to get the ordeal over with.

"Thank you, Momma," Bryce said, rolling her eyes at Harmony across the table.

Rachelle headed back to the kitchen. "I'll go see if your grandma has any more fish back there."

"We can hardly wait," Bryce snarled. As soon as their mother was out of ear shot, Bryce started complaining. "This stinks and it's making me sick. I should've stayed at the hotel and taken a nap."

Harmony leered at Bryce. "While Lucky and I clean a ton of fish? I don't even think so."

"I know that's right," Lucky said nastily.

"It really is making me sick," Bryce continued. "Whoever thought up the idea of going under the water and pulling these skank things out to ingest into the human body was a psycho."

"Is that why you're always the first one in line with a plate at every family reunion fish fry?" Harmony asked jokingly.

"Maybe, but it doesn't stink as bad when it's cooked," Bryce said defensively.

Harmony had had enough of Bryce's whining. "Maybe you should try cooking your coochie then because I can smell it all the way over here. It's drowning out the fish smell."

Bryce pointed a scaling knife at Harmony. "Harmony, you better be glad that I was raised better than to act a fool in Grandma's house. Otherwise, it would be on."

Harmony picked up a handful of fish scales and flung them at Bryce. Bryce flung some back. They all fell out laughing.

"What are you all laughing about in here?" their Grandmother asked, coming into the room to check on their progress.

They all got quiet and started wiping up the scales with paper towels.

"Nothing, Grandma."

"Are we going to stay up here all day?" Robbie asked, swatting gnats away from his face.

Chester gazed at him like he was foolish and replied, "Looks like it."

The bear had given up on trying to get to them up in the trees and had moved on to rummaging through the backpack containing the 8-piece of Bojangles chicken and half a dozen biscuits they'd bought on the way up there.

"Why don't you just shoot it?" Troy asked, afraid that if he stayed in his current position much longer, he wouldn't be able to use his legs well enough to make it back to the truck. Not to mention he was scared shitless and wasn't trying to be caught out there after dark.

"Who me? I'm not shooting a poor, innocent bear," Chester stated adamantly.

"Poor, innocent bear?" Troy asked incredulously. "Don't bears maim and kill?"

Chester chuckled. "If you get close enough to them, I suppose they do."

"Troy, you shoot it. You're crazy, anyway," Robbie suggested.

"I might be crazy, but I don't know how to shoot a gun." Troy glared over at Zachary, three limbs over from him. "You shoot it, Zachary."

"I can't."

"Why not?"

"Because I'm shaking too damn much," Zachary confessed.

"This is insane. We can't stay up here forever," Robbie said, shaking his head in dismay and wondering why he didn't listen to Lucky and stay behind. "Somebody's going to have to shoot the damn thing."

The three younger men started bickering amongst themselves while Chester looked on, trying to suppress a laugh. They were amusing to him, even though the situation wasn't. Chester really had no intention of shooting the bear. That wasn't what he came out there for, but he quickly changed his mind when he spotted it ripping into his Timberland boot that fell off when he'd started climbing.

"Damn, the stupid thing just ate my boot!" Chester yelled out and started blasting away.

The fish fry was really getting crowded. Whenever someone fried fish in the country, you were likely to see friends and relatives that you thought were deceased show up to barge in line with a plate.

Lucky was pacing back and forth in the yard, glaring at the street whenever she heard an engine. "I wonder where they could be."

Bryce and Harmony were sitting at a card table covered with a plastic tablecloth, totally exhausted and overheated from doing all of the fish preparation.

Rachelle had just come outside with a fresh pitcher of lemonade.

"Daddy had no business taking them hunting, Momma," Bryce said accusingly, as if her mother had something to do with it.

"I'm sure it was some sort of intimidation tactic, Sweetie," Rachelle responded hesitantly. She'd been worried herself, but trying not to let on. She hadn't even met Troy or Robbie yet and Chester had them who knows where, more than likely torturing them in some form or fashion.

"Well, he could've intimidated them here," Bryce countered.

"Yeah, over horseshoes in the backyard or something," Harmony added, in total agreement.

A fifteen-passenger van pulled up and Rachelle was relieved. She was dying to get her daughters' minds off their men and she knew the new arrivals would do just that.

"Look, here comes your cousin, Sally," Rachelle said, pointing in the direction of the van.

Their cousin, Sally, was in her mid-thirties and had a ton of children. Bryce, Harmony, and Lucky never missed an opportunity to voice their opinions.

"And her fifty-eleven kids," Bryce said, the first to make a lewd comment.

Lucky giggled. "All I can say is that must be some potent stuff Gary has between his legs. He couldn't possibly be shooting any blanks."

Harmony, Bryce, and Lucky cackled while Rachelle shook her head. "Hush, now. I think it's great that someone's having babies. At least your Aunt Janice is a grandma," Rachelle said, referring to Sally's mother.

"Yeah, at least ten times over," Lucky added, wondering how in the hell Sally could stand to push that many babies out of her pussy.

The three sisters shut up as Sally approached with a set of stair step kids surrounding her and one on her hip.

Rachelle gave her a hug and kiss on the cheek. "Hey, Sally. Wow, how your kids have grown."

"Yes, they sure have," Harmony said, rubbing one of the girls, about five, on the head. "You must be little Alexandra?"

Sally corrected Harmony. "No, actually that's Alexis. Alexandra's the one in the blue."

"Oh, okay." Harmony searched for the one in the blue and spotted her hiding behind Sally's sundress. "How many do you have now?"

"Eleven with one in the oven."

Bryce giggled. "Dang, that's a lot of breastfeeding."

"Bryce!" Rachelle exclaimed, totally ashamed of Bryce's behavior.

"Where's Gary?" Lucky inquired, wanting to see how the bow-legged stud muffin was holding up after working his thing so hard.

"Parking the van. He's letting Gary, Jr. help him," Sally replied.

"Is Gary, Jr. old enough to drive?" Bryce asked.

"He has his permit."

"Dang, I feel old now," Bryce said, smacking her lips. She remembered when Gary, Jr. was in diapers. Scary thought.

"Me, too," Harmony agreed, having the same exact flashbacks of the child in diapers.

"So is the one you're carrying now the last one?" Lucky asked, still cringing at the thought of pushing out one baby, rather less damn near a dozen.

"I'm not sure. Gary says that if we have thirteen, we don't have to pay taxes."

No one made a comment about that statement. It was too easy to lay into her about it, so they just watched her move on to talk to some other relatives. Rachelle went back into the house to get some more cups. She figured they would need an extra pack just for Sally's family alone.

"That's just downright trifling," Bryce finally said with disdain, once Sally and her entourage were out of earshot.

"And stupid," Lucky agreed.

"Mega-stupid!" Bryce hissed.

Harmony spotted them first. Chester and Zachary were in the cab of the pick-up while Robbie and Troy were on the flat bed. They all looked like they had been to hell and back.

"Look, here come the four stooges." Harmony giggled.

The three of them walked down to the dirt driveway where Chester was backing up against a tree.

"What took you all so long?" Lucky asked, getting to them first.

"Long story," Robbie answered, jumping down off the bed without even bothering to lower the rear gate.

Bryce went to the opposite side to help Troy down. THE MAN or not, she didn't want him busting his ass trying to dismount. A country man he was not. She was about to take his hand when she spotted the mound of bloody fur. She jumped back. "What the hell is that on the back of the truck?"

"Is that a bear?" Harmony asked, peeping over the side to see what Bryce was referring to.

"Yeah, it's a bear," Zachary replied, getting out of the cab and stretching his arms and legs. They were still sore from being stuck in the same position for so long in the tree.

"I thought you were hunting deer," Lucky said to Robbie.

Robbie laughed. "We were until the bear started hunting us."

Lucky poked him in the shoulder. "I told you not to go."

"Ya'll had no business out there with Daddy," Bryce stated with sarcasm. She knew something damn ridiculous would happen with the four of them together.

Chester looked at all three of his daughters individually as they went on and on talking trash to their men. Finally, he intervened and, as usual, his word was law. "Look, the boys and I had a good time. Now, we're starving. Let's go get cleaned up and get our grub on."

Bryce, Harmony, and Lucky shut up and watched all the men walk off into the house with Chester in the lead. They were like a colony of ants, traveling in a single file line.

"What is he supposed to be, Papa Walton or something?" Bryce asked.

Lucky shook her head. "For real. They're following him around like he's the man."

Harmony chuckled. "Maybe he is the man."

"Whatever," Bryce said and then walked off with her mind set on a hot fish sandwich.

After dinner, it was time for Bid Whist. Of course, Harmony and Bryce whipped serious ass. And, of course, they were cheating big time.

"I see you two are at it again," Lucky said nastily, upset about the three hundred to eighty-five score.

Bryce rolled her eyes at Lucky. "Lucky, don't be a hater. Harmony and I are just the better team. Just face facts, heifer."

"Oh, I have your heifer, Bryce!" Lucky shouted, pulling Bryce's pinky finger until she squealed.

"Enough of that," Rachelle demanded. "It's only a game."

"I agree, Momma," Harmony said before breaking out into laughter. "It's amazing that we practically come to blows every year over a card game."

Harmony and Bryce winked at each other and got back down to business. No one had ever been able to figure out how they cheated and they preferred to keep it that way.

Chester had his potential son-in-laws playing dominoes, along with several other male relatives. They didn't fare much better, especially when people started placing bets. Even though it was a miniscule amount of money, people were getting highly upset when they lost.

Everyone stayed up most of the night, doing whatever tickled their fancy, and the sun was almost up before Troy drove everyone back to the hotel to crash.

Chapter Twenty-Eight

The Speedway

The main event of the family reunion, a Saturday night dinner/dance, was taking place at the Charlotte Motor Speedway Banquet Hall. While the staff was still setting up inside, Harmony, Bryce, Lucky, and their men all ventured out into the clubhouse to watch the test driving that was going on at the track. Most of the kids were out in the clubhouse as well watching the action. Normally, on actual race days, people paid a bundle to sit in the enclosed area instead of out on the bleachers enduring the unrelenting sun. However, the air was off in the clubhouse and it was extremely humid, almost unbearable.

Still, they stayed out there and watched the cars speed past them at well over a hundred miles per hour. Zachary, Troy, and Robbie were all the way in the front row with their faces pressed against the glass, totally mesmerized by the action while Harmony, Bryce, and Lucky sat in a row further towards the back.

"Look at them," Lucky said, pointing at the three of them. "They're worse than the kids."

Bryce giggled. "That's because they are kids."

"No, they aren't, Bryce," Harmony stated sarcastically. They're men. Our men."

Lucky blushed and slapped Harmony a high five. "Thank goodness we all have decent men now."

Harmony shifted in her seat. The heat was really beginning to get to her. "I second that thank goodness."

"I third that billy," Bryce agreed.

Harmony turned to Lucky and gave her a love-slap on the knee. "Remember that bama Bryce used to date? The one that drove the happy face car."

Lucky and Harmony fell out laughing while Bryce rolled her eyes up to the ceiling of the clubhouse.

"Harmony, why did you have to bring Rico's trifling ass up?" Bryce asked nastily. She'd hoped that Rico would never cross her mind again in life.

Rico was a half Puerto-Rican/half African-American brother she'd messed around with in high school. He drove a 1975 big-ass Lincoln with stupid happy face stickers covering every available inch except the tires. Bryce used to be totally ashamed whenever they went out, often urging him to park around the corner from their destination so her friends wouldn't see her get out of the car.

"I brought him up because he's unforgettable," Harmony replied, still trying to get her laughter under control.

Lucky was on the brink of tears. "That car was unforgettable. That's for damn sure." Robbie turned around, taking his eyes off the race cars just long enough to blow Lucky a kiss. She blew one back before asking, "Could you even see out of the windshield when you were cruising with him?"

Bryce reached over Harmony's lap and punched Lucky in the arm. "Leave me alone, dammit. Stop teasing me. Both of you."

Harmony tried to lean over and kiss Bryce on the cheek. "Aww, give me a kiss."

Bryce moved her head so that Harmony couldn't reach her face. "Bite me, Harmony."

"No, thank you. I'm on a hooch-free diet." Harmony giggled.

Bryce had heard enough. Two could play that. "Okay, okay, you want to tease me. What about Angelo?"

"Angelo?" Lucky asked, not recalling the name.

"Lucky, you remember that fool. The one Harmony used to date before she hooked up with Zachary. The one that used to take her to do some fine-dining at McDonald's every weekend."

Harmony couldn't help but admit that Bryce was right on the money about Angelo. "Bryce, you ain't never lied. What killed me is that Angelo used to stand there at the counter staring at the damn menu board like he had never been there before. He would take forever to order sometimes."

"Sheit, as much time as you two spent up in there, you should've had not only the menu but also the prices memorized down to the penny."

"Dang, I haven't thought about Angelo in ages. I wonder if he's still taking sistas to McDonald's."

"Probably. I wouldn't doubt it. He was past cheap."

Lucky let Harmony and Bryce's voices drown out as they went on and on about past relationships. She was caught up in her present one. Robbie was everything she could ever ask for all rolled up into one. She watched as he exchanged lively conversation with Troy and Zachary about the cars speeding around the track so fast that you couldn't make out the numbers on the sides of them. Yes, she was in love. Amen to that!

Later on, inside the elegantly-decorated banquet hall, people found seats around the twelve-setting tables and got ready for the program to begin. A teenage boy walked around with a basket for donations for the Whitfield Family Scholarship Fund, which was equally divided between two high school seniors every year. There were close to two hundred people there, more than double the amount at the fish fry.

Everyone quieted down when Parker Whitfield, a distant uncle, took his place at the podium and tested the microphone.

"Welcome to the 23rd Annual Whitfield Family Reunion! Those of you that missed the fish fry last night, really missed a special treat!"

He pointed to his left, where a little girl about the age of nine stood bashfully in a pink dress with ruffles.

"Little Marcette is our Mistress of Ceremony so I'm going to turn the microphone over to her. I just want to remind everyone to get their index cards together for the burning bowl later. There should be plenty of index cards and pencils on every table."

Robbie leaned over and whispered in Lucky's ear. "Burning bowl?"

Lucky tried to explain as quietly as she could. "It's a tradition that a lot of churches follow on New Year's Eve, but we do it every year at the family reunion."

"What is it exactly?"

"You write down everything that is bothering you or stressing you out on one card. Work; bills; ill health. Then, on the other card, you write down everything you wish to accomplish or change in the coming year. Everyone puts their problem card in a huge bowl and then the bowl is set on fire."

"And the positive cards?"

"They go into a separate bowl, which we all say a collective prayer over."

"Cool, I've never heard of that before."

"I hope you're not sleepy," Lucky whispered jokingly.

"Why?"

Lucky pointed to the program booklet that had been passed out when they came in. "Because this is going to be a long program and half of the people listed to do something are long-winded."

"Oh, wow!" Robbie hoped it wouldn't be too long because he had a habit of falling asleep in such situations and didn't want to see the reaction of Lucky's father if he accidentally did. "I want you to know that I appreciate you bringing me here. I've never felt as close to you as I do right now."

"I'm glad that you agreed to come. I just hope Daddy hasn't scared you off. The thought of having him as a father-in-law must be downright terrifying."

Lucky felt ridiculous and embarrassed after the words had already left her lips. The last thing she wanted was for Robbie to feel pressured into a commitment.

"Pops is cool with me," Robbie said, caressing Lucky's hand after sensing her uneasiness.

Lucky felt reassured and winked at him. "Even though he had your ass up in a tree?"

Robbie chuckled softly. "That was wild. I'm glad that's over with."

The little girl stepped up to the podium and Parker started adjusting the microphone for her height.

"Oops, here we go," Lucky said, giving Robbie a swift kiss on his lips.

After a delicious meal of short ribs, mashed potatoes, steamed vegetables, and assorted desserts, everyone was ready to get their party on.

The DJ, a.k.a. Cousin Smitty, started the after dinner music off with a bang and played *Doin' the Butt* by E.U. Bryce was the first one on the dance floor with Troy in tow. Rachelle shielded her eyes in shame as Bryce demonstrated the right way to do the dance made popular by the movie *School Daze*. She didn't have long to sit there, though, because Chester grabbed her hand and led her to the dance floor.

"Chester, I really don't want to do this," Rachelle protested.

"Aw, come on, Sugar," Chester said lovingly. "How often do we get to show our stuff?"

"Showing stuff" was exactly what Rachelle was afraid of. Chester had been mixing all kinds of alcohol for about three days straight and she knew that he was about to cut up big time.

Troy was shocked and almost froze in place when he spotted Chester doing jumping splits.

Other family members came out onto the floor and began to shake their asses as well, but none of them could hold a candle to Chester, who was doing everything from the Moonwalk to the Happy Feet as the next song, *Back That Thang Up* by Juvenile started cranking through the five-foot speakers.

They all worked it out hard for the next forty minutes, including

Lucky and Robbie and Harmony and Zachary. They did the twenty different variations of the Electric Slide and the Booty Call as a large group. It was truly a night to remember.

Bryce was outside getting some fresh air when a country bumpkin in denim overalls and a straw hat approached her in the parking lot.

"Ain't ya name Bryce?" he asked shyly.

Bryce wanted to laugh, but didn't. She was making a sincere effort to change her ways. After all, the brother was just saying hello. "Yes, I'm Bryce."

"Hey there, Baby Girl. I'm Buckwheat," he said, cracking a smile that wasn't half-bad. "I's a friend of ya cousin, Albert."

"Excuse me, did you just say your name is Buckwheat?" Bryce asked, turning her head for a moment to gain some composure. She had to call upon some serious will power to prevent herself from saying something smart about his name.

"Yessum," he said into her back. "My momma named me after that fella from the *Little Rascals*. That be her favorite show on the tellie."

Bryce turned back around to face him and said matter-of-factly, "Hmph, I see. Nice name."

"Thank ya." Buckwheat stood up straight, apparently more confident than he was when he first slunk towards Bryce looking like the poster child for bad posture. "I's seen ya dancing in there. Ya sure know howta shake dat thang, Girl."

"Thanks, I guess."

Bryce sighed, hoping he would move on so she could take in some more of the fresh air before heading back inside. She'd had a bit too much to drink and was feeling the onslaught of a serious hangover. Troy had driven Zachary and Robbie back to the hotel to get something so she knew he wouldn't be coming to her rescue.

"I's wondering if ya might wanna go fishing wit me t'morrow?" Buckwheat asked. "We pectin' great weadur."

"You's pectin' great weadur?" Bryce repeated, bursting out into laughter because she simply couldn't keep a straight face anymore.

"Yessum."

Bryce decided that she would have to be somewhat rude to get his ass away from her, so she went for it. "Look, Buckwheat, I don't know what Albert told you about me, but I have a man. Albert should know better because I've never been without a man for more than two weeks in my entire life."

"Oh," Buckwheat said, his voice full of disappointment.

Bryce continued, "I'm not trying to hurt your feelings, but I felt you should know that. In fact, my man's here with me. He just ran back to the hotel for a few minutes."

"Oh."

Bryce headed for the entrance. Fresh air was one thing, but dealing with a brother named Buckwheat wasn't worth the aggravation.

"Well, it was nice to meet you, Buckwheat," she told him coolly as she disappeared into the glass door.

"Nice ta meet ya, too!" he called after her.

Bryce caught the elevator back up to the banquet hall and made a beeline for her older sister. Harmony was standing over by the restrooms, looking totally beat. "Harmony, I say we blow this joint."

"Where are the men?" Harmony asked. She had been ready to go for quite a while also, but didn't see Zachary anywhere.

"Back at the hotel, but I'm about to call Troy and tell him to get his ass back here to pick me up. You and Lucky can stay if you want, but I'm outtie."

"*Please*, you're not leaving me here!" Harmony blared.

Lucky pranced over to them. She had a big ole grin on her face and seemed to be having the time of her life. "Why are you two standing over here looking like Tweedledum and Tweedledee?"

"Because we're mad bored," Bryce replied, propping herself up against the wall so she could help Harmony hold it up. "I'm about to call Troy and tell him to come get us."

"I can't believe they broke camp like that. What was their excuse?" Lucky asked.

"Zachary *claimed* that he forgot his contacts and couldn't see," Bryce replied nastily.

Lucky shook her head. "So it takes all three of them to go get one pair of contacts?"

"Zachary was faking," Harmony said, jumping in. She didn't realize that was the lame excuse the men had used. "He sat beside of me during the banquet and read every word of the program. They just wanted to leave and go chill."

"Well, I'm ready to chill with them," Bryce readily admitted. She loved their family reunions just as next as the much person, but there was such a thing as overkill. Kids even get sick of Disneyland after a while.

Lucky bent over the water fountain and took a quick gulp. "But Daddy's just getting started."

Bryce glanced at the dance floor where Chester was still going at it to the tune of *Big Daddy* by Heavy D. "Daddy doesn't need us to make a fool out of himself."

Harmony giggled. "I know that's right. Did you peep the shoes?"

"Who could miss the shoes?" Bryce stated sarcastically. Chester was wearing a pair of red suede oxfords with a navy blue suit. "Daddy swears up and down that he be styling."

Lucky chuckled and started dancing in place to the beat. "Shame on it all, but he's still pumped up from bringing that bear home yesterday."

"What the hell is he going to do with it?" Bryce asked.

"I don't even want to know," Harmony said with disdain. "I might throw up."

"For real, though," Lucky agreed. She couldn't even imagine digging into a bowl of bear stew or sucking on a pair of bear claws covered with hot sauce, but wouldn't put any of that past their father.

Bryce moved away from the wall slightly and started keeping the beat with Lucky by gyrating her hips. "We need to leave anyway if we're planning to get an early start tomorrow."

"True," Harmony concurred, staring at Bryce. "Bryce, I hope that you and Lucky won't fight the whole way back in the van."

"Why are you directing that towards me?"

"Because I need to."

Bryce stopped dancing and crossed her arms in front of her. "Look, I'm going to find Momma and Grandma to say goodbye.

Are you coming?"

Harmony replied, "Yes, but first I'm going to take a spin with Daddy on the dance floor."

Bryce watched Harmony saunter away. "Aw hell, I might as well go for it, too."

"Yeah, come on. It'll be just like old times," Lucky said giddily, following behind them.

"Where's the DJ?" Harmony asked. "I want to make a request."

Harmony requested *We Are Family* by Sister Sledge, a song that she and her sisters spent hours upon hours singing when they were younger. They put on a miniature talent show for the family, with their daddy in the center doing the Funky Chicken, and they were a complete hit.

"Had to come back for your contacts, huh?" Harmony asked Zachary, who was laid up in the hotel bed upon her return. He was watching *Oz* on HBO and there were two empty beer bottles on the nightstand.

Zachary eyed her seductively and reached out his hand for hers. "Well, Baby, you know I like to be able to drink in everything with my eyes."

"Is that right?"

"Uh-huh!"

Instead of taking his hand, Harmony slowly slipped out of her dress, unsnapped her bra, and let it tumble to the floor. She held her breasts in her hands and caressed her nipples with her thumbs. "Well, how about drinking these in with your eyes."

Zachary propped himself up on his elbow. "Umm, I'm drinking."

Harmony slipped out of her panties and turned around, affording Zachary a bird's eye view of her ass. "And how about drinking this in with your eyes."

Zachary grinned. "Oh, yeah, I can see clearly now."

Harmony climbed onto the bed, pushed Zachary on his back, and lowered her pussy onto his face. "Good. I'm sure you'll have no problem drinking this in."

Zachary licked his lips in anticipation. "No problem at all."

Chapter Twenty-Nine

You Go, Gurl

Fatima had just finished up her daily step aerobics class and was enjoying a refreshing glass of freshly-squeezed grapefruit juice when *he* approached her. He was tall, real damn tall, and fine as hell.

It had been months since Fatima had allowed a man, even her little dick husband, to caress her body. Sure, she had been offered some sex, mostly from Javon's trifling ass friends that had fantasized about smoking her boots since she and Javon had first hooked up at Howard. But there was no way in hell that she was giving any of them any play. She knew all about their dirt and had no intention of being one of their many victims.

She'd taken up the art of masturbation from time to time and it wasn't half-bad. She'd never experienced an orgasm until she gave herself one in the middle of a whirlpool bath and it was truly enlightening. All she could think about was all the time she'd wasted with Javon, Mr. Full of Shit.

Fatima had pretty much decided to take her time discovering love again. She wanted to concentrate on spending more time with her children, getting her body in spectacular shape, and starting some sort of business with the money she ultimately stood to gain from her impending divorce settlement. Javon was still fighting it, poor thing. He just didn't get it. His goose was cooked and there was zero chance of Fatima ever going back with him.

Even though she'd decided to hold off on men, the fine brother headed in her direction was surely capable of changing her mind. He was clearly over six-five, dark-skinned, built like a gladiator, and was flashing her a grin that could melt ice.

"Excuse me, I hate to bother you," he said when he finally reached her.

Fatima immediately blushed. "You're not bothering me. I'm just sitting here enjoying the view."

He glanced around at the array of exercise rooms and racquetball courts visible from the elevated sports lounge. "Nice view, but not as nice as the view I'm taking in."

"Oh, do you mean me?" Fatima asked, feigning ignorance.

"Yes, I mean you." He sat down beside her at the bar without even asking. "You look awfully familiar to me. Did you go to Dunbar?"

"Dunbar High School? Oh, no, I'm not originally from the D.C. area." *But I damn sure wish I were if it meant going to high school with your fine ass*, Fatima thought to herself.

"Then where are you from?"

"California?"

"Wow, I just moved back from California!" he exclaimed.

Fatima couldn't help but notice that his eyes were dancing all over her body. She also couldn't help but notice that most of the women, no matter what their race, were checking the brother out like they were envious that he was talking to her.

"Really, what were you doing in Cali?"

"Playing for the Lakers. I just got traded to the Wizards."

Things became awfully clear to Fatima. The women were staring at him because they were all gold-diggers.

"Aw, I see," Fatima said coolly. "I'm sorry, but I don't watch much basketball. I'm a football fanatic."

He held his palm over his heart. "You're killing me over here.

Not a basketball fan? Well, we'll have to see if we can change that."

"Oh, yeah," Fatima prodded. "And how exactly do you plan on doing that?"

He eyed her seductively. "For starters, I'd like to invite you to a party tomorrow night."

"A party is going to transform me into a basketball fan?"

"A party full of basketball players might."

They both laughed.

"Well, I don't know about all of that," Fatima replied, unsure about her readiness to date someone, even casually.

"Why not? You're not married, are you? That would be just my bad luck."

"Actually, I am married, but we're separated and I've filed for a divorce. We have two kids. A boy, James, and a girl, Marissa."

Fatima wanted to make sure she added her kids in there because they were a package deal and men needed to know that from jump street.

He didn't seem fazed by her announcement at all. "Any chance of the two of you reconciling?"

Fatima giggled. "There's a better chance of me being taller than you by my next birthday."

"Ouch! The brotha must have seriously messed up."

"He was a playboy," Fatima stated angrily. "You're not a play-boy, are you?"

At that very moment, a sista wearing natural locks and practically nothing else walked past and rubbed him on the shoulder. "Hey there," she cooed.

He just said, "Hey, yourself." Then he turned his attention back to Fatima, ignoring the other woman completely.

"I guess that answers my question," Fatima commented.

"No, it doesn't. I am a far cry from a playboy. Maybe in my younger years, but now I am looking for something much more sta-ble."

"Is that right?"

"Yes, that's right." He took Fatima's hand. "So, how about the party?"

"Aren't you forgetting something?"

"Like?"

Fatima giggled. "Like asking my name and giving me yours."

He chuckled and shook his head in embarrassment. "Dang, I guess I was so caught up in your beauty that it slipped my mind. I'm Hakim."

"I'm Fatima."

"Nice to meet you, Fatima. Now, how about it?"

Fatima flew into the house like a tornado and dashed up to her bedroom. Even though she had more than twenty-four hours before her date, she wanted to select the perfect outfit. She called Harmony to tell her about the turn of events and Harmony was stunned.

"You mean Hakim Sommer?" Harmony asked excitedly.

"Yes, I think he did say that was his last name."

"Damn, Sis, you've hooked a big one."

"What? Oh, you mean because he plays professional ball."

"Girl, you're living in the ice age. Hakim Sommer just signed a deal with the Wizards for more than a hundred million."

"Get the hell out of here!" Fatima squealed into Harmony's ear. "Damn, no wonder the women looked like they would suck his toes and shit up in the health club."

"You're always hooking up with the wealthy men, Sis."

"Not on purpose," Fatima said defensively, sensing that Harmony's statement wasn't exactly meant as a compliment. "There was some definite chemistry there and I just want to explore the possibilities."

"Explore them, Sis. You go, Gurl!"

"I need your help."

"With what?"

"What I'm going to wear, what I'm going to do with my hair, everything."

"Give me fifteen minutes and I'll be right over."

Fatima hung up the phone and sprawled across her bed. She

couldn't remember ever being so excited about a date. Then again, she'd never really dated anyone except Javon since high school. She had crept around and had one night stands with a few other men, but that was it. She regretted the day she ever worked that damn voodoo on Javon's ass. Now she couldn't get rid of him. Her maid had handed her half a dozen messages from Javon when she'd walked in, probably wondering why Fatima had taken off up the stairs like a bat out of hell.

His messages were always the same: "I need to talk to you. When can I come over?"

Javon was so full of shit. She allowed him to come over to see the children, but he always tried to get her to hold a conversation and that shit was out of the question. Now, she could see herself holding many a conversation with Hakim. *Intimate* conversations. She was looking forward to the date and couldn't wait for Harmony to get there so they could start working some magic.

Hakim didn't bring Fatima home until three in the morning. When he walked her to the front door, she was torn over whether or not to invite him in. She decided against it. She assumed that most women let him have some sex after the first date and, while it was about more than that with her, she didn't want him to loop her into that circle of women that were just after his money.

She was already afraid that he would think that after he'd seen her house when he'd picked her up earlier. Even though she didn't know he was wealthy when he'd first approached her, she feared he would think that she was trying to move from the comfort zone of one sugar daddy to another. Camisha had tried to hook her up with some football players since her man was pro, but Fatima would have no parts of it because the only ones she found attractive were already hooked up. As far as she was concerned, that in itself spoke volumes about her character.

"I had a great time, Hakim," she told him honestly. Truth be known, she could never remember having so much fun.

"I had a great time, too," Hakim replied, looking down at her and running his fingers through her hair.

"I would invite you in, but it's a little late for a drink and I should probably get to bed. My kids will be up in a few hours and I better have some energy to deal with them."

Hakim chuckled. "I understand. Besides, I wouldn't want you to feel the least bit uncomfortable and I have the feeling that you would be exactly that if I came in."

"No, no, I feel extremely comfortable around you." Fatima's eyes fell to the ground. "It's just that I'm not very experienced at this dating thing. At least not for a long time."

"So, when can I meet the little ones?"

Fatima's eyes lit up as she gazed up at him. She was pleased that he wanted to meet them. "How about dinner tomorrow, unless you think that's too soon?"

"Dinner tomorrow would be great. I see you have a basketball court over yonder. Does your son play?"

"He'd like to, but he's not very good."

"Well, maybe I can show him some pointers."

"I'm sure he would love that."

"Then, I'll see you tomorrow. Around what time?"

"Five?"

"Perfect." Hakim took Fatima's chin into his hand. "Just like you."

They shared their first kiss, a *long* one, and Fatima melted into his arms for a good ten minutes.

Chapter Thirty

The Truth Hurts

Colette stared at Lloyd in amazement as he meticulously shaved in the bathroom mirror. They'd just finished getting busy in the shower and he had truly rocked her world. Lloyd was her first lover since Mandingo and she had been a nervous wreck when he first entered her, praying that her pussy hadn't been stretched too much for him to get some enjoyment out of the act. Thank goodness Mandingo hadn't been in her pussy long. He wanted the ass from jump and Colette was damn sure not allowing a man anywhere near her asshole again.

Lloyd was a major client of the law firm where Harmony had hooked her up. He was an Internet phenomenon, having launched BlackSexGods.com, the largest African-American bachelor site on the web. Colette had salivated over him for weeks when he'd come to the firm to meet with the senior partners. She finally got up the nerve to make a play for him one day in the elevator.

It was the easiest conquest of her entire life. By the time they got to ground level, they were both halfway naked and ended up fucking in the back of his limousine while the driver pretended to be wiping dirt off the exterior with a handkerchief.

Colette hadn't told Bryce, or anyone else for that matter, that she was seeing Lloyd. She wanted to surprise them after he officially became her man. She wanted a commitment from him and, judging from the way he ate her pussy like a pit bull with lockjaw, she assumed she was well on her way to becoming his one and only.

She walked up behind him and ran her fingers up and down his spine, tickling him.

He giggled. "Colette, I really need to get dressed, or I'll be late."

"What time do we have to be there?" Colette asked, referring to the BlackSexGods.com Calendar Party, where the sixteen men gracing the pages would be introduced.

Lloyd eyed her reflection in the mirror and pulled away from her, wiping the remaining shaving cream from his face and walking out into the master bedroom of his penthouse.

"Colette, I never mentioned you going with me," he said coldly.

"But, I just assumed that…"

"Maybe you should stop assuming, Colette. I never even implied that I was taking you with me tonight."

"Since we're dating, I figured you'd take me along."

Lloyd sat down on his bed and discarded his towel on the floor. His semi-hard dick made Colette suddenly horny.

"Colette, we're fucking; not dating. There is a difference."

Colette forgot all about being horny. "Excuse me?"

"There's nothing to excuse. I'm just telling you like it is. You're a lot of fun, but as far as a real relationship, I need someone who is more…"

"More what?"

Lloyd buried his face in his hands. "I knew I shouldn't have done this. It's always the same."

"What's always the same?" Colette asked, moving strategically closer in case she had to end up slapping the shit out of him.

"Whenever I get involved with slutty ass women, they expect me to give them the world."

"Are you trying to call me a slut?"

"I'm not trying to call you anything. I'm telling you straight up that you're a slut. Look at how we met."

"We met at my job."

"Yes, your *job*. A *job* is not the same thing as a *career* and I need a woman with a *career*."

Colette said, "Fuck you! I'm leaving!"

"That's probably for the best. No hard feelings, but you're just a temp. You don't even have a regular job and, as far as I can tell, you have little education. I'm a rising star and I need a woman that mirrors me in every way."

"So what the hell were you doing with me in the first place?" Colette lashed out at him.

"Like I said before, I was fucking you. Pure and simple."

Colette finished dressing in silence and left out in tears. She headed straight for Bryce's house.

After filling Bryce in on everything, the fireworks began.

"How dare that mutha fucka talk to you like that!" Bryce roared, holding onto the poker from her fireplace like she was ready to break something.

"Bryce, I just can't believe it," Colette whimpered. "I really thought Lloyd and I could have something special."

"I say we fuck his ass up like we did Dean Mitchell!"

"No, Bryce," Colette pleaded, knowing Bryce was damn serious about what she'd just said. "That was a totally different situation. Dean Mitchell sexually-harassed Lucky. I was just a damn fool for thinking Lloyd would take me seriously."

Bryce thought back to the conversation she'd had with Harmony, about Colette wanting men that were way out of her league. She hated to have to go there, but didn't see any other options.

"Colette, maybe you're attracted to the wrong type of men."

"What do you mean by that?"

Bryce sat down beside of her on the sofa. "I mean, maybe you should try dating some brothers that make a lesser income and who can appreciate a sista like yourself."

Colette leered at Bryce, clearly understanding her implications.

"Bryce, I can't believe you just said that shit to me!"

"Colette, I'm just sick of seeing you get your feelings hurt. Other than Mandingo, who almost ripped you a new asshole, and that brother that insisted you bang his asshole with a strap-on, how many men have you dated in recent years that didn't make six figure incomes?"

"There's nothing wrong with dating men that have it going on," Colette said nastily.

"No, there's nothing wrong with it, but there is something wrong with it if they're only out to use you for sex."

Colette got up from the sofa. "Bryce, I'm going to leave. I came here because I thought we could have a decent conversation. I need you to support me; not diss me."

"Colette, I have supported you *and* defended you all these years. I love you, Sis, and sometimes love hurts. I would be doing you a serious injustice by continuing to ignore the problem. You've got to realize that most men should have flea collars around their necks and unless you stumble across one that is genuinely interested in you, you'll keep ending up in the same situation."

"How do you know Troy's ass isn't cheating?" Colette asked sarcastically. "After all, George damn sure was."

Bryce stood and faced her. "That hurt, Colette. It really did, but I'm woman enough to let it slide since I know your emotions are guiding your judgment right about now. Troy may or may not be cheating. There's always a possibility, but I believe what he and I have is real. While George and I were together a long time, I've never felt as content as I do with Troy. Not ever."

Colette threw her arms around Bryce and began to weep. "I'm sorry, Sis. I didn't mean to say that."

"I know you didn't, and it's cool."

Bryce wiped the tears from Colette's face with the sleeve of her shirt. "I'll tell you what? Why don't we go take in a movie?"

"You mean you can actually leave the house without Troy?" Colette asked jokingly, feeling better by the second.

"For your information, Troy is having a man's night out with Robbie and Zachary."

"Aw Lawd, not the booty clubs again!"

Bryce chuckled. "Naw, not tonight. They went to some seminar over at UDC about dealing with African-American women in relationships."

"Are you for real?"

"Yes." Bryce giggled and they both sat back down. "Those fools actually believe that some seminar given by a male author who thinks he is a relationship guru even though he can't maintain one his damn self, will give them a greater insight into Harmony, Lucky, and me."

"That's damn ridiculous!"

"Yes, it is, but let them go waste seventy-nine dollars each to learn jack shit!"

Colette and Bryce traded humor for the next fifteen minutes before hunting down the movie section of the newspaper.

Thirty-One

A Time For Goodbyes

"**B**ryce, could you open up the door sometime today?" Harmony was kicking the bottom of the door, about to drop the brown paper grocery bag in her hands. Lucky was not fairing much better with the one she was holding.

"I'm coming! Sheesh!" They could hear Bryce rumbling around with some keys on the other side of the door. After what seemed like an eternity, the door finally swung open. "What's all that crap?"

"Crap?" Harmony rolled her eyes. "Lucky and I go through all of this trouble to come over here and cheer your ass up and you answer the door with a *tude*?"

They pushed by Bryce and went to the kitchen to sit the bags on the table.

"Damn, Bryce." Lucky glanced at Bryce. "What the hell is that on your head? An Aunt Jemima rag?"

"Lucky, you are *sooooooooo* damn funny, I forgot to laugh." Bryce reached behind her head to tighten the red bandanna. "For your information, this helps keeps my hair style in place while I'm asleep."

"You wear that to bed? When Troy is here?" Lucky and Harmony both giggled. "And he does the nasty with you while you have that on?"

"Lucky, shut the hell up!" Bryce smacked her lips and then starting rummaging through the bags. "Troy's ass is out of town on business. I can wear whatever the hell I want."

"We can see that," Harmony said with disdain. "That raggedy ass T-shirt you have on says it all." She reached over and spread the bottom of Bryce's shirt out so she could see the silk-screening. "The Commodores World Tour 1977?"

"Damn shame she has that thing on," Lucky chided and they all laughed, even Bryce.

"Aiight now, enough of the snide remarks. What's all this stuff you brought over here?"

"Well, for starters, we got all the fixins we need to make your favorite dish, homemade chicken pot pie," Harmony said. "And then..."

"Homemade chicken pot pie?" Bryce chuckled. "Which one of you huzzies think you can throw down in the kitchen like that?"

"I can burn the hell out of food," Harmony snarled. "Just because I don't cook that often doesn't mean I can't."

"Whatever!"

Lucky went into the living room and tossed her duffel bag on the couch. Bryce followed and watched as she started pulling videotapes out of it.

"Great! You guys rented some flicks. I hope you got some new ones I haven't seen yet."

"Actually, Bryce." Harmony entered the living room. "We rented a bunch of old movies to watch."

"How old?" Bryce smacked her lips. "Damn, I wanted to see some new shit like that Laurence Fishburn movie, *The Matrix*, or that Denzel movie, *The Siege*."

"Not tonight," Lucky said, butting in. "We're taking you back to the old school."

"What did you rent then? My *Fair Lady* and *The Sound of Music*?" They all chuckled.

"No, we didn't get that ridiculous," Harmony responded. "However, we did get *Cooley High*, *Fame*, and *Sparkle*."

"Word?" Bryce's eyes lit up because those were some of her favorites. "What is all this anyway? You guys pop up over here unexpectedly with groceries and movies and smiles on your faces like you're in collusion. What's up with that?"

"Nothing, Bryce," Lucky replied. "We heard it through the grapevine that Troy was going out of town on business and we knew you would be lonely and over here pouting so we decided to come cheer you up."

"Aww, how sweet." Bryce gleamed. "I do miss my boo. I was about to do something stupid like call Colette and tell her to ride back out to Raoul's with me so I could slap some midgets with my knee."

"Silly ass." Harmony gave Bryce a *love-slap* on her arm. "Well, I'm about to go cook. You guys throw a movie in."

"Which one?" Lucky asked.

"Damn, that's a hard choice. Since I was so head over heels in love with Lawrence Hilton Jacobs back in the day, let's put in *Cooley High* first."

Harmony chuckled. "Yeah, I clearly remember when you were fantasizing about his ass. I used to be crazy about Michael Jackson until he turned into a white man."

Bryce and Lucky fell out laughing.

"It's beyond me why someone would want to get all that plastic surgery when everyone in the whole damn world already knows what they look like. That is defeating the damn purpose."

"Well, the Jackson family must've gotten a group deal," Bryce added. "Shame on it all!"

"You're crazy." Lucky walked over to the VCR. "Let me go ahead and throw this movie in. Bryce, you have any microwave popcorn? That's the one thing we forgot."

"Yeah, I keep some Pop Secret in the pantry ever since Troy bought me that Jerry Springer *Too Hot For TV* tape. I watch that bad boy two or three times a week."

"You have that tape?" Lucky asked excitedly.

"Yeah, Gurl. That shit is the bomb, too!"

"Let's watch that first then!"

"Aiight, let me run upstairs and get it."

"Harmony, I have to give you mad props." Bryce was laid out on the couch, rubbing her belly. "That chicken pot pie was all that and then some."

"Yes, it was." Lucky nodded in agreement. "I must admit I was shocked. I thought it was going to turn out messed da hell up."

"O ye of little faith." Harmony chuckled. "I told ya'll I could throw down in the kitchen."

Bryce started sniffling and blowing out her nose with a Kleenex.

"What's wrong with you, Bryce?" Harmony was concerned. "You miss Troy?"

"I do miss him a whole lot, but that's not it. I'm still thinking about *Cooley High*. The ending always fucks me up emotionally."

"Me, too," Lucky concurred.

Harmony laughed. "You act like you've never seen it before. I can't really talk though. *Imitation of Life* has the same effect on me."

"On a softer note, I want to thank you two for coming over here to cheer me up." Bryce was overwhelmed by her sisters' thoughtfulness. "I realize you both have men of your own and they're probably somewhere feeling neglected right about now."

"Naw, Robbie and Zachary went to an Orioles game today," Lucky informed Bryce. "Besides, blood before dick. You know that's the Whitfield motto."

"Amen to that." Harmony nodded. "By the way, Zachary and I are having a cookout next weekend so make sure you both come and bring the fellas."

"What's the occasion?" Bryce asked.

"There's no occasion. We have cookouts every summer and here it is going into fall. You know that."

"Well, you haven't had one *this summer*!"

"Because things have been hectic, but Zachary loves to entertain so both your asses better be there."

"Aiight, no problemo."

"Robbie and I will be there, too," Lucky added.

"Cool." Harmony reached for another tape. "Now, let's throw on *Fame* so I can feel sorry for Irene Cara's ass when she meets up with that leech of a photographer."

"Yeah, that's the bomb ass flick."

Chapter Thirty-Two

One Last Party Before Lights Out

"Zachary, can you bring some more steaks out!" Troy yelled. Bryce walked up behind him at the gas grill. "Baby, are you sure you know what you're doing? We want the steaks well done, not *blackened*."

"Very funny." Troy chuckled and then popped her on the ass. "I know what the heck I'm doing, woman. I've been cooking steaks since 1964."

"Hmph! That's amazing considering your ass wasn't born until 1968."

"Smart ass. Go back in the house with your sisters and friends and let the men handle this."

"Whatever!" Bryce gave him a peck on the lips and went back inside, almost knocking over the pan of steaks Zachary was taking outside.

"Umm, Robbie, you need to go outside with the fellas," Fatima said sarcastically. "We're trying to gossip around here. "

"Yeah, female talk," Colette giggled.

"Damn, why ya'll trying to kick my baby out of the house?" Lucky asked. "I want my boo right here beside me."

Robbie leaned over and kissed her cheek. "It's cool. I'll just go out there with Zachary and the other men so we can discuss politics or something."

"Sho you right," Harmony interjected. "The only thing you men are going to discuss is booty clubs and hoochies on music videos."

All the women started laughing.

"Don't forget sports," Fatima added.

"Damn, you all sure have a low opinion of men," Robbie protested. Robbie looked out into the yard, where Hakim was twirling a basketball on his index finger. "Fatima, you have a lot of nerve anyway. Your man plays sports so of course it'll come up, but still. We do talk about other things."

"Whatever," Bryce said, pointing at the patio door leading out to the deck. "Just get to steppin' and make sure my baby doesn't set himself or his *Kiss The Cook* apron on fire."

They all giggled while Robbie sulked out of the house to join the other three men.

"So what are we going to do today besides feeding our faces and sitting around?" Lucky asked.

"Well, we could always drive out to Raoul's place and stomp on some midgets." Bryce chuckled.

"You're sick, Gurl." Colette giggled. "That was cold the way you guys left Mandingo out there to fend for himself."

"I know you're not even going there!" Harmony exclaimed. "You just need to be thankful we came and rescued your ass and I do mean ass *literally*."

"I know that's right," Bryce agreed. "We went through all that shit to get you out of there and now you're talking trash? By the way, I do mean shit *literally*, too."

Everyone busted out laughing, except Colette. "Enough of the anal jokes, damn! You guys have been teasing me ever since."

"That's because it's funny as hell." Lucky giggled. "Had us out on a mission way over in the morning to get a nucca's dick dislodged from the black hole."

"Aiight, aiight, damn!" Colette rolled her eyes. "I do appreciate ya'll helping a sista out, for real though!"

"Colette, I just want to say one thing to you," Harmony said. "It's no big secret that, at first, I couldn't stand the ground you walked on."

"You're right." Bryce jumped all up in the mix. "It definitely wasn't a secret."

"Bryce, shaddup and let me finish!" Harmony snapped. "N-E-Way, I just wanted to say that since you've been working with the agency and since I've gotten to spend more time with you hanging out and such, my opinion of you has drastically changed."

"Hold up, is this an apology?" Bryce asked. "If so, I need to break out a camcorder or *something* because this happens less often than leap years."

"Bryce, stuff it." Harmony threw a seedless grape at her over the coffee table.

"Harmony, my opinion of you has changed a lot, too," Colette responded. "I used to think you were the biggest bitch on earth!"

"How delightful," Harmony replied and they all laughed nervously, hoping she wouldn't take her apology back and kick Colette's ass. "Don't get me wrong. I still think you're a hoochie, but I guess we all are in a sense. You are just more comfortable with your *hoochiness*."

"Thanks for the compliment. *If that was a compliment?*" Colette chuckled.

"Yes, it was a compliment and I meant it, too." Harmony smiled at her. "On a serious tip though, I misjudged you and for that I apologize."

Harmony got up and gave Colette a hug for the very first time.

"Aw, I'm so happy, I could break dance," Bryce said sarcastically.

"In fact, I wanted to tell all of you something," Harmony continued.

They all stared at her intently.

"Damn, you're pregnant," Bryce poised more as a statement than a question. "'Bout damn time you're gonna make me an auntie."

"No, no babies in the oven. I wanted to thank all of you for giving me the most wonderful summer of my entire life."

"I've had fun, too." Bryce got up and gave her a hug. "Every summer has been great, but there was something about this summer that was extra special. The whole female bonding thing. Fatima and I even stopped cussing each other out all the time."

"Fuck ya." Fatima chuckled and threw her the finger.

"Oh well, I may have spoken too soon." Bryce laughed and threw the finger right back at her.

"I think it's because we've all been there for each other when the shit hit the fan this summer," Lucky added. "Think about it. I had my ordeal with the dean, Bryce had her ordeal with George, Fatima had her ordeal with Javon, and Colette had her ordeal with a mammoth, elephantine dick."

"That's *tooooooooooo* funny," Colette snidely remarked. "But you're right. We've all been through something traumatic this summer and everyone had everyone else's back. I love and appreciate you guys so much for that."

"True that," Bryce said. "The only one who hasn't been through anything traumatic is Harmony. There was the little break up with Zachary, but they're closer than ever now."

"Harmony never goes through anything she can't handle," Fatima said. "That's my gurl. She's a survivor. Always has been."

Harmony jumped up from the couch and walked over to the wet bar. Her fingers trembled as she poured herself another glass of iced tea. "I'm so proud of all of you guys for standing up for what you believe in." She turned around and looked at Bryce. "Even you, Bryce. Just because all you really believe in is freaky sex, it doesn't mean I'm any less proud of you."

They all giggled.

"Harmony, I'm going to let that one slide just because I don't want to act a fool in your house."

"Chile, please, you've been acting a fool in my house since I moved in here."

Bryce rolled her eyes.

"Next summer, I think we should all take a cruise to an island. Maybe the Bahamas or Jamaica," Lucky suggested.

"I've always wanted to go to Cozumel," Fatima concurred.

"Sounds good to me," Bryce stated.

"You know I'm down," added Colette. She'd never been out of the MD/DC area and was willing to travel to Cozumel, even though she had no damn idea where it was.

"Harmony, what about you?" Fatima asked. "What island do you want to go to next summer?"

"I say we hit all of them bad boys," Harmony replied.

"I heard that," Fatima said. "I'm down for whatever."

Harmony kept her back to them as she stood by the wet bar with her eyes clamped shut, trying to prevent the tears from coming out. "Excuse me for a second. I need to go upstairs to get something."

Zachary saw Harmony running up the hallway steps. He had been in the kitchen the entire time preparing the tossed salad, unbeknown to them, and had overheard the entire conversation.

Zachary didn't hold his tears back because he knew what Harmony was doing. She was saying goodbye to all of them in her own subtle way. However, the topic of vacationing the next summer had been too much for her to handle. They both knew she wouldn't be around long enough to even see Christmas.

Zachary debated about whether or not to go upstairs to comfort her and decided against it. He didn't want to turn their cookout into an emotional afternoon and he knew Harmony would come back down in a few minutes, smiling like she was never upset in the first place.

Zachary went into the downstairs guest bathroom, sat down on the toilet seat lid and wept in silence.

"Little girl, you dropped your candy!" Harmony yelled out, holding up the piece of peppermint she witnessed fall out the overalls of the youngster when she climbed on the jungle gym.

The girl briskly ran her petite hands over her pockets, searching for the piece of candy that was no longer there. Harmony approached her and knelt down, holding it out towards her. The girl hesitated, bit her bottom lip and twisted her hips back and forth like there was an invisible hula hoop around her waist.

"You're a stranger, lady," she whispered, still twisting her hips.

Harmony couldn't get over how much the little girl resembled herself as a child. Tall and skinny, long curly brown hair in pony-tails, big brown eyes.

"Yes, I'm a stranger. You're a very good girl. I bet your mother told you never to take candy from strangers."

The girl nodded her head.

"Even if the candy is your own?"

A perplexed expression came over the little girl's face while she analyzed the question like most six or seven year olds do. Then she grabbed the candy and ran off to play, whispering *thank you* as she climbed the wooden steps that led to the slide.

Harmony found an empty wooden bench and sat down. The discomfort in her side was getting worse by the second and the pain pills no longer worked. She sat there for a long time and thought about all the things she was going to miss. Her sisters, Zachary, her parents, Fatima, even Colette's crazy ass. Watching the sun rise in the morning and set at night. Running barefoot through the sandy beaches of the Eastern Shore. Hanging out with the gurls. Making love.

She thought about all the things she would never get to do or experience. Her thirtieth birthday, motherhood, married life, vacationing on a tropical island, turning her temporary agency into a large corporation, Lucky's graduation from medical school. There were so many things she didn't get to fit into twenty-nine years. So many, many things.

"Agnes, is Fatima home?"

"Yes, Miss Whitfield." Fatima's maid held the front door wide open so Harmony could enter the foyer. "I'll go get her for you. Would you like to wait in the living room?"

"No, I'm fine here. I can only stay for a couple of minutes."

Agnes stared at Harmony, noticing the dark circles around her eyes and the paleness of her skin.

"Are you okay, Miss Whitfield? Would you like me to get you a glass of water?"

"I'm fine. Just a little under the weather. Probably a twenty-four hour virus or something."

Agnes reluctantly left Harmony in the foyer, going into the kitchen to get Fatima.

A couple of moments later, Fatima started yelling out her good news before she even turned the corner. "Harmony, guess what? Hakim's moving in with me and Javon's ass finally agreed to give me a di..."

It took a few seconds for Fatima to register the fact that Harmony was sprawled out on the marble floor and not moving. Then her screams began.

Chapter Thirty-Three

The Homegoing

"Troy, can you set the dining room table for dinner?" Bryce yelled from the kitchen.

"Sure, Baby!" he yelled back from the living room. "What are we having? Smells damn delicious!"

"Spaghetti." Bryce chuckled, glancing towards the kitchen waste basket to make sure the lid was securely fastened. *I hope this voodoo shit works*, she thought.

The phone started ringing. Troy said he would get it. Bryce put the finishing touches on her tossed salad and then picked up the enormous bowl labeled *PASTA* that was filled to the brim with her *special* recipe. She planned on faking stomach cramps the second she finished her salad and letting Troy eat the whole bowl of spaghetti by himself.

Troy came dashing into the kitchen, taking the corner in his white athletic socks like he was Chuck Berry sliding across a dance floor. As soon as Bryce saw the expression on his face, she knew something terrible had happened.

"Go throw on some shoes and a jacket, Baby," he said frantically, headed towards the stove to turn off all the burners. "We have to go!"

"What is it, Troy? What's wrong?" The bowl in Bryce's hands started trembling, a direct reflection of her own fingers.

"That was Lucky on the phone." He paused like he was dreading saying whatever came next. "It's Harmony."

No other words were necessary. Bryce started panicking and the bowl hit the floor, shattering into bits and splashing her secret recipe everywhere as she ran towards the door.

Troy couldn't drive to The Washington Hospital Center fast enough for Bryce. She blew the horn at several people, motioning for them to get out of their way, and even tried to grab the steering wheel from the passenger's seat a couple of times. She kept bombarding Troy with questions he couldn't possibly answer.

"Lucky was so upset on the phone that she barely managed to get out the few words she did," was all he could say.

The thirty or so minutes it took them to get there seemed more like three-hundred. Before Troy could even pull up to the emergency room good, Bryce had the door open and jumped out while the car was still in motion.

They didn't say a word to each other. Bryce slammed the door and ran inside while Troy went to locate a parking space in the visitors' lot.

Bryce rapped impatiently on the counter of the nurses' station. The only nurse anywhere in sight was trying to play a game of charades with an older Hispanic woman. The nurse didn't speak Spanish and the woman didn't speak English so they were using hand signals to communicate about how to fill out the admission forms.

Bryce lasted all of twenty seconds before deciding enough was enough. "Excuse me! I'm trying to find my sister, Harmony Whitfield!"

The nurse turned towards her and rolled her eyes. "Just one moment, Miss. I'll be right with you."

By the time Troy caught up to Bryce a couple of minutes later, she had the nurse yanked halfway over the nurses' station by the collar.

"I tried to be polite at first! But if you don't tell me what room my sister is in right this second, you're going to need medical attention your damn self!"

"Bryce, calm down." Troy pried her fingers off the nurse's collar.

The nurse started smiling nervously as Bryce let her go. "What did you say your sister's name was again?"

"Whitfield!" Bryce's pulse was racing and she was battling the onset of a migraine. "Harmony Whitfield!"

The nurse started pecking away on the computer keyboard while Troy rubbed the small of Bryce's back, hoping she would calm down but knowing it was a lost cause.

The Hispanic woman started flailing her arms in the air and yelling obscenities at all of them in Spanish. She obviously didn't appreciate the distraction from her own medical dilemma.

Bryce fidgeted and bit her fingernails, something she hadn't done since the age of seven or eight. Her mother had to put a stop to the bad habit by making her dip her finger in crushed red pepper and suck it off every time she was caught in the act.

The nurse looked up solemnly from the computer monitor, realizing how dire the situation was. "Your sister is in Room 517. Intensive Care."

The words *Intensive Care* threw Bryce into a tailspin. She covered her mouth to hold in the scream that was trying to escape. Her knees started to buckle underneath her. Somehow, Troy managed to hold her up.

She started looking in all directions and the nurse, who originally gave her nothing but *tude*, gave her directions instead. She pointed down the hallway to the right of the nurses' station. "The elevator's that way!"

Bryce took off running with Troy dead on her heels. The nurse yelled after them. "No running in the hospital, please!"

They slowed their gait down to a speed walk. The nurse reluctantly turned her attention back to the woman who was still yelling obscenities at her in Spanish.

When they got on the elevator, Bryce buried her face into Troy's chest, letting her sobs ricochet off his chest into the air. All sorts of horrible images raced through her mind. She imagined Harmony leaving her temp agency after dark, having worked twelve hours or more straight, only to get attacked, beaten, raped, stabbed, or shot on her way to the car. She imagined her being in a ten car pile up on the Beltway or being the unsuspecting victim of a tractor trailer driver who had fallen asleep at the wheel and jackknifed. She imagined her being the innocent bystander in a drive-by shooting or a gang war. In D.C., any and all of the above were possible.

As soon as the elevator doors parted on the fifth floor, Bryce noticed the sign on the wall that read *Intensive Care* with an arrow pointing to the left. Instead of walking fast, she slowed down to a snail's pace because the fear had truly sunken in.

She thought back to the other times she had been in the Intensive Care wing of a hospital. They had been few and far between. When she was four, she went to visit Great Grandma Whitfield at Memorial Hospital in Durham. When she was nine, she went to visit Uncle Richard at a Baptist Hospital in San Diego. When she was fifteen, she went to visit Michael, her high school sweetheart, at a hospital in Los Angeles.

Great Grandma Whitfield lost her battle with old age, Uncle Richard lost his battle with lung cancer, and Michael lost his battle with the bullet in his chest. The point was they all lost and that was the last time she'd ever seen any of them alive.

"Bryce, everything is going to be okay, Baby." She heard Troy whispering in her ear but it seemed like he was talking to someone else. She was having an out of body experience because she couldn't begin to rationalize how she went from cooking spaghetti one minute to walking down a hospital hallway scared to death the next. Whoever said that things happen when you least expect it was speaking nothing but the truth.

"Bryce!" She looked up and saw Lucky running towards her, not caring whether it was allowed or not. That broke her out of her trance.

"Lucky, where's Harmony?" Lucky's face was tear-drenched and her eyes were bloodshot. "What happened to her?"

Lucky caught up to Bryce and Troy and threw her arms around her older sister, seeking comfort and trying to give a little at the same time. "I don't know all the details, Bryce. I just know that it's bad. *Real bad.*"

Bryce gently pushed Lucky off of her so she could look her in the eyes. "What do you mean, *real bad?*"

Lucky's eyes started darting back and forth, not focusing on any particular person or object. Bryce held her by the elbows, trying to steady her from shaking so badly. "I don't know. All I know is that Fatima called an ambulance after Harmony fainted at her house, Zachary called me, and then I called you."

Bryce was frustrated, yet somewhat relieved because it meant none of the scenarios she'd run through her mind previously were true. Harmony hadn't been shot or stabbed or involved in a wreck. She had probably just passed out from overexerting herself at work or had a stress-related episode. Then again, neither one of those explained her being in Intensive Care.

"Momma and Daddy are on their way. They're catching the next plane out of Cali."

Bryce couldn't manage to keep her emotions under control another minute. The mere fact that their parents were en route to D.C. made the situation ten times worse.

Troy pointed down the hall. "There's Zachary."

Bryce and Lucky looked, spotting Zachary down the hall waving his hand in the air for them to join him. They scurried down the hallway until they got to Room 517 and he directed them inside.

The room was quiet and filled with activity at the same time. The lighting was dim, making the situation all the more depressing. Harmony was surrounded by nurses and doctors and covered with tubes leading to everything from a heart monitor to an IV.

Fatima was sitting in a chair over in the far right hand corner and didn't even look like she was breathing. Her eyes were blank and she didn't even look up when they came in. Just sat there in a state of shock.

Harmony looked extremely pale and her breathing was shallow.

Bryce could see her chest go up and down as she struggled to take each breath. Her eyes were open but had a deadpan expression. Bryce made her way over to the bed while Lucky stood by the door, too petrified to take another step.

Harmony reached out to touch Bryce's hand. Bryce trembled when she felt her cold and frail grasp.

This can't be happening, Bryce thought, looking at the night table beside the bed instead of directly at her sister. *This is just a bad dream and any second, Troy is going to wake me up. This can't be real. Harmony can't be laying up here in a hospital bed. Just yesterday, we were making vacation plans.*

"Bryce, look at me." Harmony's voice was weak, her words barely audible. "It's time for me to go home."

Lucky started wailing loudly, still glued to the wall, afraid to come any closer. Bryce diverted her eyes to Harmony's face. She was still in shock and couldn't believe it was really happening.

"Remember when Daddy used to sing *His Eye Is On The Sparrow* to us all the time?"

Bryce nodded. "Yes, I remember."

"Tell him." Harmony paused, gasping to catch her breath. "Ask Daddy to sing that song for me at my funeral. It's always been my favorite."

Bryce couldn't hold her emotions in any longer. "You're not going to die, Harmony! You can't die! If you die on me, I swear to God I will kill you!"

Harmony managed to chuckle at the irony of Bryce's last statement. "Don't worry, Baby Sis. You and Lucky are going to be just fine. I've made all the arrangements and the two of you will never have to worry about making ends meet. Neither will Momma and Daddy. My insurance money will make all of you set for life."

"Harmony, stop talking crazy! You're not dying, dammit!" The frustration showed in Bryce's tear-drenched eyes. "You're not even sick! You can't be sick!"

"Bryce, I *am* dying." Harmony tightened her grip on Bryce's hand. "I'll always be with you though. I'll always protect you."

"NOOOOOOO!!!" Lucky's screams filled the entire Intensive

Care wing. "NOOOOOOO, she can't die! She can't die!"

Fatima snapped back to reality, stood up, and took Lucky into her arms, determined to try to comfort her like she knew Harmony would if she could.

"Lucky." Harmony glanced up at her. "I want you to know how proud I am of you. I always have been. Both of you."

"Please don't leave me," was all Lucky could manage to utter before her sobs overtook her again.

Harmony shook Bryce's hand to make sure she was listening. "Bryce, you've got to be the strong one now. I bought a suit, a powder blue one, my favorite color. Zachary knows where it is. I want you to bury me in it."

Bryce feverishly shook her head. "No, none of this is happening. There's nothing wrong with you. This is all some sick joke." She looked at Zachary for some reassurance. "Right, Zachary?"

Zachary came and sat down on the opposite side of the bed from Bryce and rubbed the small of her back, trying to maintain his own composure like he'd promised Harmony he would. "I'm so sorry, Bryce."

"Okay, hold up!" It finally started to hit home. "Let's just rationalize this whole thing. What's wrong with you, Harmony? You haven't even been sick?"

Harmony bit her bottom lip and managed a slight grin. "Actually, I've been sick for a very long time. I hid it from you. I guess you were wrong about being able to read me like a book, huh?"

Bryce thought about how the last few months had troubled her because she sensed something was wrong with Harmony. *What a fool she had been not to see this coming!* That's why Harmony had been acting strange. That's why Harmony had tried to push Zachary away. That's why she slept with Javon and allowed herself to be videotaped. She knew she was dying all along.

Before Bryce could get the next question out, Dr. Dresher came in the room and practically fainted when she saw Bryce sitting there. They all had puzzled expressions on their faces, except Zachary.

"I'm sorry, Miss. You just took me off guard. The resemblance is uncanny." She came closer to the bed. "You must be Bryce. I'm Dr.

Dresher."

Lucky stepped in then. "Dr. Dresher, what's wrong with our sister?"

"You must be Lucky, right?"

"Yes, I am," Lucky confirmed.

The doctor glared at Harmony, not really wanting to break her oath but not wanting to lose a patient without a fight either. "There's not much time. There's a chance it might work."

Harmony shook her head. "No way, doctor. I meant what I said."

"What might work?" Bryce asked, standing up anxiously.

"Nothing, Bryce. Don't listen to her," Harmony stated avidly. "Nothing at all!"

"Harmony, I love you and you might hate me for this, but I have to do it," Zachary interjected.

Zachary could see the hurt in Harmony's eyes when she whispered, "You promised."

He turned towards Bryce. "Bryce, there's a *slight* chance you may be able to save Harmony's life."

"How? I would do anything for her!"

"I know you would and that's what I've been trying to tell her all along." He took Harmony's hand. "Please tell her or I will. I refuse to just sit here and let you die."

Bryce sat back down on the bed. "Harmony Whitfield, if you die on me and I find out there was something, *anything* I could have done to prevent it, they'll be giving us a double funeral. Do you hear me? A double funeral because life is too damn hard to go through without you!"

Harmony looked from Bryce to Zachary to Lucky and decided she really wasn't ready to leave them all behind. Never had she asked anyone for anything, but there was a first time for everyone. "Bryce, I need you to be a donor for me."

"A donor?" Bryce chuckled nervously. "Hell, *is that all?*"

Harmony and Bryce both giggled.

"What do you need? An arm? A foot? A leg? I could always get me a peg leg. I think they look sexy any damn way."

"Silly ass!"

"Seriously, Sis, what do you need? I'll cut out my heart for you if I have to."

Harmony looked into the eyes identical to her own and spoke the words before she lost her nerve. "Actually, all I really need is a kidney."

Bryce lifted Harmony's hand and kissed it, not hesitating for even half of a second. "One kidney coming right up."

"You don't have to do this."

"Yes, I do have to do this. Can you honestly say that you wouldn't do it for me?"

"No, you know I would do it for you."

"Then let me be the one to do something for you for a change and stop complaining because I *am* getting the last word this time. I don't care what you say."

They both giggled but the pain shot through Harmony's side again and she started gasping for air.

"We have to hurry this up, ladies," Dr. Dresher interjected. "There's no guarantee you'll match. Although, from the physical resemblance, I'm about ninety-nine percent sure you will."

"How do we find out if I match?"

"A simple blood test but we have to do it right away." The doctor went to the door and held it open for Bryce. "Please follow me."

Bryce kissed Harmony's hand again. "Don't worry. We're Whitfields and Whitfields never quit."

"Wait! I'm going, too!" Lucky screamed out.

Eight Months Later

Chapter Thirty-Four

It's About Damn Time!

Jazzlyn and Jazmin stood on the edge of the ocean, letting the waves cascade over their bare feet and touch the bottom hems of their white cotton dresses.

They giggled as the water and pebbles tickled in between their toes. They had never been to the beach before and were anxious to change into bathing suits and dive head first into the cool, brisk water.

"Jazzlyn and Jazmin, get up here right now!" Lucky yelled out to them from the top of the hill. "You're going to be all dirty before the thing even starts!"

"Coming, Cousin Lucky!" Jazmin exclaimed and ran through the sand up to the pavilion with her twin right on her tail.

Thirty minutes later, the twins marched down the red carpet in the makeshift chapel inside the pavilion. They were all cleaned up and had on white lace socks with black patent leather shoes. They scattered rose petals as the quartet of musicians played *The Wedding Song* by Kenny G.

After they were in place, Lucky marched down the aisle in her beautiful hunter green maid of honor dress. Colette and Fatima looked dashing in their bridesmaid gowns, having marched in earlier, and Robbie looked particularly handsome in his tuxedo. Lucky thought to herself, *he really is the best man. The best man for me.*

The doors swung open one more time. Chester Whitfield was grinning from ear to ear as he led his daughters down the aisle, one on each arm. Instead of a double funeral, Harmony and Bryce had the double wedding they had always dreamed about.

"Jamaica's so beautiful!" Harmony stood on the balcony of their suite. "I'm glad we decided to come here for our honeymoon."

"You're the beautiful one." Zachary walked up behind her and placed his arms around her waist. "I just want to hold you forever."

Harmony turned to face him. "Even though the island is gorgeous, I really want to make love the entire time we're here."

"You won't get any argument out of me." Zachary giggled, kissing Harmony on the lips. "But what about Troy and Bryce? We're going to have to tour the island with them and hang out *sometime*. That was the whole purpose of both couples honeymooning here."

Harmony chuckled. "I don't think that's going to be a major problem."

She wrapped her arms around Zachary's waist and whispered into his ear, "Take me to bed, husband!"

"Umm, husband. I like that word."

Zachary picked Harmony up, carrying her to bed.

"Darling, I'm going to lay it on you all night long!" Troy yelled from the bathroom of their suite as he got out the shower.

"Oh, I know you are, Honey!" Bryce yelled in return. "All night and then some!"

She heard him coming so she quickly took out the jar from her cosmetics bag and poured about an eighth of the liquid into Troy's glass of red wine. *Gotta ration this shit since Ripuoff got locked up*, she thought to herself.

She replaced the jar in the bag and stirred the mixture into his wine with her finger as he was coming out the bathroom.

She walked over to the bed, carrying two glasses of wine and making sure not to get them mixed up.

"Bryce, why do we have red wine and Zachary and Harmony are chilling over in their suite with champagne?"

"Because red wine is my favorite and I want everything about tonight to be special," she lied. "Now drink up so we can get our freak on."

"Gurl, you are in for it tonight." Troy downed the whole glass of wine, Niagra and all, in one swallow.

"We both are," Bryce chuckled.

Zachary was busy going to town on Harmony's left nipple when he heard someone screaming out, "UNCLEEEEE!"

"What the hell is that?" he asked, plopping her nipple out of his mouth.

"Umm, that's just Troy," Harmony replied.

"Dammmmmn, it's like that, huh? Bryce must be laying it on him something fierce," Zachary joked.

"More like the other way around but I'm sure she's enjoying every minute of it." Harmony grabbed Zachary by the neck and pulled him back towards her. "Now come here and enjoy every moment of me."

"Umph! Umph! Umph!" Robbie smiled lovingly at Lucky, admiring how beautiful she looked in the floor-length, off the shoulder, red evening gown. "You look absolutely scrumptious tonight, my love!"

Lucky blushed and returned the compliment. "You look mighty delectable your damn self. That tuxedo is all that!"

Robbie struck a pose, grabbing a hold of his lapels and grimacing. "Nothing's too good for my baby."

"You're too damn sweet, Boo." Lucky embraced him and planted a big, wet kiss on his lips. "Are you going to keep me in suspense or are you ready to give up the 411 on where we're headed tonight?"

"No, it's a surprise!"

"Awwwwwwww, pretty please," Lucky pouted, "with sugar on top!"

"Nope! I'm not giving in," Robbie persisted. "You'll just have to wait until we get there."

Lucky rolled her eyes and smacked her lips. "Okay, but I just hope we're not overdressed. I would hate to fall up into The Florida Avenue Grill sporting these type of clothes."

They both chuckled.

"No pig's feet and collard greens tonight." Robbie giggled. "Since both your sisters are honeymooning in the islands, I wanted to do something extra special for you."

"Soon, we'll be honeymooning in the islands."

"Most definitely, Baby," Robbie concurred. "The second we both finish med school, I plan on jumping the broom with your fine ass!"

"You mean we can have the type of wedding I've always dreamed about?"

"Of course, Baby." Robbie kissed her on the forehead. "No matter what type of wedding we have and no matter what type of gown you wear, you'll always be the most beautiful woman in the world to me." He paused, then added as an afterthought, "Even with one kidney, you're still the bomb diggity!"

Lucky threw her arms around his neck and hugged him tight, hoping that the perfect feeling wouldn't end. She was looking forward to the future. A long, happy marriage with Robbie, making a house full of babies, and saving the lives of thousands of people. If somehow, all of that wasn't accomplished, it wouldn't matter much because she had already saved one life, Harmony's, and that was the most important life of all.

Robbie broke the embrace and glanced at his watch. "We better hurry if we're going to make it to New York City in time for our dinner reservations."

"New York City?" Lucky's eyes lit up like moonbeams. "Aw damn, do you have any idea how long I've been sweating going to

NYC?"

"Well, the wait is over my love!"

Robbie opened the door and held out his hand.

Lucky blushed excitedly when she spotted the white stretch limo parked outside. "NYC, here we come and in the shiniest damn, whitest damn, longest damn limo I've ever seen. Shame on it all!"

About the Author

Zane is a professional, African-American female in her early thirties. She resides in the Washington, DC area with her two beautiful children.

Over the past two years, she has gained tens of thousands of direct subscribers to her monthly erotica newsletter, Zane's Erotica Noir. Hundreds of readers have emailed her for advice on their relationships and sex lives.

Zane can be reached at zane@eroticanoir.com or Endeavors@aol.com

Shonda Cheekes, her publicist, can be reached at shonda@eroticanoir.com

Special Preview

The Heat Seekers

Come on along and take a roller-coaster ride with two sistah-gurls and two homeboys all looking for the same exact thing; satisfaction.

Tempest is sick and tired of being sick and tired. She has looked for love in all of the so-called right places only to end up with the short end of the stick every single time. She has basically given up on love and vowed herself to a life of celibacy. She has dedicated her life and career to making sure that young teenage girls don't make the same mistakes she made in the past.

Janessa has a predilection for thugs and playas. She is destined to find out the hard way that love and sex are not always interchangeable. She would consider herself lucky if she could just land a man who wasn't doing fifteen to life in the state pen.

Geren has it all. Wealth, success and good looks. Yet and still, all he has to show in the romance department is an entourage of gold-digging women with one common goal; hooking his ass and getting him to the altar with a quickness.

Dvontè is a canine and proud of it. His reasoning is as long as he is clocking enough dollars to get by and making women scream out his name in bed, his life is complete. He makes no excuses for his behavior. In fact, he lets women know from jump street that he is all about the booty calls.

One fateful, summer evening the four of them cross paths and discover things about themselves and each other that will forever change their lives. Secrets are revealed, friendships are dismantled, and the old adage "If you can't stand the heat, stay out of the kitchen" takes on an entirely new meaning.

The Heat Seekers

Chapter One-The Seekers

Tempest

MY HAND HOVERED OVER the lighted dial pad of my cordless phone, debating about calling another sorry mofo. The first one wasn't home and it was just as well. Giorgio was this brotha I met while I was in line at Starbucks Coffee waiting on a mocha cappuccino. He was attractive, nice and the perfect gentleman. We kicked it a few times together. Everything was kewl until......I found out the nucca had six toes on his left foot. Yes, I said six damn toes. He had this miniature one hanging off of the side. I discovered it one night when he treated me to a foot massage and I decided to return the favor. Normally, I would never venture to caress a man's feet but I was being daring that night and the shit will never, ever, ever, ever happen again. It freaked me out, that sixth toe, and it reminded me of that Stephen King flick, The Dark Half. I came to the conclusion Giorgio was genetically conceived as a twin but he somehow swallowed his other half up. For days after the gruesome discovery, I had nightmares about marrying him, waking up one morning, and seeing him standing there with a hatchet in his hand and grinning like Jack Nicholson in The Shining. No, that nucca had to go. I know it sounds shallow but I would rather be safe than sorry.

I flipped through my version of the little black book, a tattered and worn 4"x6" plastic pink phone book with a black poodle on the cover. The only letters left from the word address were the a,

the r and the e. As I eyed the pages, a feeling of disgust over-whelmed me. So many names, so many sorry ass mofos. And to think, I had allowed these nuccas inside my world, catered to their every desire and even performed all the fellatio techniques I learned from that Monica chick's book, The Complete Guide to Tongue and Jaw Maneuvering, on the parasites.
Let me break it down for you.

Sorry mofo number one: Trent, a twenty-six year old systems analyst. Fondest memory: practicing earth-shattering Tantric Sex with him and basking in the afterglow of the numerous yoni(clit) massages he bestowed upon me. Most traumatic memory: walking in on him bestowing the lingham(dick) massage on his roommate Bill. I will never forget that day for as long as I live. Mostly because I hurled up my partially-digested lunch, Kung Pao Chicken, all over the two of them and my favorite suit, a black wool number I snagged a great bargain on from a one-day sale at Macy's in Pentagon City Mall. I loved that suit. Damn them two homie-sex-uals for ruining my shit.

There I was infatuated with what I thought was a prime candi-date for The Pussy Eater's Hall of Fame when all along I was giving all my sweet loving to a booty bandit, a rump wrangler, a sword swallower. No wonder he knew how to eat a pussy so damn good. Any man who can deep throat 9-10 inches ought to be able to suck the lining and ovaries out of a pussy.

Shame on it all. I shook my head in disbelief at the very thought of him, muttered an expletive, and then scratched his name out with a red magic marker. Good-ness knows I would spread my thighs open for a three-legged baboon with one eye in the center of its forehead before I ration Trent another millimeter of puntang.

Sorry mofo number two: Hezekiel, a thirty-two year old pro-duce manager at the friendly neighborhood super-market. I know what you're thinking. What woman in her right mind would date a brotha named Hezekiel? Sheeitttt, every sistah I know wanted to break a piece off to his fione ass. As for you brothas, you shouldn't even fake the funk. If a sistah looked like Halle Berry but her name was Kizzy Kunte, you would be screaming out "Work it, Kizzy! Work it!" in the bedroom.

N E Way, enough of defending myself. Back to the matter at hand. Fondest memory: the way he used to like to get freaky and suck on my fingers, toes and everything in between. I don't know if it was due to his grass roots upbringing in the foothills of Kentucky or not but the brotha was born with a platinum tongue. He told me once that he had a nipple fetish because it reminded him of milking his Papa's prize-winning cow, Bessie. To hear him tell it, Bessie won the blue medal at every Kentucky State Fair for ten years in a row. Whatever it was, the brotha had mad skillz. Not skills, but *skillz*. Used to make me scream out his name in forty-two different languages. Most traumatic experience: letting him have $800 to get his BMW fixed. I gave him the money out of the goodness of my heart. It wasn't even a loan, mind you. It was a straight up gift. Okay, I will confess. I was whipped. Tongue-whipped. At least until I found out the BMW wasn't even his but this bean pole anorexic bitch's. I saw the two of them cruising down at Haines Point in it while I was jogging. The bastard had the nerve to almost run me over after his nerves got riled up from spotting me. I cussed his ass out but all he did was haul ass and leave me in a cloud of exhaust. Even though the money was a gift, I contemplated taking his skank ass in front of Judge Judy and perjuring my ass off by claiming it was a loan so I could recoup my money. Trick ass!

Needless to say, the chances of me ever letting him suck on anything else, even my asshole, are slim to none and Slim's scandalous ass is out of town kicking it with some hoochie at 135th and 5th Avenue in Harlem. I put my magic marker to work again and my phone book began to look like a toddler's drawing pad.

Sorry mofo number three: Scott, a twenty-nine year old graduate student. Fondest memory: having him recite his original poetry to me on our romantic five day vacation at Hedonism II in Jamaica, making love in the sand under the island moon, erotic dancing to Reggae music, and seeing if he could fuck me in every position known to modern man without breaking my back or putting himself in traction. Most traumatic memory: receiving my

American Express bill and finding out the trifling ass son of a gila monster charged the whole damn escapade on my card and neglected to mention it to me. That vacation cost me a grip and if I ever see his venomous, hideous black behind again, I will unload my entire three-ounce can of pepper spray in his beady little eyes and finish him off with my stun gun. Twelve thousand volts to the head of his dick will set his ass straight but good. I scratched his name out so hard, I ripped the page.

Sorry mofo number four and you are going to absolutely love this one: Kenny, a twenty-five year old bum extraordinare who also happened to be my high school sweetheart and the one who busted my cherry bomb. Fondest memory: discovering the joy of sex together, sitting on the balcony of my Aunt Geraldine's apartment after cramming some of her delicious soul food into our guts and making plans for the future together. Most traumatic memory: finding out from my best friend Janessa that Aunt Geraldine and Kenny not only were knocking boots but had gotten hitched by the justice of the peace the day before hc was supposed to take me to our senior prom. I figured Kenny must have been out of his fucking mind so I asked him, "Are you out of your fucking mind?" You know what that stinking, malicious relative of Godzilla told me? He said the only reason he chose Aunt Geraldine over me was because she was on public assistance and therefore, food stamps would keep him from starving and their rent would only be $20 a month. The really sick part is that Kenny is three years younger than my cousin Marcus, Aunt Geraldine's son. I am *tooooooo* through with both of them. I hope her old ass gets a leg cramp one night while they are fucking and ends up stuck in a pretzel shape from now until Armageddon. I ripped his old number out my book and hers, stomped into the bathroom and flushed them down the toilet.

I was still holding the cordless in my hand when I came back out into the living room. I tossed it on my black leather sectional and headed to the kitchen in search of the pint of Haagen Daaz Double Chocolate Chip Ice Cream I kept hidden in the back of my freezer especially for nights when the maggots invaded my thoughts. I don't know why I let them bother me. They were all out of my life, somewhere getting their freak on with another woman, or man in Trent's case. Yet, I was working myself into a hissy fit over the fetid shit they did to me.

I found my ice cream, grabbed a spoon and a Pepsi, and headed to my bedroom to drown myself in sorrow. I flipped on *Jerry Springer*, got undressed, and threw on one of my home alone nightgowns, a tee I picked up in New Carrolton Mall with *I Just Can't Stand A Broke Ass Man* imprinted on both the front and back. I saved the good supply of nighties for when there was a man in the house, a rare occurrence. I laughed at the women who were fighting over sorry ass mofos on a talk show but I am not sure whether I pitied them or related to them and was really laughing at myself. Whatever the case, I tore into my unhealthy snacks and settled in for yet another boring Friday night.

Janessa

Friday night. *Millennium* night. There were only two shows I was absolutely crazy about, other than *Jerry Springer* of course cause everyone loves *Jerry*. *Millennium* and *The X-Files*. Something about that supernatural, alien, not-of-this-world shit gets to me. It was the season premiere and I was as excited as a virgin teenage boy in a whorehouse about to get some. I waited all week to see the show, listening to plugs for it on WPGC 95.5 and catching a few of the previews on FOX. I even stopped by Giant Food on my way home to pick up some Pop Secret Movie Theater Butter popcorn for the big night. *Don't you know someone in my family had to ruin it for me!* Most of the time on Friday nights, my parents turned in early since Momma was the type who still got up at 5 AM even though she had been retired for more than ten years. Pops preferred to pass the hell out after he got in from his maintenance job. My lard ass brother Fred pissed me off though. His ass is so big, he could shut off a water main eruption with the crack of his anus alone. There he was, laid out on the couch, snoring and sounding like an off-key chorus of hyenas. He had his shoes and socks off and the *au natur-*

al odor emitting from them bad boys was stronger than the butter flavoring on my popcorn. I turned the TV up louder with the remote and held my nose with one hand while I shoveled popcorn in my mouth with the other. I made a mental note to definitely get a tube for my bedroom on my next payday cause something had to give.

It was hot as hell up in the crib that night. Felt like Satan was breathing down the nape of my neck. I hated living in the projects. No central air. Roaches as big as rats, rats as big as dogs, and enough hoodlums to fill a state penitentiary. For months, I had considered asking Tempest if I could crash at her place. I knew she would say yes, but I also knew she would go into her mother figure mode and get all in my grill about shit. I got enough of that from my real mother so I didn't even go that route. I give props where props are due though. If it wasn't for Tempest, I never would have gone through with night school and gotten my GED. If it wasn't for her, I never would have taken the postal exam and landed a job as a clerk at the local branch.

Millennium went off. The part I heard of it over Fred's snoring was pretty damn good. I was going to watch *Jerry Springer* but the baked beans Fred had eaten for dinner kicked in and the farts emitting from his ass could have been bottled as weed killer. I couldn't take the madness one more second.

I went up to my bedroom and tried to crash but I had to leave the window open so I wouldn't suffocate. All hell had broken loose outside and the noise was way past ridiculous. It was the first of the month, the busiest day of every month for the liquor stores and drug dealers. That's when all the junkies and addicts cashed their welfare checks to pay for their habits instead of providing for their children. The crack house across the street, the one run by that homeboy of Ripuoff's, Lewis, was jumping that night. I hear Ripuoff is doing twenty years to life in Lorton for manufacturing that Niagra shit. Too bad I didn't get a couple of grape jelly jars full before he got sent up the river. I know some brothas who could use that shit for real.

I couldn't sleep, my nipples were harder than ping-pong balls, and my beeper had not gone off all day. Where were all my dicks? Where was the beef? I knew the answer. They were out getting their jollies off with some hoochie mommas or hitting the clubs with their boys.

I needed a car bad. I was willing to settle for a hoopty if I had to. I didn't care if the ride was held together by duct tape and sounded like Chitty Chitty Bang Bang as long as it could get me from point A to point B. I sat up in the bed and said, *"Fuck it!"* I knew Tempest would be pissed if I called and threw her a guilt trip about leaving me at home with Fred's stank ass, but I just had to get out of there. I was bored, I was lonely, I was horny. I had gone without getting my kitty kat stroked for more than four months and I was reasonably sure Tempest hadn't had sex since Kangol hats were the bomb. We needed to get out and explore our horizons. We needed to do the sistah-gurl thing and hang out. *We needed to find some fione ass men.* I got up off the bed and headed back down to the living room, which smelled like a natural gas explosion, to find the phone.

Geren

I'm still trying to figure out why I let Dvontè talk me into going clubbing that night. Looking back at it now, I realize it must've been fate. I was exhausted after a long day at the firm and the last thing I needed to do was deal with a smoke-filled room full of desperate women. That's all I seemed to run into, desperate women in all shapes and sizes and from all walks of life.

Some of them were subtle in their endeavors, but most of those kind frequented churches and cabarets looking for Mr. Right. The ones at nightclubs generally came right out with it and held nothing back. Tits and ass busting out of dresses two sizes too small, brushing up against me and sneaking a feel of my dick on the dance floor, whispering nasty thoughts in my ear. Sure, I slipped a few times and took advantage of the sexual favors they were offering. The only problem was they would expect me to fall in love or lust with some imaginary bomb ass pussy in the span of one roll in the hay and a hundred pumps when all I ever wanted was a quick sexual release.

I had decided there would definitely be no more of that. Times are hard and penicillin no longer cures every-thing. Frankly, I preferred taking care of business myself somewhere between flipping through the pages of *Ebony Male* or *Sports Illustrated* on the toilet and hopping in the shower to get ready for work. It was safer and my palm never expected me to propose to it afterwards with a three-carat diamond.

Dvontè, on the other hand, was a hoochie-loving man. His philosophy was the more punanny the better. I used to tell him he was going to run up on some lethal pussy one day and pay the piper but he always replied, "We all have to go someday. I want to die laid up in the bed with my dick inside some hot, juicy pussy!"

Dvontè was my boy but his playa behavior was getting old and our outlooks on women and relationships were far from mutual.

All I ever really wanted was one woman who could satisfy all my needs and not just my sexual ones. I'm an avid believer that once there's an emotional bond and friendship, everything else falls into formation. Unfortunately, most of the sistahs I had dealings with weren't on the same wavelength. I've never been anyone's fool and my eyes were wide open to the fact that women were after me for two reasons. My looks were above average and I had money. Lots of it.

There were a few sistahs who I honestly believed were genuine until they started asking me for things right and left. One even had the nerve to ask me to buy her a Lexus after the third date. She never heard from me again and I suspect she's still catching the Metrobus unless she lucked out and hooked up with a *so-called* successful drug dealer who simply didn't give a fuck. Any self-righteous man who attained his wealth the honest way, through hard work and perseverance, wouldn't fall for an obvious gold digger like that. Although, I must admit that sports figures and entertainers do have a tendency to do that very thing. They're so overcome by the legions of pantiless groupies flinging themselves at them that they fall for the game. Fools, I tell you because Geren Kincaid would never go out like that.

Looking around the club, I spotted all the various categories of women. First, there were the spandex queens. You know the type. Sistahs who have the nerve to squeeze into a size 6 spandex outfit when they really wear a size 26. More breast meat hanging outside of their tops than inside. Pants so tight that it makes a brotha want to break out an ink pen and play connect-the-dot on the rolls of cellulite protruding through the material. Sistahs who have to take a deep breath before they even attempt to sit down because the outfit is so tight they can't bend their legs. I'm not saying I have anything against large women. I love *all* my black queens, but I prefer women who carry themselves with class. If a woman puts on high heels in the morning and they're flats by the afternoon, common sense should tell her she has no business whatsoever sporting spandex. That's all I'm saying.

Then there were the pedestal women. Sistahs who think they are so damn fine that a man better not even attempt to approach them. They come to the club early and take up all the good seats at the bar or at the tables by the dance floor so they can sit there and talk trash about other people all night. So worried about what other people are doing, what other people have on, how people are dancing, that they don't even want to take a potty break for fear of missing something. *They are not even fooling me!* Half of them sit there sipping on the same drink the whole damn night because they can only afford one and still make their rent payment. Often times, you only see these type of sistahs at clubs around the 1st and 15th of the month after they've cashed their paycheck. Ninety-nine percent of them get paid on Friday and are pinching pennies by Monday morning.

Then there are the leeches. Hitting up every brotha they can grab by the elbow for a drink. All the young hustlers love those kind of women because they automatically think if they buy a couple of drinks, the sistah will give them an obligatory fuck. Most of them end up sitting in the bucket seat of their Ford Explorer or Chevy Blazer by the end of the night whacking off to Puff Daddy and the Family. Mind you, with about fifty dollars less in their pockets at that.

Let us not forget the video queens. Sistahs who have more fake stuff on them than real. Weaves, colored contacts, acrylic nails, gold caps on their teeth, silicon breasts, the whole works. Inside the club, under the dim lighting, some of them look fine as all hell. Wait till you get them outside though. Some of them are straight up hurting. *I mean hurt!*

I stood there, leaning on the bar and sipping on a Hennessy and Coke, trying to keep my self from busting out laughing at Dvontè. Speaking of hurt, the sistah he was trying to mack looked like she could play the lead in *A Bug's Life.* He was sinking low, even for him. Brotha man must have wanted some bad to be talking to her. She had eyes that looked like they were about to burst out of her head and was so skinny, if she swallowed a marble you would have swore up and down she was nine months pregnant.

I saw him glance over at me, darting his eyes down at her breasts trying to get me to size her up. The only problem was there was nothing to size up. My twelve-year-old baby cousin Rhonda had a better-built body than the sistah he was trying to get up on. She was so skinny her nipples were touching.

I pulled up the sleeve of my navy Hugo Boss suit and glanced at my watch. It wasn't even midnight yet. We got there about eleven. I was ready to go by ten minutes after, but I promised Dvontè we could hang out. If nothing else, I'm always a man of my word.

Dvontè

Geren was getting on my last damn nerve. Always trying to playa hate. Like they say, "Don't hate the playa. Hate the game." He was just mad because the only woman who had tried to step to him looked old enough to have an autographed copy of the Bible. I mean she looked older than my grandmother. The sistah was probably a waitress at the Last Supper. I chuckled because he had some ugly woman eyeing his ass. I know he sensed her but I don't blame him for not looking her way. She was so ugly, it looked like her neck threw up. Truth be known though, if she could give good head I would have closed my eyes and let her suck me like a lollipop.

I never in my life used a woman. They use me. I just happen to get a little ass in the process. Hell, if it weren't for men like me, there would be hundreds of thousands of lonely sistahs in the world. I make a woman's life complete. Give her something to look forward to after a long, stressful day at the office. Put a little pep in her step.

Let's face it. Most women, and men for that matter, spend the better part of every day doing something they hate to do; working. The majority of people work to pay bills and make ends meet. The only time they really get a chance to live it up is after work. I'm there waiting for these ladies when they come home with wet lips *and* a savory dick. What more could they ask for? .

I'm a precious commodity these days. A black man with a job, a place and no secrets hiding in the closet. I'm heterosexual, drug free, and I'm not a convicted felon. That alone makes me worth my weight in gold. Add to that the fact that I work, have my own crib *and* car and what you get is a man's man. That's me. Dvontè Richardson is a prince among men.

I've always been straight up with the sistahs. I want to get some ass and then roll out. I never fake the funk. If they don't want to play by my rules, then they can get to steppin' and tell their story walking. Sistahs always blame the man when something goes wrong as if they weren't even present when the shit hit the fan. Like they were having an out of body experience and were witnessing the whole sorted mess from afar. Who the hell are they trying to fool? *I know my rights!* I have the right to remain freaky as I want to be for as long as I want to be. *Simple as that!* Looking back on things now, I should've kept my ass at home that night. Most of the sistahs were tore up from the floor up and the one I ended up getting with almost ruined my whole damn life, even though she was fine. There's something to be said for making it a Blockbuster night. No doubt I would've been better off watching rented flicks that night.

ORDER FORM

Use this form to order additional copies of *Strebor Books International* Bestselling titles as they become available.

Name:_____

Company _____

Address: _____

_____

City: _____ State_____ Zip_____

Phone: (_____)_____ Fax: (_____)_____

E-mail: _____

Credit Card:☐Visa ☐ MC ☐ Amex ☐Discover

Number _____

Exp Date: _____Signature: _____

	ITEM		PRICE	QTY
1.	*The Sex Chronicles*	by Zane	$ 15.00	
2.	*Shame On It All*	by Zane	$ 15.00	
3.	*All That and a Bag of Chips* by Darrien Lee		$ 15.00	
4.	*Daughter by Spirit* by V. Anthony Rivers		$ 15.00	
6	*God's Bastards Sons* by D. V. Bernard		$ 15.00	
7.	*Luvalways by Shonell Beech & J. Daniel*		$ 15.00	
8.				
9.				
10.				

SHIPPING INFORMATION			Subtotal	
Ground	one book	$ 3.00	shipping	
each additional book		$ 1.00	5% tax (MD)	
			Total	

Make checks or money orders payable to
Strebor Books International
Post Office Box 10127
Silver Spring, Maryland 20914